WEL(
WALLOPS

THE WALLOPS BOOK 1

for Shure

Gill McKnight

Gill McKnight

Copyright © 2020, Gill McKnight
Second Edition, Revised
Dirt Road Books, Inc.

Cover design by Jove Belle
Cover photo © @Danussa

ISBN 978-1-947253-48-3

CHAPTER 1

Jane Swallow freewheeled down Main Street in Lesser Wallop, her bicycle wheels whizzing, strands of dark hair tugging loose from under her hat. Her messenger bag bumped against her hip and her spectacles misted up in the drizzle. A few passersby raised a hand in greeting, but she'd barely time to nod an acknowledgement before she flew past. She was late. She should have been at the office five minutes ago and Colin did not like to be kept waiting.

She hopped off her bicycle before the wheels stopped spinning, gravel cascading around her feet. Hastily, she propped the bike against the red brick wall by the door before barrelling through, hurling her hat and coat on a nearby bench.

"Colin." She burst into her tiny office. "How are you? Sorry I'm late." She ran her fingers through her mussed hair, accepting it was going to look like a wind bush, no matter what she did.

Colin Harper turned slowly from the window from which he'd been peering out, no doubt witnessing her scattered arrival. His hands were deep in his pockets and he looked relatively relaxed until Jane noticed the sour set of his mouth. Colin was a handsome man with a moody face, and the mood was always sullen.

"Yes. Well. Nothing we can do about that now," he said. He glanced pointedly at the wall clock. "I have another appointment at half-past so I'll keep this brief. I think it's safe to assume that now we have a publicity officer, this year's festival will probably be much bigger. So I suggest we move it to the High Wallop cricket field. We've better facilities up there."

Jane was prepared for this. Colin tried to hijack the Beer and Cheese Festival for High Wallop every year. Some attempts were clumsier than others, some stealthy and sleek. This was a clumsy year. "Not really a publicity officer, Colin. More like a travel writer passing through, who owes the Bishop a favour—"

"Hardly passing through. I heard he was settling in here for the foreseeable," Colin spoke over her as usual. "Bishop Hegarty has bent over backwards for this. It's a coup for The Wallops to get this sort of exposure. We need all the tourism we can get and the festival is our best chance to drag people in. This guy writes for the national newspapers. We'll be inundated with visitors, so we need more space, Jane. Surely, even you can see that?"

She tried not to bristle. "I think you're being a little over-optimistic. Traditionally, the festival is hosted on the village green in Lesser Wallop. It's been like that since medieval times. I'm surprised at you—of all people—wanting to overthrow tradition when we don't have any actual numbers to work with. We've not even printed the tickets yet."

"So you agree then, that it depends on the sales figures

and we'll review when we hit, say, 500 sales?" Colin pounced and Jane saw the trap. Again, this was a none-too-subtle year.

"No," she said evenly. "If we sell tons of tickets, then we'll have to extend the budget for facilities in Lesser Wallop. This is where the festival has been held for over seven hundred years and I see no reason to change things now. If it was good enough for Edward III, then it's good enough for us."

There was a moment's silence as both took stock. Colin's lips thinned in disapproval but the hands on the clock ushered him towards the door. "I'm afraid I have to go. We'll discuss this again later. Goodbye, Jane." He walked out without waiting for a reply.

"Goodbye, Colin," Jane called after him with relief. He was not the best way to start the day because he was always sniffing around looking for something to "improve" or meddle with. Why couldn't he simply let things be? Not everything needed his micromanaging, and especially not Jane's business.

Colin Harper saw himself as a genuine man of the Wallops, but the truth was, his main concern was always High Wallop, and he would never stop machinating until he'd sneaked the Beer and Cheese Festival out of Lesser Wallop and up the valley onto his home turf.

Her stomach rumbled. It was 9:30 a.m. and she was meeting Wendy for coffee at the Potted Crab cafe. A quick rifle through the morning mail stacked on her desk and she was through with the office. She preferred working from home anyway, and people always knew where to find her if she was needed. A perk of being the boss…well, almost. She stuffed the letters into her messenger bag, re-shouldered it, and was good to go.

The soft June rain was still falling as she pedalled back through the hedgerows to the village green. Wood anemones and mallow dotted the sides of the lane, and the air held the sharp, clean smell of wild garlic. Where the lane widened at the crossroads, she paused. Raindrops hung like tiny crystals from the four-fingered road sign that told her Lesser Wallop was a half-mile to the south. Twelve miles beyond that, right down on the coast, lay Cross Quays, a small fishing port and thriving town. Behind her, three miles to the north, stood High Wallop at the crown of the Wallop Valley, a quiet rural town, once famous for its wool before foreign imports destroyed the market. And finally, London, seventy-four miles northeast of everything. Jane wiped the mist from her glasses and smiled. She had come here from London and it gave her the greatest happiness to be reminded of the distance between the capital and herself.

She pushed onwards, leaving the lane and merging with the narrow road that led into her village. Fields soon gave way to houses with picket fences and well-maintained gardens, and then, rounding a gentle curve, the centre of Lesser Wallop opened up with its shops—a butcher, the grocers, the newsagent with its post office branch, two pubs, and a bakery. All were grouped around the village green and its pond, where mallards and call ducks quarrelled and rattled the reeds. The smell of fresh bread wafted from the bakery, and the door of the Potted Crab tinkled as someone pushed into the café's warmth.

Jane's spirits lifted. A spot of brunch was exactly what she needed, along with a chat with a very good friend.

"…and we found it in the fruit bowl." Wendy concluded, not entirely satisfied with her denouement. For a tall and somewhat awkwardly angled woman with slouched shoulders, constant finicking, and the perpetual worried crease to her brow, Wendy had the air of a perplexed church mouse. Her soft brown eyes glowed with an ever-present anxiety mixed with a healthy dollop of trust and basic human decency. That's why Jane loved her friend. She always strove to see the best in people. And in Jane's opinion that made her wonderfully suited to her job.

"So it wasn't a mugging after all?" Jane asked.

Wendy fiddled with the salt cellar. "No. Seems she got confused with a CSI episode from the night before."

"Wendy, does Mrs Ford need to see the doctor again?"

"I've had a word with her son. He's coming down from Oxford to visit next weekend."

"Okay. Maybe I'll pop by and say hello. I haven't seen Trevor in ages."

"That'd be good," Wendy agreed, relieved. She picked a piece of lint off her uniform sleeve, then tucked a stray strand of sandy coloured hair behind her ear. "Because last time, she was seeing penguins in the koi pond, but we blame the National Geographic channel for that."

Their coffee and toasted sandwiches arrived. "Tuna?" the waitress asked, and Wendy raised a finger in acknowledgement, "Here you are, PC Wendy. And the three cheeses must be yours." This was set before Jane.

"Thanks," she said. But Brenda, their waitress, had already bustled away.

"It's Police Community Support Officer Goodall when I'm on duty," Wendy muttered huffily after Brenda. "PCSO Goodall, not PC Wendy. That sounds like a puppet show character. People have no respect for me. It's because I grew up here, isn't it?"

"No. It's because you fit right in and they're relaxed and happy around you. The best thing for an authority figure to be is approachable."

Wendy paused to consider this and decided to be pleased. "Yeah, I *am* an authority figure." Then her shoulders slumped into her usual slouch. "I just never thought police work could be so boring."

She took a healthy bite, then puffed her cheeks to blow the heat out of her mouth. "God, this is molten. Gimme your water. Gimme, gimme." She lunged for Jane's glass and gulped it down.

"You do this every time. Why don't you ask for your own glass of water? Or eat slower?"

"I'm hungry."

Jane rolled her eyes. "So, Colin was badgering me about the festival again." She nibbled the crunchy edges of her sandwich, waiting for the contents to cool.

Wendy rolled her eyes, too. "When will he ever give up?"

"Not until the festival is hosted by High Wallop and they erect a statue to him in the cricket field."

"He wants everything up there. If he could, he'd shut down this village and march us all up the valley in a blink."

"He thinks it'll be a big event this year, as we have a sort-of publicist."

"Publicist? I thought this guy was a writer. A mate of the Bishop's."

"That's what I understood, but several times now, Colin has stated there'll be newspaper articles and travel pieces and whatnots. That's why his knickers are in a twist. He really thinks this will be a massive year for the festival and he wants it all for himself up there." She waved a finger at the hills outside, where the church spire and wet rooftops of High Wallop peeped through the mist at the top of the valley.

"Maybe I should give him a traffic ticket. I'm sure I saw him driving while using his mobile phone the other day."

"Wendy," Jane admonished gently, "isn't that an abuse of power? Something you were sworn not to do. Are you absolutely certain he was on his phone?"

"No." Wendy's expression fell. "I was on my bike and couldn't catch up to see him proper. Stupid bike. Why can't I have a squad car with lights and sirens and everything? I'm toothless."

Jane patted her hand. "It's the cutbacks. One day you'll get one. Not that you need it, because you represent law and order in this valley, Wendy Goodall. Everyone respects you, even Colin Harper."

Wendy stared glumly out the window.

"Are you prepped for the quiz tonight?" Jane changed the subject.

"Pretty much. Amanda says she might be late. Her babysitter's messing her around." She took another bite of her sandwich, which seemed to perk her up a bit. "Oh, Moira's gagging to know who your new neighbour is."

Jane laughed. "Of course she is. Can't say I have much to tell her, though. Haven't had much time to get a sense of things in that regard."

"Hmm. Want me to do a stakeout?"

"Wendy…"

"Kidding." She shrugged. "Kind of."

"Oh, Lord," Jane muttered as they slipped easily into small talk while rain tapped against the Potted Crab's windowpanes.

Jane cycled home to Rectory Row, glad of her water-proofs. The rain, while light, seemed never-ending. It had rained intermittently for two weeks now and everyone was getting sick of it.

The lane to her cottage was narrow with barely enough room for a car to pass, which was nice for a bicycle owner but problematic for the other residents in the row of tiny cottages. They had to park wherever they could farther down the lane and lug all their shopping to their doorsteps by foot. Most of Jane's neighbours were elderly and she helped where she could, carrying bags of groceries and sometimes parcels from the post office.

She pedalled around to the rear of Rectory Row and followed the path past the back of all the other cottages to her own on the end. She was hemmed in on one side of the pathway by rows of quaint country gardens, brimful with flowers and vegetable patches, and on the other side by the Sturry, a little stream that dilly-dallied around the outskirts of Lesser Wallop to finally join with the Wallop River as it made its way down to Cross Quays, and on out to sea.

After she pushed open the gate, she wheeled her bike up the path and stowed it in the garden shed, making a promise to come and hose the mud off later. For the moment, all she wanted to do was get inside and switch the kettle on for a brew.

"Hello, boy," she announced when she got inside and peeled off her waterproofs on the kitchen doormat. Whistlestop raised his long, woebegone greyhound face in greeting and stared at her with wise and thoughtful eyes. His whip of a tail slapped the lino twice before he lost interest and his head slumped back onto his bed.

"What have you been up to this morning, eh? Dreaming of rabbits? Do you want to go out for a widdle? I'll leave the door open for you."

He reviewed the weather conditions outside and decided against a widdle, for he yawned and curled into a tight ball, shuffling even closer to the radiator.

"Okay. You had your chance." She closed the door and was soon halfway through her second cup of tea when a mechanical rumble brought her to the kitchen window. Even Whistlestop raised his head in query for a split second before the effort was too much.

Jane hugged her teacup to her chest and blatantly snooped. *Look at me. I'm a curtain-twitcher. Never thought it would come to this.*

A small Bobcat digger had turned up. It chugged up the back entry of Rectory Row belching fumes and too much noise. A white tradesman van squeezed along behind it snapping branches and cutting up the grass verges. "Bill Gerrard & Son, Builders" was emblazoned on its side in large red lettering. Jane's heart sank.

The Bobcat digger spun around violently, then heaved itself onto the picket fence next door like a mating buffalo, flattening it completely. The white wooden railings crushed to splinters in seconds even as the Bobcat drove over the dahlia bed, churning up muddy twin tracks, and pushed through onto the wet, overgrown lawn.

Poor dahlias. Jane absentmindedly sipped her tea. They had valiantly withstood a springtime of neglect, and despite a weed invasion and early spring drought, had still managed to put on a colourful, if slightly droopy, display. Now they were squished to bits. John had loved his dahlias. He'd won prizes in the village fete for them, and it hurt to see his flowerbeds ploughed into the mud. He would have been appalled. Well, maybe not. If anything, he had also been a pragmatist. "Life goes on, m'dear," is what he would say if he were looking down on all this mayhem from above.

She let the curtain drop. If she watched anymore, she'd become genuinely upset. One by one, the cottages on Rectory Row were losing their elderly tenants. The sweet little stone-built homes, once owned by the church, were being snaffled up at exorbitant prices by wealthy Londoners looking for shrewd investments doubling as weekend getaways. Rectory Row had fifteen cottages, and only four were lived in year-round by long-term tenants. The others were only ever used for a few weeks here and there, especially in early July when Lesser Wallop held its festival. And now John, her neighbour, was gone and his cottage sold in a blink to some rich ignoramus who at this very moment was crushing the old chicken coop to matchsticks.

She wished the church could afford to hold onto the cottages and lease them out to its elderly parishioners. But the church needed money, too, just like everyone else, and so the quaint little homes were sold off one by one.

The kitchen clock said 11:22 a.m. Time to get some work done. Jane washed her cup and went to her small study. She preferred it much more than the stuffy little office she'd met Colin in. Just stepping into her cool, cream-coloured study relaxed her and settled her mind onto a soothing trajectory. Rows of white bookshelves lined the walls, along with exotic knickknacks from her various travels. Her desk, with its open laptop, looked out over her small front garden, resplendent with delphiniums and cape daisies, bellflowers and foxgloves, and, of course, her glorious roses. The petals shone like coloured gemstones under the soft patter of raindrops, and with a last lingering look at the swaying peonies, she settled down to work on her piece for *The Rosarian* gardening magazine. It was a relief to become lost in the colourful world of Chinas, floribundas, and noisettes, and, at least for the moment, forget the carnage next door.

At twelve fifteen, the drilling started seeping through the connecting wall—a deep, unpleasant whine that put Jane's teeth on edge. She could hear the dull echo of the workmen's voices through the empty rooms, bouncing off bare floorboards. They were installing a new kitchen and it felt like the work was dragging on for weeks. She scowled but soon got lost in the petaled mysteries of *Rosa hybrida* "Gruss an Aachen."

Lunch break brought a surprise. The Bobcat was still there but parked up out of the way and the "Gerrard & Son" van stood at the bottom of next door's garden. The van doors lay open and three men sat in the back out of the rain smoking and doing little else. Jane recognised Bill Gerrard, Junior, the "& Son" part of the company, and slunk outside for a quick chat over the hedge during a break in the rainfall.

"Bill," she called. He dropped his cigarette butt and ground it into the decimated dahlias before ambling over.

"Hi, Jane." Bill Jnr was a cheerful young man, and always

glad of any distraction from actual work.

"What's going on?" She nodded at the Bobcat. "Are you landscaping, then?" She looked around the pulverised garden wondering that there hadn't been something worth salvaging.

"Hard standing for a garage," Bill Jnr answered.

"A garage?" She hoped her horror wasn't obvious. "It's the first I've heard of it. When did permission for that go through?"

"Dunno." Bill Jnr scratched the stubble on his chin. "Ask me dad. He'll know."

Bewildered, she looked along the leafy lane with its picket-fenced gardens. Potting sheds and greenhouses, and bobbing banks of flowers swathed the backyards of Rectory Row. Birds sang, and butterflies flitted around champion-sized marrows, onion beds, broad beans, and compost heaps. Willow trees swayed along the banks of the Sturry, their branches tickling the meandering water, and above them, the narrow, slightly crooked steeple of Saint Poe's church rose needle-thin towards the slowly brightening skies.

It was an idyll. A small part of rural Sussex that clung tenaciously to the last century, and maybe even the one before that. Ladies in crinolines twirling parasols could wander down this lane and pass milkmaids with yokes and wooden pails, and neither would look out of place. It was a Constable painting, an Austen novel, a film set, and the new owner wanted to build a garage in the middle of all this bucolic loveliness?

"The old man will be along soon." Bill Jnr spat indifferently onto the ground. "He's coming with the Hi-lift to rip out the trees."

Jane's gaze fixed on the beautiful trees in John's garden. "The fruit trees?" She pointed out the small orchard of apple, cherry, and plum trees.

"And the willows, too." Bill Jnr nodded at the banks of the Sturry where a copse of willow hung dreaming over the stream. He didn't look impressed at the amount of work coming his way. He was the antithesis of his hard-working father.

"Who bought it? Do you know?" Her anxiety rose within her like a tide. The sale of the cottage next door had completed several weeks ago. The new owner hadn't even shown his face in the neighbourhood and already he was tearing up the garden and decimating the willows?

Bill Jnr shrugged. His interest was waning. She'd never known him to last long in any conversation unless it was about football.

"Would your father know for certain?" she pressed. Bill Snr was much more switched on than his son.

He shrugged again and dropped a marked look at her teacup. When she didn't offer to make him one, he strolled off. Jane was damned if she was going to provide drinks for him and his lazy workmates. She turned for the house just as Bill Snr arrived and she closed her kitchen door on the earful Bill Jnr was getting for having done very little prep work in the time he'd had before the Hi-lift arrived. She was more interested in the poor trees than the Gerrard family saga and stared forlornly out her window. The willows were huge and drooped gracefully over the heads of those walking along the lane. They hugged the banks of the Sturry like good, caring friends. The view from the back of her house would never be the same. Jane felt an old ache in her chest. She hated change in her small, safe world. She'd had more than enough of it.

The Tuesday night bar quiz was always held at The Winded Whippet. The ten percent off house ale and chicken wings made it a popular evening and brought in an eclectic mix. It was also the best place to hear the local gossip. Jane's team was called God Only Knows and was joint second with Piston Broke, the local petrol heads, and three points behind the leaders, Let's Get Quizzical, whose members all worked at the local medical centre.

"So." She slid into her seat, careful not to spill a drop of her Bouncing Badger real ale. "Does anybody know who my new neighbour is?" She peered hopefully over the rim of her glass at her teammates and was met with blank stares and shaking heads.

"No idea." Wendy buried her nose in her own pint. "Though Moira certainly wants to know."

Moira's head bobbed in agreement, shaking the twenty-something coiffured curls on a fifty-something head. "I heard he's famous and rich." She gave a lewd wink, which was nonsense, really, as she was happily married to Barry, the local butcher. Though that didn't stop her pretending to be a flirt. Moira was extroverted and gossipy and kept up with the latest fashions, courtesy of her daughters, even though half those fashions were too young for her. "So, you haven't set eyes on him yet?"

"No, but I'd like to," Jane shot back, thinking about the garage going in next door. "I know he's a famous writer, but I can't remember his name."

"Black. Something Black." Ranjeet piped up from the neighbouring table. Ranjeet was a clerk at the local solicitor's and sat with the rest of his colleagues from the Can I Get A Witness team.

"Is this the guy working for the Bishop?" Moira asked. "What writer do we know with the surname Black? A travel writer, isn't he? Well, I go nowhere so I wouldn't know."

"Anyone can be an author nowadays. Just ram something up on Amazon and suddenly you're Stephen bleedin' King." Una was always blunt. A junior solicitor, she worked with Ranjeet.

"Joe Black." Wendy was excited. "He's Stephen King's son. And he's a writer. Horror stories, like his dad. I tried to read one but it was too scary and I had to put it down."

"You mean Joe Hill. *Meet Joe Black* is a movie," Jane said. "And I hardly think Stephen King's son is moving in next door to me."

"Name Stephen King's son, that would be a great question for the quizzes," Una said.

Jane was about to respond when Steve Burr, the quiz compere, called them to order.

"Okay, ladies and gentlemen, round one." He paused for dramatic effect. "Kings and Queens of England."

"Damn." Wendy picked up her pencil. "Amanda's late and she's our history whiz."

"All right. First question. Who brought the Magna Carta into English law?" Steve barked into the microphone.

Wendy chewed her pencil top and looked at Jane and Moira wide-eyed. Moira shrugged.

"King John," Jane said a little doubtfully.

"Edward the First." Amanda appeared beside her as if conjured. "It's a trick question. John signed it but Edward made it law in 1297. And sorry I'm late. Babysitter probs." She looked flustered and quickly wriggled out of her raincoat and hung it on the back of the chair before sliding her slim figure into her seat. "Have I missed much?" She rolled the sleeves of her chunky jumper up too-thin arms. Raindrops dappled her long, mousy hair and she wiped them away, dabbing a tissue at the moisture on her pale, tired face. She had walked over, and as usual, exuded her patented mix of exhaustion and excitement. Amanda drew short straws but used them to sup the good out of life, and Jane loved her for that. Her positivity that things would get better shone out of her clever brown eyes, as wise as an owl and as fleet on the wing, too.

"We've only just started," Jane said, noting how haggard her friend looked and made a mental note to invite her and her kids around for dinner that weekend. Amanda looked like she needed a large meal and an even larger glass of wine.

"Who was the last Stuart on the throne?" Steve boomed.

Wendy scored out John and scribbled in Edward I. "Glad you're here. These are hard questions."

"Queen Anne," Amanda whispered. "They're not too bad."

"Not if you have a degree in history," Moira pointed out. Already she was scrummaging through her handbag for her cigarettes, preparing for the first fag break.

"Actually, she's a PhD in history." Jane smiled at Amanda.

"And you're a cleaner?" Moira tutted, shaking a disposable lighter to check it for fuel.

"Well, there's not much call for doctorates on how gender, class, and social action contributed to the Suffrage agenda." Amanda gave a rueful smile. "Nell Gwynn," she said, giving the next answer. "And cleaning is the only work I can get at the moment. It's not bad, and it fits around the kids' school hours…nineteenth of May 1536."

"What?" Wendy blinked.

"Anne Boleyn was beheaded on nineteenth of May 1536. Are you even listening to the questions?"

"Oh." Wendy picked up her pen and filled in the answer sheet.

"You should go to London. Get a job at a university or something," Moira continued.

"George the Third," Amanda said in response to another question. "It's not as easy as that, Moira." There was a practised patience in Amanda's voice, as if she'd had this conversation a million times over. "There are no jobs there, either. And besides, the kids love it here. I couldn't uproot them to London. It wouldn't be fair. Battle of Bosworth."

Wendy quickly scribbled the answers down. "Yeah. It's all youth gangs and knives up there." She sighed and went misty-eyed, no doubt thinking about all the police work she could be doing in London.

"Well, I think you're doing great," Jane said. "You've got all those holiday homes contracted for cleaning work, *and* the town hall offices. You've practically built an industrial empire." She squeezed Amanda's hand and got a weak squeeze back. "Did you see that job advertisement I emailed you for part-time lecturers for the Open University?" She hated how Amanda had to struggle for every penny. She was a clever, conscientious young woman who deserved much more.

"...survived five purported assassination attempts?" Steve boomed.

"What'd he say? I missed it again." Wendy hissed.

Moira shrugged. "I wasn't listening. I hate history. Lot of nonsense."

Amanda rolled her eyes but she was smiling, too.

"Ask him to repeat it," Jane said.

"No." Wendy ducked her head. "I'll look stupid."

"It has to be Victoria," Amanda said. "There were a lot of attempts on her life."

"What? Queen Victoria?" Jane was shocked. "I thought everyone loved her."

Amanda laughed. "She was quite contentious for her time."

The following round was The Weekly Wallop, where all the answers came from that week's issue of the local newspaper. An easy round, as they had all read it.

"We'll take a short break now so everyone can replenish their glasses," Steve announced. People queued at the bar or dashed outside for a cigarette.

"We've just heard someone called Black has bought next door to Jane." Moira immediately launched into the latest gossip, even as she gathered her cigarettes and lighter to leave. "And he's digging up John's beautiful garden to build a garage. It will ruin Rectory Row."

"Oh, no." This was obviously news to Amanda.

"It's beautiful along the back lane." Wendy added her sympathy. "Now there'll be cars driving up and down it all day long. *Londoner* cars. Massive four-by-fours and the like."

"You think so?" Jane frowned. It hadn't occurred to her that this might start a precedent for the absentee owners farther down from her.

"Yeah," Moira said. "It's bound to. And soon that lovely old lane will be dug up and tarmac put down." She sighed heavily. "It's such a pity."

"Ouch." Amanda pulled a face. "Has anybody got any good news?"

"The new neighbour is rich and famous." Moira offered compensation before heading for the door with the other smokers.

"We don't know that for sure," Jane told Amanda.

"Is he the guy the Bishop is hoping will write about the

festival?" Amanda asked her.

She shrugged. "Colin thinks so. But I'm not sure. I would have heard if he was moving into the Wallops, never mind right next door." She frowned again as she considered it, then shook her head. "Nah. I'd have heard. Bishop Hegarty would have said something. I'm the head judge at the festival and I'd have been told for sure."

She spotted Bill Gerrard Snr over by the bar. "Excuse me a moment," she said as she grabbed her glass, then went and joined him.

"Hey, Bill."

"Hello, Jane." He turned to greet her. "Here, what'd you put down for that one about the assassinations?" He was on the Barnstormers team, a mish-mash of sixty-something farmers and builders who always came last. They only showed up for the discounted drinks and chicken wings. "I said Richard the Third 'cause everybody hated him."

"Um, good a guess as any, I'd say." Jane wiggled out of welching on the correct answer. "But I was wondering more whether you know anything about my new neighbour. Besides the garage thing?"

He looked grim. "Not really. Never met 'im. Some guy called Barrack. Pity the town planning went along with the Bishop and allowed him to build. There'll be a whole rash of garages down your back alley now. All 'em Londoners will want one." Despite his criticism of the planning department, he looked keen on the idea, especially if he got to build them all.

"The Bishop okayed the planning permission for this?" Jane hid her irritation. The church had avoided a rash of objections from the remaining tenants of Rectory Row by sidestepping them as their landlord. It was a sneaky move, but legal. Then it dawned on her that Bill Snr had used another name. "Barrack, you said, not Black?"

He shrugged. "Never said his name was Black. It's Barrack, or something like that." The barman appeared and Bill gave his drinks order. "I've only dealt with his architect, not him."

She waited patiently behind him for her turn, thinking that it seemed no one was sure about her new neighbour at all.

"Some bad weather coming in." Bill Snr turned back to her. "Forecast is for a big storm later this week. A bad 'un. Gale force winds and torrential rain. Then it gets better and summer begins. At last."

"So I heard," Jane replied. "But, Bill, what about the willows you were uprooting today? Will they be replaced? The Sturry needs them to bind its banks. You can't go hacking away at the vegetation willy-nilly."

Again, he shrugged. "It's not my job to replace 'em. Ask the Wallops Valley Council, Jane. All I know is they okayed me to cut 'em back for the machinery to get in. They'll grow back in a year or two."

"Not if you uproot them." But the conversation was cut short by the barman asking her what she wanted to drink, and Steve Burr simultaneously booming out the start of round three, The Animal Kingdom. She sighed and put in her order, then returned to her table with her fresh pint.

Bishop Andrew Hegarty was as vague as ever. "Jane, Jane." He slapped his hand on her knee with no regard for social mores, and shook it in a hearty manner until she thought her kneecap would detach. "I know you're upset about the trees, but I have assurances from the council they will be replaced. They were very old and losing their integrity. Why, if any of them fell into the Sturry, it could cause a terrible commotion in the village. The whole place could be flooded, just like that last time."

"That last time was over a hundred years ago and that's why they planted the willows along the Sturry in the first place, to prevent flooding." Jane was patient with the Bishop. He was white-haired and whiskery with the kindest eyes she had ever seen, and he did his best to make everyone happy, which was impossible in a community this size, where everyone contradicted each other.

He sighed. "The church needs to sell off its assets. Gone are the days we could sit on our pots of gold. Now we have to be seen tightening our belts like everyone else. Congregations are fading away, Jane. Churches are closing down all over the country." His expression saddened and she followed his gaze out her kitchen window across the Sturry towards Saint Poe's. The small church stood awkward and naked now that its skirt of willows had been removed. Roses billowed around its doorway and a Virginia creeper, lush and green, smothered the south face up to the worn slate roof with its short, bent steeple. She busied herself refilling his cup and offering another teacake.

"About my new neighbour." She pulled the subject back to more pertinent and less troubling topics. "Is this the writer who will publicize the Beer and Cheese Festival? Black, or Barrack, or something?"

Bishop Hegarty looked at her blankly. "How on earth did you know that?" He stirred himself out of his surprise.

"I *don't* know. That's why I'm asking you."

"My dear girl, the rumours fly around this valley faster than the crows."

"If tongues were wings, we'd *all* fly. So can you tell me what's going on?"

"Well, nothing's going on. No contract has been signed as yet, so I'm not at liberty to say. Though, I've admired this writer for some time and we've corresponded over the last several months—" The telephone in the hallway rang and she excused herself to answer it.

"It's Colin for you." She came back and handed over the phone, exasperated at Colin Harper's ability to pick his moments, and under no illusion it was a deliberately timed intrusion. Andrew Hegarty always forgot his mobile phone, proving that Colin monitored the Bishop's visits to her if he knew where to call to find him.

"Yes, Colin...I see."

She moved away and gave the Bishop some privacy. When she returned, he handed her the phone and reached for his jacket.

"I'm sorry, Jane. Colin finds himself in a bit of a pickle, so I'll have to leave you. I know that as head judge, you and I need to sit down and discuss the publicity for the festival, but until the contract is actually signed, my hands are tied." He bustled towards the door as he spoke, nearly tripping over Whistlestop, who chose that moment to stand in the open doorway and look thoughtfully at the clouds.

So, was the building permit for the garage a sweetener for your writer friend? The thought depressed her. She knew more was being heaped on Bishop Hegarty's sagging shoulders than he was able to cope with. In fact, she fully expected him to announce his retirement within the next year or so. The world was a faster, more vicious place than when he first took his orders.

She washed up the dishes as rain began to pitter-patter against the window. It never seemed far away these days. The wind had also begun to rise and, clearly, the predicted storm was coming in early. Whistlestop came up and pressed against her leg. He looked up at her with inscrutable, ink-dark eyes. She gently kneaded his knobbly head and smoothed the worried furrow between his brows with her thumb.

"You're always there to comfort me, aren't you, Whistlestop?" In answer he kicked his empty food bowl against her shoe.

"Oh, fine. I see how you are." She gave him another few pats and picked up his bowl, wondering again who the new neighbour was and what the fate of Rectory Row would be.

CHAPTER 2

The storm arrived full force that night.

Jane had lain awake listening to the wind howling down the valley and rattling her windows until the wee hours. At some point, she must have drifted off, for now she awoke with a start at the crack of a tree branch breaking away. At first, she thought it was gunfire and her heart raced, then full awareness of where she was and of the storm outside kicked in, and she guessed immediately that the rotted chestnut tree had finally lost a branch.

Whistlestop padded over to the bed and laid his head on the quilt and gave a soft snuffle.

"You don't like storms, do you, boy?" She reached out and stroked his bony head, ruffling his ears before dropping a kiss somewhere near his nose. The bedside lamp clicked uselessly when she tried it. The branch must have taken the power lines down with it and her immediate thought was for her elderly neighbours. They'd all be tucked up in bed, and maybe, with luck, the power would be restored early next morning with hardly any inconvenience to anyone. Right?

She knew better. With a sigh, she grabbed her emergency flashlight from the bedside cabinet and made her way along the hall to the bathroom. Whistlestop plodded along behind. He was scared of the dark, too, and she usually kept a small plug-in nightlight on for him near his bed.

Outside, the wind rattled and roared, its sounds mixed with the distant clang of garden ornaments, seats, dust bins, and Lord-knew-what-else being blown about. Jane ran through her mental checklist for the umpteenth time. The greenhouse was as secure as she was ever going to make it. She'd staked up the taller plants but accepted they'd be blown to bits by morning. The watering cans, empty flowerpots, and anything moveable were all tucked up in the potting shed out of harm's way. So what was that banging? It was almost rhythmic, like a door slamming back and forth in the wind. She did another run-through of her list. There was nothing she could think of that could be making that noise. She'd tied everything possible down.

At the rear of the house the banging was louder, and she realised with alarm the noise was coming from next door.

"Don't tell me the builders didn't lock the house up," she told Whistlestop. A very loud bang came back as an answer. Whistlestop groaned, as if, on some level, he knew what this all meant.

"You can moan all you want but we have to see what's making that noise." She could easily imagine Bill Jnr sloping off early as soon as the weather worsened, and not stopping to make sure the cottage was secured properly. Quickly, she dragged on her waterproof coat and Wellington boots.

Opening the back door was like entering some post-apocalyptic maelstrom. The wind nearly tore the door from her hands and she had to use her entire body weight to stop it from slamming behind her. Rain cut at her in horizontal ribbons and her pyjama legs were soaked in seconds, clinging coldly to her skin. "Bloody hell!" she shouted into the storm.

Whistlestop didn't even make it to the doormat. From the corner of her eye, she saw his tail disappear back down the hallway. Three steps out and she splashed ankle-deep into water. It surprised and frightened her and it only got deeper the farther she went. She hesitated, as her flashlight showed a scene of carnage.

Her flower beds were flattened, but given the conditions it could only be expected. At least she had no structural worries from what she could see. Next door was another matter. The Bobcat digger at the bottom of the garden stood waist-deep in water, its windshield shattered. The corrugated tin sheeting they'd pulled off the old chicken coop roof now whipped around the yard in great gyrations, screeching against every possible surface like horrendous banshee wails.

She swung her flashlight about to assess the damage. The lane at the rear of Rectory Row was chaos. She could make out the inky ripple of water under her zigzag of light. The Sturry had burst its banks and flooded the lower part of Jane's garden, which meant the gardens on the other side of her were in even greater danger because the land rolled gently downhill from her house.

They should never have taken away those willows, she

thought, but the gratification of being right was short-lived compared to her shock at the damage. There was a gap in the bank where the trees had once stood, and the earth had washed away, taking part of the lane with it. A surge of flood water cascaded onto her garden and the neighbouring ones. It hissed and gurgled and swirled threateningly, casting everything safe and familiar into heinous unfamiliar shapes and patterns. It was sucking and unstoppable. Rectory Row was sinking, or looked like it was about to.

She retreated inside and picked up the phone. It was dead, probably because power lines were down. She called Wendy on her mobile and got a fuzzy, "Hello?"

"It's Jane. The Sturry is flooding. My house is all right, but I'm not sure about Mrs Agnew and those farther down the lane." She could hear the thud and rustle of Wendy clambering out of bed.

"Right. I'm on my way. I'll check in on the old ducks at the far end, okay?"

"Thanks. I'll try and see what's up at my end. Be quick or they may quite literally be old ducks because the water is still rising, as far as I can make out. And there's no power over here. The lines are down."

"None here, either. The whole village must be out. See you later. Get the primus stove out for a cuppa," Wendy said cheerfully, no doubt pleased by the midnight adventure and the use of her police skills.

A great gush of wind increased the banging from next door. Jane couldn't ignore it any longer. She grabbed her flashlight again and went back outside. This time she focused her attention on the neighbouring cottage and could clearly see two windows swinging crazily open and shut as if trying to wrench themselves off their hinges. Rainwater drove through the openings and Jane could only imagine the damage done to the new interior.

She contemplated straddling the fence versus plodding down to her back gate, wading along the partially demolished lane, and coming in through the decimated neighbouring garden. She considered that leaping the fence might be a little beyond her tonight, especially with corrugated tin whipping about like a guillotine blade. Mincing through cold floodwater was probably just as dangerous, however, so she awkwardly straddled the fence, water sloshing wetly around her calves.

It was deeper on the other side, where the recent excavations for laying new water pipes had left deep trenches in the ground that were now awash. Jane's heart sank as the water topped her boots right up to her knees. From here she could see that the back door of the cottage lay wide open, and the muddy swill had run inside. The new kitchen, and probably the whole ground floor, was under several inches of water. All the expensive carpentry was ruined and the kitchen destroyed before it had even been completed. She walked into the house and fastened the windows shut. The water wasn't as deep as it was in the garden, but it had gotten in everywhere. Her flashlight spilled crazy patterns over the wet walls and rippling floor.

The wall between the kitchen and the main lounge had been removed. No wonder the work had been going on for weeks. But the effect was lovely—if it hadn't a tidemark of muddy water lapping up the walls. The beautiful honeyed oak cabinets were ruined. The original quarry tiles had been prised up and a new wood floor laid. It was ruined, too. The newly plastered walls—forget it. The only thing in the kitchen not destroyed were the beautiful granite worktops. Jane ran appreciative fingers over the smooth surface and gave a little hum of approval.

Okay, so the kitchen was a goner, but what about the other rooms? This was just outright snooping now. With water swilling around her shins, Jane pushed on through a layout more or less identical to her own. Everywhere was waterlogged and the oak floors and plasterboard would all have to be replaced. She shook her head. The new owner would not be pleased.

There was nothing Jane could do but return home, make some tea, and wait for Wendy. The morning would bring a world of pain for Bill Gerrard & Son. She began her exit when the blaze of a flashlight much larger and stronger than her own momentarily blinded her, bringing her to a halt by the back door like a rabbit on a highway.

"Who the hell are you? What are you doing in my house?" a female voice snapped.

"Can you turn that thing away, please, you're blinding me." She raised a hand to block the light. The slash of rain whirled in dizzy patterns in the glare.

"Watch your step or my dog will go for you."

Jane cocked her head, and around the haze of light haloing her fingers she saw the dark shadow of a woman mercilessly drilling a flashlight on her and beside her stood the angular, and slightly fuzzy outline of a tall, scrawny, windblown animal.

"That's *my* dog," she said, recognising Whistlestop, who chose that moment to turn and meander off, dismissing them both.

"Oh?" The flashlight dropped away. Jane blinked several times in relief, trying to banish the bright spots of colour behind her eyelids. "He just wandered up to me," the woman said. "Is he a watchdog? He's rubbish if he is."

"He's mostly a nosey bystander. You get them a lot around here." Jane wiped the rainwater off her face only serving to smear her glasses more. They were both standing in water, getting soaked. This was ridiculous. "And you are?"

The flashlight zoomed up to dazzle her again. "I'm the owner of the house you have been looting. What are *you* doing on my property?"

Her property? So, the famous writer had a wife. "What's there to loot? As you can see, the Sturry has flooded your home." Jane shielded her eyes again, not caring that there was a snap to her words. This woman was rude. "And as I live next door, I came to check on it, not loot."

"We're neighbours?" There was no joy in the words.

"Apparently so." Jane surmised this was a rather hardnosed individual. She was just about to deliver a quick report on the damage and then get off home when Wendy rolled up.

"Hullo there!" The cheerful call was accompanied by a flashlight brighter than both theirs combined. It burnt holes in Jane's retinas. She could hear the other woman's gasp of shock as she fell victim to it, too, and revelled at her getting a taste of her own medicine.

"Turn that thing off, Wendy, before you blind us permanently," she said.

The light swung away and she could hear the sloshing of Wendy's rubber boots as she crossed the garden.

"All's well down the far end." Wendy reported, straddling the fence. "It's worse here because they dug up the garden to lay pipes. You're both standing in a great big hole." She pointed out good-naturedly. Her flashlight wavered towards the river. "And ripping out the willows didn't help. It looks like the bank collapsed and took part of the lane with it. There won't be any ugly old garages being built here for some time."

"Who are you? Another helpful neighbour?" This earned the newcomer another full-on blast from Wendy's supernova torch. Jane winced and looked away. Splashes of colour swirled before her eyes.

"Hi, there," Wendy said. "I'm Police Community Support Officer Goodall. And who are you?"

"Will you get that bloody thing out of my face? I own this property, and I found this woman trespassing." The stranger's flashlight swept across Jane's face, making her blink wildly.

"Look," Jane said. "Can we stop standing in a hole blinding each other? Why don't we go back to my house and have a cup of tea and Officer Goodall and I will explain everything. It's obvious you have flood damage but there's little you can do until the morning. Can we please get in out of the wind and rain?"

"I'm freezing. A cuppa would be lovely." Wendy moved toward the fence dividing Jane's garden from the neighbours.

"After you." Jane waved vaguely at the fence for her new neighbour to follow. A strange feeling of unease had been tugging at her for the past several minutes and she could see something similar in the other woman's hesitation towards her. "There really is nothing that can be done here," she reiterated. "You'll be able to assess the damage for yourself in the morning." She was tired now and her unease was giving way to a general grumpiness. She was up to her knees in cold river water trying to do her best by her neighbour, and had been met with nothing but rudeness and suspicion.

With a quiet "humph," the newcomer mounted the fence and slid over to the other, just-as-boggy side. Jane followed, the nagging in her head now becoming the beginning of a headache. Light flowed out from her kitchen. Wendy had lit her storm lantern and the yellow oblong of gaslight spilled from the window and illuminated the stranger's rain-whipped face in a steady stream of light.

Jane gasped, the air wrung out of her by the sudden constriction of her throat. Her legs trembled and then gave out bringing her down in an unhappy, uncomfortable slump halfway over her fence.

"Are you okay there?" A hand reached out to her and she recoiled. Then, as the light played across her own face her new neighbour stiffened and a look of abject horror flitted across her face. "Fuck." The whisper was hard and brittle from a mouth twisted in distaste.

"You alright out there?" Wendy called out from the kitchen. "I found your camping stove and got the kettle on. Hurry up, you two."

"Jane Swallow," the stranger said. It sounded like an accusation.

Jane swallowed the lump in her throat.

"Jane, is that you?" The woman asked, and again Jane's voice was too constricted to respond. "Bloody hell. You bitch."

The hissing tones scalded her ears.

"Milk? Sugar?" Wendy was oblivious to the tension in the room.

"Black. Black as the heart of a betraying lover." The newcomer gave her order.

Wendy blinked.

"Okeydokey." She poured a cup of tea and handed it over. "You'll be the writer moving in next door, then?"

"Renata Braak." She held out her hand with stiff politeness.

"Braak. See, Jane? Not Black and not Barrack." Wendy shook hands. "Isn't it weird that everyone got the name wrong?"

"Yes, very weird." Jane moved around her kitchen, keeping to the darkened fringe of the camping light and feeling like she was in a dream. One of those bad dreams after she ate too much cheese.

"So…" Wendy plodded on, determined to make conversation. "You're a travel writer then, Ms Braak? That must be fun."

"Renata," she corrected and sat down at Jane's kitchen table, her face in part shadow from the lantern on the counter. "And I'm not a travel writer. I write about metaphysical issues, such as high consciousness and self-actualization."

"Ah." Wendy's conversation ran out abruptly. "So…" Or had it? Because she started right back in. "You picked a bad time to drop by, didn't you?"

"I don't think there was ever going to be a good time, do you?" The question was directed towards Jane, and again Wendy's face cramped with confusion.

"Do you two—" she began to ask.

"How do you know Bishop Hegarty?" Jane lurched into action. She flung herself into the seat opposite and poured tea with a shaking hand. She was aware her question sounded sharp-edged. Wendy looked at her curiously.

"He's a fan." The answer was just as clipped.

There was an awkward silence for a few moments that

Wendy felt obliged to fill. "Bishop Hegarty likes meta... thingies?"

"He read a few of my books and we started a correspondence. He'd like me to look at the ley lines running through the Wallop Valley. He suspects there's a lot of healing energy in the area."

"I thought you were the publicist for the festival?" Wendy looked to Jane for some sort of verification but got none.

"Yes. That, too," Renata added a little belatedly, causing Jane to switch to an even higher level of alertness. She could sniff the lie from the other side of the room.

"Did you get to talk to Mrs Agnew?" Jane abruptly changed the subject and, thankfully, Wendy followed peaceably.

"No. All the occupied houses were in darkness, so I left them alone. The only water damage I could see was the bottom end of the gardens. I can pop back in the morning if anyone needs anything once they're up and about. And I've already informed the electricity and phone companies the lines are down, though they knew about it already." She stood and rinsed out her cup. "I'll head on home now. Are you okay, Ms Bra—Renata. Where are you staying? Can I give you a lift anywhere?"

"I'm staying at The White Pig in High Wallop."

"Oh, posh," Wendy said.

"If you say so. I dumped my bags and drove on down here, so I've no idea." Renata didn't look at Wendy as she spoke. Her gaze was fixed on Jane.

"I'm not sure how safe the roads are." Wendy dithered by the sink. "There are trees down everywhere. I could show you a farm track back up the valley. It might be okay."

"Thanks, but I think I'd like to stay and chat with my old friend."

Wendy slapped back down in her seat. "I knew it! I just knew you knew each other. The conversation was so hinky."

"I feel extremely hinked," Renata replied.

"We were surprised to see each other, that's all. Especially under the circumstances," Jane said.

"Especially under the circumstances," Renata repeated.

"Weren't you heading home, Wendy? Tomorrow's a busy day." Jane shot her a look.

"Yeah. Weird, eh? So where do you know each other from?" Wendy ignored her and poured herself a second cup of tea.

"Oh, ages ago." Jane felt a cold sweat form on her body. She darted a furtive look at Renata that was met with a steely gaze in return.

"Where was that, then?" Wendy persisted.

"I can't quite remember. It was so long ago." Jane cleared her throat and decided to plunge right on in with further hedging. If she skated around the truth gracefully enough, it wouldn't be so much lying as a winter sport. "We've lost touch, so you can imagine my surprise to find out Renata is my new neighbour."

"I can barely believe it, either. It's like one big universal joke." Renata spoke with borderline bitterness and Jane stiffened.

When it was obvious Wendy was struggling, Renata elucidated. "Not a belly laugh. More a snide snigger."

"Ah." Wendy nodded in false understanding. She drained her second cup and stood. "Well, I best be on my way. Nice to meet you, Renata. I hope to see you around."

"Oh, I'm sure you will."

"Sorry about your house."

"Yes, it's a real tragedy."

"I'm sure Bill Jnr didn't mean to leave all the windows and doors open."

"He did, did he?" Renata's head snapped up. "Well, I'm sure his father will be very proud when I call him first thing in the morning about the mess."

"Um. Yes." Wendy bumbled her way out of the kitchen, and Jane felt for her—in a way. She was glad Wendy's blatant snooping had gleaned little information, but sorry that her friend had been made to feel awkward in her home. That had never happened before, but the atmosphere Renata brought with her blended perfectly with the storm surrounding them. The woman could brood. Jane remembered that very well. Poor Wendy had picked up on the forecast, but was too unversed in emotional meteorology to understand what had just blown in.

"See you tomorrow," Jane called belatedly as the door closed, before turning to face her guest.

She was greeted with, "You fucking cow. You left me. You abandoned me on that Godforsaken island!"

"You're hardly Robinson Crusoe. I simply went home.

For me, the holiday was over. It's not illegal to go back to real life and get a job."

"What's that supposed to mean? You didn't even leave a goodbye note. You just fucked off the minute my back was turned. That was dirty, Jane."

Jane stood. Her hands were shaking and she pressed them to her sides to try and stop. "I'm not going to talk about it now," she said, ignoring the waver in her voice. "I'm exhausted and I'm going to bed. I'm not sure if it's safe for you to drive back to The White Pig. If not, there's a couch in the front room you can use." She turned away and almost tripped over Whistlestop, who had slunk back into the kitchen and was watching their visitor with wary eyes.

"And please don't shout in front of my dog. He's a rescue animal and his nerves are frayed. When he gets upset, he becomes incontinent."

Renata dropped her gaze to Whistlestop and her face softened slightly. "Why a greyhound? I see you as more the lap dog type."

Jane shrugged. "He was there and he needed me. I got him from a shelter for retired racing dogs, but it turned out he didn't race that much. He kept fainting. He suffers from neurasthenia."

"You mean he's neurotic?" Renata gave Whistlestop a dubious look. His tail slunk between his legs and he gave her a squinty, skittish look back.

"He gets a little depressed from time to time," Jane said, defensive. "He's had a hard life."

An awkward silence grew between them. With both sets of eyes on him, Whistlestop ducked his head and sloped out of the room.

"We need to talk." Jane said abruptly. "But not now. I can't get my head around this and I'm too exhausted to try." The sigh that fell out of her rattled her bones. She was dead on her feet and emotionally drained. She pointed through to the lounge. "You can crash there if you need to. I'll leave out a towel and new toothbrush for you in the bathroom. We'll talk in the morning, if that's okay."

There was Codeine in the bathroom cabinet and Jane was going to gulp two down as soon as possible.

"It's going to have to be."

Jane was glad to close the door on those words. There were plenty of cushions and throws on the couch for Renata to make herself comfortable. Jane needed to sleep now, to remove herself from reality and hide away. Tomorrow, recharged, she would begin to repair the damage, no doubt along with half the village. Though her damage was more than watermarks and mud. Her damage was damning, and she didn't want to think about that day all those years ago when she'd made the choice to leave Renata behind. Not tonight.

It was just after eight o'clock when she awoke. Sunlight streamed through the bedroom window and it wasn't until she looked out and saw the garden and lane all torn about and strewn with leaves, branches, and displaced things that she could believe there had been a terrible storm the night before. The morning looked so innocent. She checked the light switch. The lamp came on, so power had been restored.

Normally, she'd slop about in her pyjamas until she'd had at least two cups of coffee, but this morning, she dressed for battle in her favourite jeans and comfy sweater, and drew her dark hair back with a barrette. She hoped she looked collected and calm, though her insides felt like jelly.

The battledress was for nothing. The lounge was empty. Renata had gone. Whistlestop sat on the couch in a curl of warm blankets and looked startled by Jane's appearance.

"What have you got there?" She pulled away the silk scarf he was chewing on. "Oh, Whistlestop," she said, dejected. "This looks expensive." His eyes rounded into huge wells of guilt.

"Okay, let's get you some breakfast." She stroked his muzzle. "At least it wasn't her hair." Though that looked expensive, too. She smiled inwardly at the thought of Renata fast asleep on her settee with Whistlestop gently nibbling on her platinum blonde, hundred-quid hairdo.

She gave him his morning biscuits with warm water, and had started making coffee when Mrs Agnew rapped on the kitchen window, then came straight on in.

"Hello, Jane. What a night that was."

Jane smiled, knowing Mrs Agnew had slept through the worst of it. "Yes. We were lucky. Did you see next door?"

"I did. Terrible, just terrible. Poor woman. I saw her driving away this morning." Mrs Agnew turned hawk-eyed and skewered Jane with an inquisitive look that seemed to bore right into her. "She was out your back on the phone with Bill Gerrard. I could hear her all the way down the gardens." Mrs Agnew paused, and Jane wondered why she wanted a prompt. Usually, she talked nonstop once she'd cornered a listener.

"Oh?" Jane obligingly prompted.

"The language, my dear." Mrs Agnew rattled on, now that she'd been primed. "It was fearful. I bet Bill Gerrard got the rudest awakening of his life."

"There does seem to be a lot of damage." Jane was careful with Mrs Agnew. She was a shrewd and artful old widow, who lived on the opposite end of Rectory Row from Jane, and seemed to think it her place to police the comings and goings of her neighbours.

"She said it was all his fault. But, I mean, a flood's a flood. Lord knows, we all have to bear up and do our best. It's not as if Noah had a builder to phone up and complain to, now is it."

Jane privately noted no damage had been done to Mrs Agnew's cottage for her to "bear up" to. If there had been, Mrs Agnew would be first in the complaining queue, complaining that the queue itself was not moving fast enough.

"But the back door and kitchen windows had been left open, letting all that water in," Jane pointed out, immediately annoyed with herself for defending Renata Braak.

Mrs Agnew's face mottled with a flush of surprise and irritation. "Well, I never. What a thing to happen. I'll wager it's that son of his. He's a no-good wastrel." And she effortlessly changed sides.

Jane kept silent on her own opinion of Bill Jnr. "Coffee?" she offered instead.

"No, dear. I'd better be getting along. I'm going over to the shops." That meant she had gossip to share. Jane hoped she'd keep her news about next door in context but knew it was a wasted hope. In Mrs Agnew's hands, it would be an Oscar-nominated movie script by lunchtime.

Whistlestop wandered in with the silk scarf in his maw, slobber trailing from it. Mrs Agnew hesitated and watched avidly as Jane disentangled the thing from his mouth. She set it on the countertop without a word, ignoring the inquiring gaze Mrs Agnew pinned on it.

"Have a lovely morning, Mrs Agnew," she said calmly.

"You, too, dear," she said, and finally left.

Jane poured her delayed first coffee of the morning and sighed into the fragrant steam rising from her cup. Her stomach was still unsettled, and out her window, the clouds were rushing in from the east, bullying the weak sunshine into submission. More rain was on its way and her mood sank to greet it. It felt like a troublesome day was brewing.

She must have missed Renata's departure by perhaps twenty minutes if Mrs Agnew had seen her go. She turned on the radio, always set to the local station down at Cross Quays. The local news bulletin told her the flooding had been minimal and all power had been restored. The telephone cables would be repaired by tomorrow, though several felled trees still blocked many minor roads. So it was a good thing Renata had stayed and not followed Wendy's advice to take the back road up to High Wallop. She'd never have made it.

On her second sip of coffee, it hit her—low and hard in the pit of her stomach: Renata Braak was back in her life, hovering like a wraith. Their "talk" had been postponed, and with no regard or manners as to informing her when it would be resumed. Renata had left without a word. She clearly had bigger fish to fry, and secretly Jane was glad. She didn't want to talk, didn't want to explain why and how she had made her decision all those years ago. It was too exposing, and especially at a time in her life when she felt more inclined to hide than ever.

Her hand trembled around her coffee cup, making the liquid ripple across the surface. She had dodged a bullet but there was a missile still to come. She headed to her study. At the front of her house, she saw the Gerrard & Son van obstinately squeeze down the narrow street and was relieved that next door was no longer any of her business.

She'd spend an hour working and then head out to do her own shopping. She refused to dwell on the fact that this was avoidance. Renata was doubtless going to return and stand over Bill Gerrard and his erstwhile son, whip in hand, while they carried out her repairs. Jane wanted to be well out of the way when that particular whip cracked.

CHAPTER 3

Renata Braak fixed the collar of her blouse and checked herself in the mirror. Her eyes held a dark, crazy expression. She was so frazzled, she was surprised she didn't curl at the edges. Her brain was fried in her head.

Jane Swallow. After all these years, Jane Swallow had popped up out of fucking nowhere and was her freaking new neighbour! What sort of joke was that? What sort of twisted, evil... She sighed and snapped her mind off that particular trajectory. The Universe was just another bitch, that's all she needed to know.

She'd lain festering on that couch last night surrounded by Jane's things, by her books, and cushions and throws and home comforts, by her smell, and by her flaky dog, who eventually crept close enough to lie on her legs until her feet went numb. The storm had swilled around the house and her stomach had swilled right along with it. Her skin had itched, her mind had itched, and her tongue had itched to run to Jane's bedroom and scream out her anger and frustration. But the dog had begun to gently nibble on her fingertips and she'd found the sound of the storm strangely cathartic. She was not alone. A lot of things were being tossed about that night, inside and out.

Around seven o'clock, the storm had abated and weak sunlight poured across the sky. She got up, punched Bill Gerrard's number into her phone, and gave him a wake-up call about her house being left open to the elements by his workmen.

A fallen tree had blocked his driveway but he'd sworn he would be there in just under two hours to look over the damage with her. That gave her time to head back to The White Pig and shower, change clothes, and grab a bite to eat.

She'd been glad to leave Jane's house. She didn't want to talk, not now that the Gerrards had seeped the anger out of her. Jane could stew a little longer, but she'd get hers soon enough.

Renata looked out her bedroom window. The White Pig stood in the town square of High Wallop, but from her vantage point, she could see straight down the valley. The high peak of Gyfu's Coyne stood testament to the old Anglo-Saxon goddess it was named for, and facing it on the other side, the grassy lumps and knolls of an Iron Age hill-fort. *Healing ley lines, my ass.* What was Hegarty thinking?

This was a landscape riddled with old scars and scores yet to be settled. It was prehistoric. People had clubbed each other senseless here over the millennia, and that was the only energy she could pick up on. And now, here she was, with a great big stick of her own.

She checked her reflection again before leaving her room. Pristine as ever. She had worked hard on her cool, blonde Nordic looks. It was a great front, and it sold books.

Even so, she was startled by the wildness in her eyes. There was fear there, too. She knew herself well enough to see it lurking. She blew out a slow, calming breath and counted for five heartbeats. First things first. She'd tear a strip off this half-assed builder, then deal with Jane Swallow later.

"R.B. Braak is a renowned pioneer of the global phenomenon for self-actualization and self-development," Jane read aloud from the Amazon author page. "She has dominated the *New York Times* best sellers list with *Self-Life: Prolonging your Soul's Expiry Date. Heart Hunting: How to Manifest True Love.*" Here Jane snorted rudely. "And *Power Up Your Yin-Yang for Sexual Healing.* Good Lord, Whistlestop, have you ever heard anything like it?" He looked like he hadn't, so she read on.

"R.B. Braak was born in Utrecht and has lived all over the world, calling herself a nomad of the Spiritual Path." She snorted again. "More like one step ahead of the law," she muttered. "She currently lectures in over sixty international cities and offers several online courses for personal manifestation and development."

She glanced up, startled. "I think I've read one of her books, Whistlestop." She swung out of her seat and lurched for the bookcase, avidly examining the contents. "In fact, I'm sure of it. Ah-ha!" She pulled out a tattered paperback and waved it triumphantly at him. Whistlestop slunk around the back of the couch to peek out at her from behind the armrest.

"*Ancient Healing: A Forgotten Art.* See? I told you I had one." She looked at the book with a mix of awe and distaste. It wasn't hers. She remembered Bishop Hegarty pressing it into her hands yonks ago. Renata had bragged he was a fan. Jane had delved into the pages once or twice but found it rather trite. He hadn't wanted it back so it had gathered dust on her bookshelf for the last two years. The author's name, R.B. Braak, hadn't registered. Why would it? Renata had always been Renata to her. Not that she thought of her much.

Well, not that much.

"So now she writes self-help books. Of all the…" Jane couldn't think of anyone less likely to be helpful to her fellow man than Renata Braak, much less be a pioneer of a global phenomenon for self-development. The woman was a con artist. A borderline criminal. A scam artist who had struck it rich somewhere along the way.

"Well, blow me down, Whistlestop. This is where she gets her money from." Jane was confounded. "But why the do-goodery all of a sudden when she could be swindling old ladies out of their pearls?"

The moment she said it, she knew she was being extra mean. Yes, she had excellent reasons to lack faith in Renata, but did she really think her capable of preying on the weak? Her beef with Renata was over a particular issue. She knew the exact day and hour she'd found out the truth about her wonderful, intoxicating girlfriend. *Ex*-girlfriend, she automatically corrected. The exact moment when her world had tilted on its axis and all the wonder drained away.

Even now, thinking about it, the ache of that disillusionment made her stomach feel bruised. She had been cowardly that day. She knew she had, and she understood Renata's anger, but the lack of responsibility went both ways. If Renata couldn't see that, then why was it Jane's burden alone?

The phone rang, demonstrating that the lines had been restored.

She reached for it automatically. "Jane?" She winced as Colin Harper's clipped tone filled her ear. "What's this I hear about our publicist arriving yesterday, *and* it's a woman, *and* you know her?" He sounded peeved. Wendy hadn't wasted a minute. A casual word to Moira and the valley was resonating with gossip. "Does the Bishop know you know her?" Ah-ha, the crux of his problem: had Jane an inroad to the Bishop he had not? She smiled, a little vindicated.

"Yes, Renata's an old acquaintance." She couldn't bring herself to say friend, or anything else remotely pleasant. Even the name stung her tongue. "And I think Bishop Hegarty has been drawing the wool over our eyes. Renata may be here to publicize the festival but mostly it's because they're both ley line fanatics." That was her take on it, anyway. Renata had another agenda other than the festival, so no surprises there.

Colin groaned. "Not that hocus-pocus again."

Jane didn't comment. The Bishop's interests were his own. She only regretted he knew Renata Braak at all. *That* was the only hocus-pocus, as far as she was concerned.

"That's all I know." She began to wind down the conversation. "Sorry I can't help you, Colin." Her favourite words tasted sweeter than ever this morning. It was none of his business that Renata was her new neighbour, or that her house was now a tributary of the Sturry. Colin Harper was another snake in the grass. There were so many of them around these days she'd have to watch her step.

A mechanical hum vibrated through her walls from next door. Bill Snr must be pumping the water out.

"I need to go, Colin. Nice to chat." She quickly got rid of him and put the phone down. If the Gerrards were working on the house, then Renata couldn't be too far away. Time to get up and out. Her war mood from earlier had completely dissipated and she found she didn't want to talk just yet. She was still processing the events of last night and struggling with her own disbelief. One more glance at the open Amazon page did little to dispel her incredulity.

Life had just thrown her a massive curve ball and she was completely unprepared to catch it.

The butcher shop fell silent the moment Jane entered, and her heart fell, too. She'd just walked into a gossip session and she was the theme. All the signs were there. Mrs Agnew was flushed and brazen-faced while Moira held her gaze with an inquisitive stare from behind the meat counter. Amanda and Una, the only other customers, both had the grace to look guilty as they turned to greet her.

"Wendy's just been in with the news," Moira stated baldly.

"She's just an old friend." Jane felt her cheeks heat into two angry spots of colour, making her feel like a painted ragdoll. She cursed Wendy and her blabbermouth.

"Who?" Moira asked.

"Yes, who, dear?" Mrs Agnew pressed.

"My new neighbour," Jane answered perplexed. "I thought you were talking about her?"

"Your new neighbour's an old friend? You mean the writer? Did you know she was moving in next door?" Moira asked.

"No." Jane was properly confused now. "Obviously not."

"Wow. That must have been a surprise," Amanda said.

"A terrible surprise. We've been out of touch for ages."

"You never told me this." Mrs Agnew gave her an accusing stare.

"Well, the subject never came up." Jane knew she was becoming defensive but couldn't help but bristle under Mrs Agnew's slit-eyed look.

"So your friend is this famous writer the Bishop wants to sex up the festival?" Una honed her question into a cutting blade as only an up-and-coming solicitor could do.

"And you never mentioned it before? How could you not know it was her?"

"Because the Bishop never mentioned a name. I only knew as much as you did." When Una raised her eyebrows, Jane glowered. "You're the one who told me it was a man and the surname was Black," she pointed out.

"That was Ranjeet."

"What is her name?" Amanda asked.

"Renata Braak," Jane said and sighed inwardly.

"Renata Bra— Not R. B. Braak? But I love her books!" Amanda made a squeaking noise.

"I've seen your bookcase," Jane muttered.

"Renata Braak is here, in Lesser Wallop? Oh, my God!" Amanda gushed.

"Who's this Renata Braak, then?" Moira asked.

"She's a world-famous self-actualisation author," Amanda continued, gushing. "I love her. She gives spiritual guidance that helps people turn their lives around."

She certainly has me in a spin. Jane was growing glummer by the minute.

"Can I have two pounds of lean mincemeat, please, Moira?" She tried to steer the conversation onto firmer ground. If she got her order quickly, then she could get away sooner.

"You mean she's like a guru?" Mrs Agnew turned her suspicions onto the village newcomer.

"I wouldn't call her a guru as much as a spiritual advisor," Amanda responded.

"It's all new age devildom!" Mrs Agnew announced with a sniff of outrage.

"No, it's not. She's a counsellor for self-development that involves asking the greater good in the Universe for help." Now Amanda was becoming defensive, and Jane empathized.

"So…" Una said slowly. She had her thoughtful face on, and Jane didn't think that was a good sign. "You are best pals with this new age guru who is working for the Bishop on the Beer and Cheese festival that you're head judge of, and she moves in next door to you and gets permission for an ugly garage to be built in a local beauty spot, a building that you highly disapprove of, by the way… And you knew nothing about it?" Her eyes narrowed. "What are the odds?"

"She's not my best pal. I told you, she was an old acquaintance," Jane said.

"Friend," Una corrected. "You said she was an old friend."

"Did I? Just generic. Friend can mean acquaintance, too." She really wanted to melt into the ground.

"Uh-huh." Una raised her eyebrows. "The odds are astronomical," she continued. "Totally astronomical that this situation is playing out this way."

"Has to be the greater good of the Universe," Amanda broke in, sounding a little giddy.

"*She* said 'new age guru'." Mrs Agnew pointed out Una's use of words to Amanda. "And *she's* a lawyer, so *I* must be right."

"I don't care how astronomical the odds are," Jane said, frustrated. "I didn't know it was her next door until last night." The Universe was not working for the greater good. As far as she was concerned, the Universe was being very sneaky.

"Well, *I'm* a doctor and *I* read her books and if *I* say she isn't a new age guru, then she isn't!" Amanda squared up to Mrs Agnew.

Jane looked from one to the other, wondering how she could quietly exit this stand-off.

"Why here?" Moira asked, a question that served to break up the sparring.

"Huh?" Jane turned to her.

"Why'd she come here? I mean, she bought a house here, so she must know the area," Moira continued.

"Um." Jane actually had to think about this question, and it resurrected a hazy half-formed memory she quickly reinterred. This was not the place for an autopsy. "Ages ago—and I mean ages, like maybe sixteen years ago—we were passing by on the coastal hiking path and we came up into the valley and thought it was the most beautiful place we had ever seen." She shrugged, awkward. "I suppose she liked it as much as I did. That trip was why I chose to come and live here. I suppose it must have been the same for her." Another shrug. "But again, we lost touch over the years and I had no idea she had bought the place next to mine. I don't know why you're all so fascinated with her. Aside from her being famous, I mean."

"We weren't at all fascinated until you came in and told us all about her." Mrs Agnew sniffed again. "False prophets is what the Bible calls them."

Wolf in sheep's clothing, more like, but Jane didn't voice that. "So, what did Wendy say, then, if she wasn't on about Renata?" This conversation had totally confounded her since the moment she set foot in the shop.

Moira threw her a dark look that put her on alert. And Amanda and Una moved away, obviously uncomfortable. Only Mrs Agnew stayed put, staring at her avidly.

"She was talking about Tinker's Field," Moira said bluntly. "How the Travellers have returned."

Jane's vision went white, then sparks flashed across it, pulling her focus back to the slabs of meat under the glass counter.

"She went over to your place. You must've just missed her," Moira continued, but Jane wasn't listening. She was already out the door, ignoring Moira calling.

"Here, what about your mince?"

"The wind could've rattled them open," Bill Snr said over the hum of his cranky old water pump. His use of the "could" meant Renata had him beat. His workers were responsible, and he knew it. He just didn't want to make the call to his insurance broker.

"Funny how it rattled open only the windows of the room your men were in," she answered drily. "The door was wide open, too. The next-door neighbour had to go in and close them all in the middle of the night. You can imag-ine the fun." If he put up a fight, she'd cudgel him with a two-by-four. She was in such foul form, she almost hoped he would.

"Jane?" he asked, and his cheeks mottled with ugly red blotches. He deflated before her eyes, all the bluster hissing out of him.

Renata gave him a look. *Oh, so you think well of her, then? Her word means something around here, does it?*

"Ben, fetch that other pump," he yelled. "I'll get it all cleaned up and we'll see to the damage." The water had re-ceded slightly, but the trenches dug all along her backyard were not helping it seep away. Her garden resembled the Somme in winter. It was hard to believe this was her dream, the little corner of the planet she had decided was her next, and, hopefully, final home.

"Good morning!" Officer Goodall came sloshing along the lane, then switched to hopping over the garden fences where the lane had disappeared into the Sturry.

"Good morning, Officer Goodall," she said, and was sur-prised by the bright smile she received.

"Hello, Renata. I'm looking for Jane. I thought she might be around the back with you. God, what a mess. It looks worse in daylight."

"You were here last night, then?" Bill Snr asked.

"Yeah. I had to check on the lower row, but it was okay there. This end caught the worst of it. I mean look at it, it's a midden," she carried on affably, oblivious to Bill's reddening face. "Your guys dug up the lawn and left no sandbags. You even left the house open. Just look at Jane's place, and she did all she could to protect it and she knows what to do in a storm around here."

Renata glanced over at Jane's garden. It looked like wildebeests had migrated through it. It was clear where the excess flood water from her own property had gone. She noticed a long, woebegone face at the window. Jane's greyhound eyed her warily. He dropped out of sight only to momentarily return with her silk scarf in his mouth and continue his unblinking stare. Renata was disconcerted at seeing her thirty-quid scarf in his slobbery chops, and only managed to tear herself back to the conversation in order to witness a high point.

"And since when do you know anything about building, PC Wendy?" Bill Snr huffed.

Wendy's expression darkened and Renata realised she hated the nickname, though she didn't think it was deliberately used to annoy her. Rather, it was probably more the village norm.

"I bet I know more than your son," she replied, snippy. "I mean, tearing out the willows was daft. Anyone can see that."

Bill Snr ignored her and concentrated instead on two of his workmen struggling along the lane carrying a heavy pump between them. "Get that over here quick," he bellowed.

Renata had seen enough. There was nothing she could do here. It would take several hours for the house to clear of water, and Lord only knew how long to dry out. Her schedule was shot. Her builders were clowns and her kitchen would have to be torn out and redone—at Gerrard & Son's own expense, of course.

"I'll be back tomorrow once this mess is cleared," she said, and headed off, not waiting for his reply. If Bishop Hegarty hadn't recommended Gerrard & Son as the best builders in the valley, she'd have kicked them off the job, except she had no idea who to replace them with. She was in a foul mood and was not pleased when "PC Wendy" popped up at her shoulder, walking along with her over squelching lawns and lopsided fences out onto the derelict back lane.

"Jane's not in," she said and looked at Renata as if she could spread light on the mystery.

Renata grunted and preferred to concentrate on where she stepped next in the mire underfoot.

"Is he going to fix it, then?" Wendy asked. "Your kitchen?"

"Damn right he's going to fix it."

"Looks like a tear-it-out-and-start-again job to me." Wendy kept pace with her. "If I buy one of your books will you sign it?"

Again, Renata grunted in a noncommittal way, a little irritated at her switch to that topic.

"Which one should I get? Do you have a favourite?"

She forced herself into less prickly author mode. "How about my latest, *Motivation and Success: Finding the Right*

Mindset for Satisfaction at Work." She guessed "PC Wendy" needed to read that one most. Then, because Wendy was actually a nice person, she felt mean and softened her words with, "I should have a complimentary copy somewhere you could have."

"Wow. I could do with a book like that." Wendy actually chuckled, and Renata wondered why she'd worried. Wendy wouldn't recognise a snub if it bit her on the ass.

"I'm going this way." She nodded to the left, at where she'd parked her car, and began to peel away.

"Me, too." Wendy pulled her bicycle from off the hedge it was propped against and began to wheel it along the pavement, still glued to Renata's side. "I must have missed Jane by minutes. She's probably out shopping."

"Probably." And she didn't care if she was. In fact, she didn't care if she never saw her again.

"You didn't see her this morning, did you?" Wendy asked casually.

"No."

"So, you drove back to High Wallop last night, then? That must have been quite a journey."

Renata hesitated. She was unsure what was being asked here. Alien abductors probed with more delicacy than Wendy Goodall. Did she want it known that she had spent the night on Jane's couch with her bony, awkward-angled dog? Did Jane want it generally known? Renata had a feeling Wendy wasn't the most discreet person. And why was she worrying about what Jane wanted, anyway? It wasn't

Renata's problem. This was Jane's problem. Wendy wasn't Renata's snoopy friend.

"It was okay," she said, wondering why she bothered. She knew Jane to be a reserved, private person who would not approve of Wendy's questioning. Renata knew to stay out of village politics and a vague response felt like the better option.

"You must have had tons to talk about," Wendy prattled on. "My God, Jane's face. I've never seen her look like that in all my life. It's hard to believe neither of you knew you were going to be neighbours. What a laugh."

Renata considered playing this inherent inquisitiveness to her advantage. What that advantage was, or why she felt she needed it, she didn't know. She was acting on instinct now. Sneaky predator instinct. She was a lioness circling a blinking, baffled ostrich. The comparison was just, because Wendy seemed to walk through life with her head buried neck-deep in sand.

"Have you known Jane long?" She began her approach through the long grass.

"Since she arrived." Wendy's face lit up.

Oh, ho, a little bit of a crush, have we? Renata's inner lioness gave a victory growl.

"And we've become the best of friends," Wendy continued. "I wouldn't have gone for the community police officer job if she hadn't encouraged me. I tried for the regulars but failed the entrance test. Jane helped me go for this." She gave her bicycle a little shake as it rolled along beside her.

Renata was slightly moved by her honesty about her failings and the earnestness in her voice. But only slightly.

"Jane says if I do a good job here, then it will help my chances applying to the police service again later on," Wendy said. "It builds up my résumé, Jane says. And because I'm a local, the people around trust me as their representative of the law."

By the second "Jane says" Renata was zoning out. "So, you're a local?" She grappled for another topic. Why had she parked her car so far away?

"Yes. Lesser Wallopian through and through. My parents own The Winded Whippet. You should drop by, it's a lovely place. Very *oldey worldey* with a big fire and great homemade food. My mum's a fab cook." Wendy was very enthusiastic. "The tall, skinny bloke behind the bar is Will, my twin brother, though we don't look anything like each other. He works there on the weekends. Through the week, he has a job in one of the micro-breweries in Cross Quays. If you go there and have your lunch, tell him I sent you." Her face was wreathed in smiles at the idea.

"Maybe I will." Her hire car came into view and she relaxed. Soon she'd be on her merry way. "Do both your parents work there?" she asked casually. She was in an inquisitive mood this morning. Or maybe masochistic.

"Yes. Mum will be in the kitchen and Dad does the later shift on the weekend so Will can go out with his girlfriend, Jill. They got engaged at Christmas. Why are you laughing?"

"Nothing. No reason. I'm just in an astonishingly good mood despite almost having my new home washed away." And this Wendy person was so open, it was hard not to like her.

"You've a good attitude. That's why you write all those books, I suppose. To teach others how to be as happy as you." Wendy swung her leg over her bike saddle. "Well, I better be off and find Jane before someone else tells her about her dad."

"Is there something wrong?" The question was out before she could stop it. She buried any concern at once.

Wendy hesitated. The tremor of an inner struggle crossed her face. "No. Nothing major," she said. It sounded forced. "Nothing much at all."

"Okay." Renata nodded and looked through her handbag for her car keys.

"I just don't want her to get upset."

Renata looked up, it seemed Wendy's inner struggle wasn't over. "That's understandable." It was the only thing she could think of to say. She really wasn't that interested. Really, she wasn't. Right? "Why would she get upset?" she found herself asking.

"Her and her dad don't get on. Hasn't she mentioned it?" Wendy sounded surprised that she knew this about Jane while her old friend didn't.

Renata bristled but disguised it well. Why was she even having this stupid conversation? "You're the one mentioning it. Jane said nothing about it last night." And that was not a lie.

"She didn't know last night. I only found out this morning."

"Found out what?" She almost pleaded, desperate to end this interminably silly, interminably circular conversation with something sensible.

"That he was back in Tinker's Field."

"Ah." Still no sense out of her, but it had always been a high hope. "I'm not a local, remember? Where or what is Tinker's Field?"

"It's a mile down the road towards Cross Quays." Wendy obediently pointed towards the south and the coast. "Where the Travellers' camp is. The council allocated them a special site and built a shower block and electric hook-ups and everything. Keeps them out of the lay-bys and the beach car parks. The tourists don't like 'em"

Renata vaguely remembered a mish-mash of caravans and camper vans behind a high hedge as she drove into the Wallop Valley only the other day. God, only the other day? It felt like years ago. She had definitely aged since her arrival.

"Her dad's Roma?" *That* was news.

"Not quite. He's a Traveller. An Irish tinker but not a gypsy. The Roma are an ethnic minority who represent a segment of the diversity that underscores the social and cultural pluralism today's police force faces." Wendy began quoting from some community policing policy, and Renata quickly interrupted her.

"Okay, he's a travelling hippy. Nothing wrong with that. Or with being Roma." So Jane had become a snob, as well as a first-class bitch.

"No, there isn't. As long as we recognise the homogeneity such overarching terminology invokes and the potential stigmatising—"

"Yes. Yes. I get it. He lives in a caravan and moves around. If he owned a camel, he'd be a nomad." It was a decent enough joke but Wendy only blinked at her. Renata didn't mind. PC Wendy had just made her day even brighter.

"Oh, he hasn't been moving around," Wendy said, expression serious. "At least not for the last two years. He's been in prison and already he's breaking his parole."

CHAPTER 4

Jane rode into Tinker's Field and headed for the top left corner and the grottiest caravan on the lot. The field rose sharply, so she had to push her bike the last few yards past the burned-out bonfires, the totem pole strung with dream weavers, the sweat hut, and the kaleidoscopic graffiti on every nonmoving surface.

Despite the affectations, it wasn't the best site for a travelling community because it wasn't flat enough, but the council had felt obliged to build one and this field was the only place anyone could agree on. And so it was tacked onto the edge of a permanent mobile home park, much to the disgruntlement of the residents. The result was a travelling community dissatisfied with what they had been begrudgingly provided with by a council that wanted them gone anyway.

"Tipper," she called at an ugly, dark green camper constructed out of a twenty-something-year-old transit van. "Tipper." She banged on the side with the flat of her hand. There came a deep porcine snort from inside that told her someone was about. Then a grumbling girl's voice. Jane rolled her eyes. Typical.

The stained curtain at the window pushed aside and the

scrunched-up, sleepy face of a young man appeared and stared at her through sleep-caked eyes. He gave a wide yawn that revealed too many fillings and said, "Hey, Aunt Jane. Wassup?"

His bed companion, thankfully wrapped up to the chest in a dirty duvet, sat up to peek out, too, and Jane was treated to another wide yawn, this one with less dental work, followed by a grunt. "What bleedin' time is this to come banging around people's homes?"

"Good morning, Zoe," Jane answered, then got down to business. "Tipper, can I talk to you for a moment?"

"Sure, the door's open."

"Can you come out here for a second?" Jane did not want to enter that camper van under any circumstances. She had made that mistake once before. Plus, she wanted privacy for what she was about to say. She didn't want to share her family business with Zoe. She may be Tipper's latest squeeze, but he'd more squeezes that an accordion, making Zoe nothing special despite her pretensions.

A few minutes later Tipper Swallow emerged from his camper wearing an orange vest and zipping up his camouflage pants. His feet were bare. The first thing he did on hitting the fresh air was light up a cigarette, then cough his lungs out.

"When did my dad arrive?" Jane got straight to the point.

"Wednesday night. He got a lift down with a load of others." He indicated some vans at the other side of the field and dragged a hand through his dreads. Tipper was white and his dreads were his pride and joy, but he was oblivious to any possible cultural appropriation he might be engaging in.

"And you didn't tell me?" She was genuinely dismayed.

"I thought *he* did," Tipper defended himself. "He had to go down to Cross Quays to arrange for his dole and see the parole officer. Then the storm came and it was too rough to go anywhere. He bedded down here for a few days."

"Where is he?" Jane looked around the camp site. There was an eclectic assortment of vehicles, some so rusted up and broken down that they would never leave. At least not under their own locomotion. The field was beginning to look like a scrapyard. Dogs wandered about and a few children hung out around a play area that was covered in graffiti and litter. She warily eyed the caravan behind Tipper's camper. She knew it was his. The windows were all blacked out. He used it for storage, he'd told her, and she wondered if her father was currently was inside it, snoring off his last bottle of whatever. Tipper casually inserted himself between her and the caravan.

"He's not in there," he said, as if he'd read her mind. "He went into town early. Had to go to the post office to collect his dole money."

"Look—" She paused. What was she to do? "Look. Tell him to call me, okay? We need to talk."

Tipper shrugged. "I'll tell him, but you know how he is."

She did, so she changed the subject. "The Sturry flooded last night. If I ask Amanda about the cleanup for the back gardens, would you be interested? Those Londoners will pay a decent rate to get things back in order."

He visibly brightened. He was a good kid. Maybe not the brightest spark, but not afraid of hard work, either. If he'd had the opportunities in life of, say, Bill Gerrard Jnr, he'd have taken off running. Instead, he was a Swallow and at nineteen, he already had a police record for possession. She hoped those days were behind him. She hoped that by coming down here and getting away from that council estate in Hackney, his luck would change.

"That would be great, Aunt Jane. Say hi to Amanda for me, will you?" He didn't know he wore his crush on his face.

"Of course."

"Tipper." Zoe bellowed from the camper door. She had pulled on one of his tee shirts, though it barely made her decent. "Where's the fags?" she asked. Jane suspected she had been listening in and made her appearance as soon as Amanda's name was mentioned. Zoe was older than Tipper by several years, insecure, and insanely jealous. Jane wished he had never taken up with her. She was one Traveller Jane wanted to see keep on moving.

And there was no reason for Zoe to prickle. Much as she liked—no, loved—her nephew, Jane was realistic enough to realise Amanda would run a mile from a lad like him. Becoming a single mother with two kids had greatly refined Amanda's taste in men.

She waved her goodbyes and wheeled her bike back down the field to the road, accompanied by several barking dogs.

The Winded Whippet was cosier than she had expected. It was nearly empty, too. Renata found a table near the huge inglenook fireplace, where a small fire burned, even though it was June. The inclement weather for the last few days had left a chill in the air and it was hard to believe this was supposed to be the British summer.

The tall, thin lad behind the counter did look a little like Wendy. He had the same brown eyes and sandy-coloured hair that was dry and crinkly and determined to do its own thing. Except his was already thinning. He was polishing glasses, and behind him, a blackboard displayed a huge "Bill of Fayre." If all that it offered was homemade, then Wendy was right—the menu was great, and Renata was impressed.

Her phone beeped and she checked the text message. Andrew Hegarty was running late but would be there soon. She had invited the Bishop to lunch with her, as good a time as any to sift through his theories, though she had little interest in ley lines and the modern earth mysteries movement.

Since her celebrity, there had been an endless chain of authors, would-be authors, and publishers all wanting her to endorse their latest brand of whack-out. These days, she was very choosy who and what she aligned with. She'd struggled all her career against snide "witchy-woo" commentary, and she didn't need to embrace the stuff now. She was a psychologist with a very lucrative side-line, not some wicca chick collecting berries and praising blackbirds. She was, however, beholden to Andrew Hegarty, as he'd actively helped in the purchase of her cottage direct from the church estate. He was a crafty old goat, and now she owed him and his retirement project at least a hearing.

"C'mon, lazy arse. Yer slow." The growling voice drew her attention from her phone back to the bar. Will Goodall seemed to be as good-natured as his twin sister if his response to such an ignorant request for a pint was anything to go by. A misshapen, scruffy man with over-long, greasy hair and an unshaven face had slouched in from the pool room demanding a refill for the glass he slammed on the counter. The Winded Whippet may be *olde worlde*, but it still had an annex full of the usual pub money-spinners—a pool table, juke box, and slot machines, this older and original part being the restaurant and bar area.

Will congenially complied and made small talk as he poured the pint. His reward was a grunt with a fiver tossed at him. Renata was pleased to see him slap down the coins of the man's change in a casual but warning gesture. He would only take so much of the gruff stuff.

She went back to examining the blackboard, trying to decide on her lunch order, when the scruffy man was back. "That machine of yours stole my fucking money."

"It's a blackjack machine. Of course it stole your money." Will laughed.

"No. I mean it took it and didn't let me play."

Will shrugged. "Yes, it did. I can hear it dinging all the way from here."

"Liar. You give me money back."

"I can't do that, Winston. You played the game and lost. I know you did."

The swearing and finger-pointing started. Will's face flushed with anger. He stood tight-lipped and stalwart as the tirade continued. Renata looked around, a little thankful that she was the only one in the bar at this moment, and thereby the only witness to this drunken unpleasantness. A middle-aged woman bustled out from the kitchen, bringing a waft of aromatic smells and the clatter of kitchen noise with her.

"I can hear you all the way back in my kitchen, Winston Swallow," she scolded. "I'll not have you in here causing trouble and using language like that."

Renata sat up straighter. *Winston Swallow?* This must be Jane's father! She felt a little twinge at judging Jane so harshly earlier in that regard.

"What yer gonna do? Call yer girl? PC Wonder," he jeered.

Renata watched fascinated. Jesus, what a wreck he was. And that must be Wendy's mother, who looked nothing like her lanky offspring.

"I don't need to call my girl, or any of the police for that matter, I can toss the likes of you out by myself." She was a plump, rounded woman with massive forearms and broad shoulders that backed up her statement. She looked more than capable of delivering on her promise. Winston was already unsteady on his feet and a sour look of uncertainty flashed across his face.

"Mum," Will said in a warning voice. He looked more than willing to take over from his mother given the word. Winston seemed to realise he had angry Goodalls fore and aft and began to deflate.

"I want me money," he persisted, but in a less nasty tone.

Already Will's mum was shaking her head and thumbing towards the door. "Out. I know what you're like with drink. One too many and you're nothing but bad news, and already you're on the turn. Out before you break something."

"Yer all thieves."

She snorted.

"It's always people like me get banged up while the likes of you thinks you can get away with it with yer hoity-toity pub. Yer all fucking thieves." His voice was rising but he was making his way to the exit. The door swung open and Bishop Hegarty came in. There was an instant—almost comedic—when both men stood face to face in the door-way, unmoving. Then Winston lurched past the Bishop, almost knocking him over.

"And you can fuck off, too," he growled before slamming the door so hard, one of the glass panels cracked.

"I see Winston is back," Bishop Hegarty said, examining the glass with a tut.

Will's mum sighed, and turned for her kitchen. "They should have thrown away the key. He'll be nothing but heartache until he's locked up again. The usual is it?"

"Yes. The chicken and ham pie and a pint of Black Bess, please, Paula."

Will began to pour his pint and Paula disappeared behind the swing doors into the kitchen, letting out another waft of mouth-watering aromas.

"Ah, Renata. I didn't see you there." He came over to join her and tapped a couple of books under his arm. "I have your latest for you to sign, if you don't might indulging an old cleric. And I brought a few books and maps of my own on ley lines and the local archaeology." He patted the bag at his side. "I thought we could peruse them over lunch. Have you ordered yet?"

Inwardly Renata sighed. A lunchtime spent with an advocate for ancient wisdom was the last thing she needed. What she wanted to do was sit quietly and mull over the unpleasantness of Winston Swallow and somehow relate him back to the simple compassion of the woman she had once, a long, long time ago, loved so fiercely that the betrayal still hurt.

"I've not ordered any food yet. I'll have another glass of Chablis and I think I'll order the chicken and ham pie, on your recommendation." It took little effort, the way she moved from dismay to mannerly, but Renata could always swing it. Her thoughts about Jane and her father would be her own. With a smile, she opened the first book he handed her and got out her Montblanc to sign her name.

"So, tell me, Andrew, why am I supposedly here to write about this local beer festival? Is the work you wish to do so delicate, I need a disguise?"

"Maybe *I* need the disguise." He smiled, at ease with the

question. "My research would not sit easy with some of the local parishioners. It's a little too esoteric for some of them. The festival is what it is—a joyous, rambunctious affair, though a line or two from you in a national rag would not go amiss. But the real work is in these." He indicated the books and maps he'd set on the table. "The Wallops hold a mystery, and I need your help in unpicking it."

"And over there is a Bronze Age megalith, just on the rim of Aled's Beacon." Bishop Hegarty held onto his hat in the heightening wind and pointed across the valley. Renata followed his direction with her binoculars, squinting through the light summer rainfall that had caught them off guard.

"You mean the standing stone?"

He nodded. "Now look to the south. See how it lines up with the ruins of Castle Mewley?"

"Mew-*ley*. The 'ley' referring to the waypoint the ley line is guiding you to or from?" She wiped the damp from her forehead.

The rain didn't matter. It was persistent but light and she was happy to be up here on the high ground with a skilled guide. The valley was as beautiful as always, and now she was seeing another side to it, and she was excited. She felt like an initiate and extraordinarily lucky.

"Exactly. Mew-*ley*, Swan-*lee*, Bur-*leigh*, all spelled differently but essentially they are all names for ancient places connected with ley lines, or the old paths. Now, Mewley lines up with that hill over there."

"Yes."

"Well, the name of that area is Saturn Fields and on it are the remains of a Roman villa, and underneath it they found a Bronze Age settlement. It was only discovered a few years ago, but do you see what it means? Do you?" His voice bubbled with excitement.

"You have a triangle," Renata answered, trying to tamp down her own excitement. She hadn't meant to get sucked in, and she'd been determined not to, but Andrew's enthusiasm over lunch had been catching. They had sat on for another hour or so with their coffee and cheese board, examining his books and maps, and talking about his theories.

Andrew Hegarty's intention was to retire within the next eighteen months and move back to the Wallops. As Diocesan for the counties of East Sussex and Kent, he had an official residence in Royal Tunbridge Wells, but had already bought a modest bungalow near High Wallop, where he and his wife, Susan, could enjoy rural life while he pursued his hobby in amateur archeoastronomy.

Looking down from Gyfu's Coyne, the beauty of the Wallops stretched before Renata like a Renaissance tableau. June rainfall tickled her cheeks, but she didn't mind. The breeze was strong yet warm and the rain merely passing over, leaving a promise of good weather for the better half of the day.

Below her she could see the shadow of a raincloud

rolling over the grassy hilltops of the winding Wallop Valley, matting the backs of sheep in misty cobwebs and hanging in jewelled droplets from the barbed wire fences. She swung her binoculars in the direction Andrew instructed and found herself focussing on the ancient oak copse on the western slope, watching it grow darker as its dusty leaves were washed clean. The meandering streams that crisscrossed the gentle meadows were now swollen and purposeful and flowed past small hill farms, through sodden fields down to the Wallop River to run south to the sea.

"And then, through it all, see the old Roman road running directly north to south?" Andrew continued, drawing the collar of his raincoat closer around his chin. "And the cairn at Cross Quays—"

"Wait a minute. That's more geodetic datum than a triangle. What are you saying you've got here, Andrew?" She pulled her face away from the lens and looked at him, sensing this was the crux of almost four years' conversation between them.

"I'm saying they all converge at the church in Lesser Wallop. Every ley line I can find in a sixty-mile radius travels straight through it. Hundreds of them, all at seven degrees of separation. It's uncanny."

She turned to look down the valley towards Lesser Wallop and its small church, its thin steeple crookedly pointing up to a brightening sky.

"St Poe's was built on the site of an ancient pagan temple. It must have been very important in its time to have so much traffic passing through, and so much energy pointed towards it," Bishop Hegarty said.

"Like an ancient nuclear reactor." Renata raised her binoculars again and pointed them back to the rise opposite and above the church. It was a local beauty spot, renowned for its views out to sea. The sweep of her binoculars didn't quite make it to the top of the slope, where hikers would stand to admire the view. Instead, part way there, her gaze fell on a secluded patch of woodland.

Her heart beat harder. She remembered sheltering there from the rain, many years ago, to share a picnic with her companion. She remembered they'd made love until the sun came out and warmed their flesh. She remembered the smell of the damp earth and the wet oak leaves. Angelica and bluebells had surrounded them, and dog-rose and sweet cicely was their bed, and bees had droned around wild honeysuckle as they kissed. A broad-leaved canopy of chestnut and sycamore had kept them dry on the one wet day in an otherwise idyllic summer. A halcyon summer etched deep onto her heart. The summer she fell in love and lay under those very trees cradling Jane Swallow in her arms.

Abruptly, she scanned away, out to sea, the sky, the horizon, a seagull—anywhere and anything to break the spell. Why was this so hard? It shouldn't be, since people fell in love and broke up all day long. The dirty polygamous human race had been doing it forever. She watched the swoop of a white wing. Seagulls mated for life, didn't they?

Maybe she had a seagull heart. The bird suddenly dropped. It plummeted forty feet at twenty-odd miles an hour to be swallowed by the sea. And there you go, she thought. Right as usual.

"It would take a lot more research to corroborate my findings," Hegarty said, sounding anxious. "And then produce the book. I'm talking about years, Renata."

She watched the ripples left by her diving gull for a moment longer. Years stuck here, in this valley next door to Jane. Carefully she put her binoculars away and, forcing a smile, said, "I'm on board, Andrew. I think you've got something here."

And maybe I do, too, though God only knows what it is.

CHAPTER 5

He was sitting at a picnic table smoking a cigarette. "Hello, pet."

"Hi, Dad." Jane slid onto the opposite seat. "How are you?" She averted her head slightly to avoid the cigarette smoke. She'd been cycling over to the office when she'd spied him by the pond on the village green and pulled up.

He shrugged. "As good as expected in the circumstances. It's taking them forever to get me dole money sorted, lazy bastards."

She knew from Tipper that he'd already got his benefits and this was a ruse to borrow money from her. Jane decided she'd lend him some anyway. She reached into her handbag and brought out her purse. He blew a long exhale of smoke off to the side so as not to annoy her while she opened her purse and checked out the notes. She'd stopped off at the bank on the way over knowing she'd need a little extra.

"Here." She handed over fifty quid in tenners. He took it quickly, his eyes never leaving the remainder of the bank notes peeping out of her purse.

"Good girl." He broke his gaze to check the amount then stuffed it into his trouser pocket. Then he stubbed out the butt of his cigarette and pulled a fresh one out of the packet by his elbow in one fluid move.

"How's it been living at Tipper's?" she asked.

"Not my thing." He sniffed. She was surprised at this. He'd lived in caravans all his life. "Got my name down for an assisted living place in Penge."

"Oh?" She wasn't sure why he needed assisted living. She'd contacted the Prison Fellowship in Hackney. They'd offered him a room in a special hostel for ex-offenders, which he'd obviously turned down if he was living in Tinker's Field. She was unsure why he'd done that. "What about the room I got you in Hackney?"

"Don't want it."

"But the people at Hackney can help you. They're specialists. They can sort out a job and—"

"Don't want it."

There was a second of silence while she digested this. "All right," she said. "So, what do you like about Penge and this assisted living setup? Don't you have to be ill, or infirm, or something?"

He shrugged. "I am ill." He coughed violently. The hoarse smokers cough she'd listened too most of her youth. "I'll need a bob or two for the flat. Like a deposit."

Jane frowned. "Usually you don't need a deposit for assisted living. There'll be a waiting list for places like that. And when it's your turn, you get a flat."

"No. It's not like that with this one" He was adamant. Angry, even. "With this one you give 'em the money. The deposit, see? And you jump the queue. Just a couple of grand and I'll be out of yer hair. Can't stand it down at Tipper's place. He's driving me mad, all that jungle music, reggae, whatever."

"Look," Jane began, but she was thinking this through. So the deal was he'd go away if she paid him this "deposit?" Yeah, she knew that wasn't going to happen. "Why don't you send me the details and I'll talk to them?" It was always best to defuse rather than outright deny him. It made things less ugly. This was how she usually dealt with his wilder notions. Ask to see the evidence, some paperwork, something that made sense before she handed over the hundreds or thousands of pounds he was always demanding.

His face went sullen, and suddenly he was pushing his cigarette packet into this jacket pocket and rising to go.

"You're going already?" She was surprised, as it had barely been ten minutes. She'd hoped there'd be more to it.

"Yeah. Gotta meet Zoe. She's giving me a lift down to The Bear," he said, and started walking away without a backward glance or a word of thanks for the money.

She stifled a frown. The Dancing Bear was an unsavoury pub near the docks at Cross Quays. Nobody good went in and nothing good ever came out. She sat watching him leave and considered the conversation. There was no way he was going to get that much money out of her. She was okay with padding out his dole cheque once in a while, and she expected no thanks for that. The day he gave her a genuine "Thank You" was the day she'd keel over.

When she could no longer see him, she got back on her bike.

When Renata and Andrew finally came down from Gyfu's Coyne, it was late afternoon and the sun threw long shadows across the fields. They reached their cars and said goodbye. Andrew turned right for the coast and the A27 back towards Kent, and Renata decided to turn left and head down the valley towards Lesser Wallop. She wasn't ready to sequester herself in The White Pig just yet. Laden with Andrew's information and theories, St Poe's intrigued her.

Once the rain had stopped, Andrew had pulled out his ordinance survey map and shown her how, over the years, he had composed a delicate web of lines from all over the surrounding counties. Each ley line traversed a sacred or ancient site of some sort. The lines cut through medieval castles, Iron Age forts, many churches and even, in one instance, a cathedral. Ancient markers also dotted the filigree design, standing stones, stone circles, cairns and other burial sites, and the core of it all seemed to be the small church of St Poe's.

Bishop Hegarty was definitely onto something, and Renata could feel the thrill of it skipping along her skin and sizzling her synapses. The writer in her itched to peel back the ages and expose the secret.

St Poe's had pride of place in the centre of this mystery. Folklore had it that the ancient site once held a healing water spring, but the well had long ago been bricked up and forgotten. Now the tiny church was struggling for survival in these days of declining congregations and religious apathy. *Empires and gods come and go, determined by the fickleness of man.* Renata mulled that for a bit.

She drove along the road, no more than a lane, really, that led to the church. The Sturry ran behind the fields to her right, and through what remained of its flank of willows, she could see glimpses of Rectory Row opposite and the white picket fences of her neighbours' gardens with the yellows, pinks, and blues of flowerbeds, along with smooth, green lawns passing in a colourful blink.

The air breathed in clean after the cloudburst. Birdsong filled the early evening and the fading sun's rays enlivened the wildlife in the hedgerows. Sheep bleated, and she thought she saw the white flash of rabbit tails darting across the fields. Linnets and yellowhammers chased insects while above them, blackbirds and song thrushes chorused in the slow, sleepy end of the day.

Renata was meant to live in this valley. She knew it, and it soothed her soul. This place was so right for her, destined for her, promised to her—so why was Jane Swallow stuck in the middle of it all? She was the blot on the landscape, she was the anomaly, the alien, the one thing that didn't fit.

St Poe's drew near. Its spindly, twisted spire rose over the squat church and the yew trees that surrounded its walled graveyard. Why would such a nondescript village church have such an unwieldy, wonk-eyed steeple?

Something wriggled under the hedgerow up ahead. The greenery rattled and rustled, and leaves cascaded as the hedge slowly and painfully gave birth to a long brindled, boney backside.

Renata slowed down and watched as Whistlestop righted himself, shook the debris from his coat, and ambled out into the lane in front of her vehicle, as if moving vehicles held no threat for him. She pulled over, got out, and approached him carefully, in case he took it into his head to bolt.

"Whistlestop," she asked gently. "Are you lost?"

In answer, he peed on a clump of oxeye daisies, all the while regarding her patiently until he'd finished his toilette. Then he strolled over to sniff her shoe, peed again on her car tyre, and finally wandered off into the church grounds, seeming very happy with his current state of affairs.

Intrigued, she followed, wondering if she should try and bribe him into her car but also worried about his expensive chewing habits. She didn't fancy paying the car hire company for slobbered seatbelts or lumps missing out of leather headrests.

Maybe it was best to leave him to his own devices? He seemed to know his way around, and the Sturry was through the hedge he'd emerged from, and across a small field. He'd be home in no time. Anyway, it wasn't any of her business what Jane let her stupid dog do. However, while she was here, she might as well investigate the church. Andrew had piqued her interest in the place.

The sturdy wooden gate into the churchyard lay ajar and scraped over the gravel path as she opened it farther. Whistlestop was off to the left in the graveyard, reacquainting himself with his favourite tombstones. Renata decided to follow him into the small cemetery. It was obviously very old and no longer in use. Lichen covered the gravestones, their carved letters so softened by age and the elements that they were almost unintelligible. The most recent graves were in a far corner where the end of day shadows stretched the longest. Two simple, identical tombstones, side by side, for local boys lost in World War II.

Sparrows fluttered from tree to tree and she could hear crickets in the long grass and the drone of honeybees buried head-deep in cowslips and wild thyme. It truly was a restful place, all the more so because nature had been left to soften the edges and gather in the dead.

The tension seeped from her and she felt a queer harmony with the people under her feet. It had been a day of contrasts and her head spun with new and exciting information while her heart contracted horribly at unwelcome memories. It soothed her to stand in the stillness of this place.

The click of a door latch cut through the peace, the scratch of metal upon metal an unnatural intrusion.

Driven to investigate, she returned to the front of the church, where the slowly setting sun painted the stonework a soft rose, and the coastal breeze that wandered up the valley was still warm and gentle. A narrow, mullioned side door lay open, the word "Private" painted on the black oak panelling and, seated on a stone bench off to the side, Jane Swallow raised her face, eyes closed, soaking in the last rays.

Renata hesitated, wanting to draw back and disappear, but the crunch of footsteps on gravel had given her away. She found herself pinned by Jane's clear grey, startled gaze. Renata stepped forward.

"Hello." She felt weak and underprepared for this encounter. She'd wanted to be a raging bull when she next met Jane. An angel with a flaming sword. She wanted to bowl her over with the righteousness of her anger. Instead, she was mellow, relaxed even, and perhaps a little anxious at seeing her so unexpectedly. Not only anxious for herself, but also for Jane, now that she'd seen that train wreck of a father.

Jane had been somehow exposed by him, and a part of Renata felt sorry, as well as guilty, to have witnessed it. Winston Swallow was a man who would do bad by you as quick as blink. It had to have been a hard twenty-four hours for Jane. First her ex and then her father turning up on the doorstep. So much unresolved emotional business to be dealt with all at once. Perhaps some sort of Universal justice was at work? The idea pleased Renata. Jane had been horrible to her and deserved a Universal reckoning. And she felt qualified enough in this area to recognise a big dollop of divine "serves you right" when she saw it.

"Hi," Jane said back, guarded and none too happy at seeing Renata, either. Her eyes went a dark, slate grey, with a worry of her own. "What are you doing here?" It wasn't quite an accusation, but there was suspicion in her voice.

"Andrew told me about this quaint little country church, so I thought I'd take a look." She shrugged and looked around her. "It's sweet."

"Andrew?"

"Bishop Hegarty."

The answer did not seem to please. "Ah, yes. Your great fan, the Bishop. Well, I hope the developers like this place as much as you do. It will make lovely apartments."

"Apartments? He said nothing about apartments. What are you talking about?"

Jane stood to move away, her interest in talking over.

"Wait," Renata called. "I don't understand."

Jane sighed. "This valley has too many churches. St Poe's is under-attended, and between it and St Dunstan's in High Wallop, one of them has to go. There just aren't enough parishioners in the valley to warrant two churches." She cast a despairing look around her. "It will be snatched up for development in a heartbeat. Londoners can't get enough of this valley." She sounded tired. "Now if you'll excuse me."

"And Andrew has to make the decision if the church closes?" This was laughable. Andrew Hegarty was in love with St Poe's. Unpicking its mysteries was to be his life's work, his greatest achievement. This place was a cash cow but in different ways than what Jane thought. No way were developers going to get their hands on this little gem.

"*Andrew* has no say in it. It's down to attendance figures, community interaction, pastoral leadership, and whether St Poe's is seen as an essential ministry. The final decision is an ecumenical one that considers the constitutional by-laws, and this particular church's strengths and weaknesses against all others. The Archbishop will take council and then make the final decision, not Bishop Hegarty."

"Ah." Renata wondered if Andrew was secretly as worried as Jane seemed to be. He'd not mentioned this little speck of sand in the cogs of his retirement plan. And why was Jane so upset? Did she attend church here? Renata almost laughed aloud at the thought. Jane the goody two-shoes churchgoer. Had her wild lesbian lover—*ex-lover*—reinvented herself so she could integrate into this sleepy valley with its simple farming folk? Ridiculous. She had to be in some sort of witness protection programme or something.

The laughter swelled up inside her. *Jane Swallow a holy-roller.* Jane Swallow, who had run around the beaches of Greece naked as the day she was born. Loved outdoor sex, smoked pot, and drank wine like it was water. More unwanted memories that made her stomach cramp.

"What's the big joke?" Jane's voice was tight. Renata wondered if she'd read her thoughts.

Well, read this. "I saw your father today. That was a joke."

Jane stiffened, but Renata had her attention and ploughed on. "They were chucking him out of The Winded Whippet. He almost took the good Bishop with him on this trajectory out the door." It was a nasty thing to say, but anger fuelled it. The peace she'd had in the graveyard dissipated like soap bubbles, popping one by one until all that was left was a bitter residue in her mouth.

"If that was meant to hurt, then you missed the mark." Jane turned on her full force. "I also saw my father today. Do you really think there is any snide comment or humourless quip you can make that could embarrass or hurt me more than growing up with a man like that?"

Renata felt her face burn, and her anger burned along with it.

"As much as I hate his pollution of the place I call home and all the garbage he brings with him," Jane said, "it's still not half as distasteful as seeing *you* again. Obviously, I have somehow, inadvertently, kicked over a rock." Jane flung her hands up in disgust.

"I'm not here because of you," Renata said. "Please get that idea out of your head. I was approached by—"

"I have no idea why Bishop Hegarty invited you here. The Beer and Cheese Festival does all right on its own, thank you very much. We don't need a publicist." Jane pointed directly at Renata, who took an involuntary step back and was at once annoyed with herself for doing so.

"If there's money to be made, then people like you won't be far behind," Jane continued, "so don't play dumb with me over the developer's thing. I know you're up to something, Renata Braak. Your type is always up to something."

Renata was completely blindsided by this argument.

What the hell was Jane going on about? There were no developers, just a barmy old bishop and a hell of a good book to write.

"And understand this," Jane said. "I am disinterested in our past, or in discussing any aspect of it. I owe you nothing and I expect nothing from you. Do you understand me?" She finally fizzled out, the fireworks display well and truly over. "So, as long as you're here, let's at least try and be cordial towards each other." Her last words came out lamely, as if she didn't believe them, either.

"And this is how you plan to start? This is your idea of cordiality?" Renata exploded. "You have one hell of an opinion of yourself. Poor Jane wanting the peaceful life with all her dirty laundry shoved away in some deep, dark closet. Well, surprise, surprise, I didn't come here to out you. The Universe, in its infinite wisdom, plonked you into the middle of *my* life. My—up until yesterday—very prosperous, happy life!"

Jane snorted. "I thought manipulating the Universe was what you were all about. You manipulate everything else."

"I'd rather my house washed into the Sturry than live beside you."

"The house I did my best to save?"

"If you'd have known it was mine, you'd have let it drown and me right along with it."

"That's nonsense. And as usual, here we go with the drama."

"This is not drama. This is emotion and I have a right

to own it and to express. You said some pretty hurtful things."

"Is that one of your worldly, wise platitudes for your gullible public—own your emotions?" Jane came back at her. "And I think you're forgetting, you started this by laughing at my father."

"You hate your father."

"No. I am disappointed in my father. I hate *you*. Now go away. I'm not going to shout on church grounds." She looked away and her face contorted into a look of shame. "Oh, Whistlestop. Oh, darling, I'm sorry. I'm so, so sorry. I didn't mean it. We didn't mean it."

Renata looked over to where Whistlestop cowered, backed up into a corner of the doorway. He sat in a puddle of his own urine, his tail between his legs and shaking all over. There was a look of abject fear in his eyes. Guilt ricocheted through her and she automatically followed Jane's lead in comforting the dog. They brought him over to the bench, where they sat side by side and stroked his head and flanks until his trembling eased.

"Easy, boy. Easy. I'm sorry your mummy's a shrill harpy," she crooned.

"People are stupid, Whistlestop. Don't listen to them." Jane whispered in his silky ear. "Especially her. She'll steal the biscuits out from under your nose and tell you the Universe did it."

"You really care for this old duffer, don't you?" Renata said, seeing a spark of someone she used to know.

Jane had her face buried in his neck. "Yes." Her voice was muffled. "We all need something to love. That pearl of wisdom's in one of your books, isn't it?"

"You read my books?" This was surprising, but already Jane was shaking her head.

"The Bishop gave me one. I dipped in and out." She made it sound like a cold bath.

"Are you friendly with Andrew?"

"Of course. He's my boss."

"Boss?"

"Don't pretend you don't know. That's what all this storming around and shouting has been about, hasn't it? Your one little piece of power in my life and of course you abuse it."

"What are you talking about?" Renata felt herself bristling again and tried to push it down so as not to upset Whistlestop, but he'd already sensed her darkening mood and began to shift away from her petting hands.

Jane stood in disgust and drew him with her towards the gate. "For whatever reason—revenge, spite, malice— you want to ruin the life I've built for myself in Lesser Wallop. My father does it because he can, and at least he doesn't pretend to have a reason because he's just mean-minded. You, however—you need an excuse. You need to feel wronged so you can pretend to be righted through your own spiteful methods. I know you want to hurt me, but in doing so, you'll destroy St Poe's. But, then, what do you care? You probably have an investment in developing it."

"For the last time, what the hell are you on about?" Renata rose to her feet, angry and unable to hide it.

Jane pointed to the hand-painted board by the church gate. The sign Renata had walked past when she'd followed Whistlestop into the graveyard.

It read:

Saint Poe's, Lesser Wallop. Founded, circa 1348.
This building, dedicated 1793.
Sunday: Morning Service 11.00
Evensong 7.00
Eucharist: Wednesday, 7.00 p.m.
Rector: The Reverend Jane Swallow

CHAPTER 6

*R*ector: *The Reverend Jane Swallow.*
Rector: The Reverend Jane Swallow. Renata had to read it several times before it sank in.

Rector: The Reverend Jane Swallow.

Jane is a priest! No, a rector or reverend, or whatever. She's a fucking rector!

Then she became aware she was standing alone blinking up at the signboard. Jane and her dog had gone. She could see them across the field walking slowly back towards the Sturry and Rectory Row. There had to be a bridge or crossing point somewhere along the riverbank to access the back lane to their houses. Renata wanted to call after her. To run after her and talk more. *You're a rector now? What the hell happened in the time since we parted?* But as usual, Jane had run away before Renata could find out anything.

Deep in thought she returned to her car and headed back to her hotel. Her life these last few days had been the utmost weird. The Universe was telling her something, or maybe some god somewhere was telling her something, and so far, she was clueless as to how to interpret any of it.

She dined alone, though not room service. She wanted people around her—not to interact with but more to observe.

This silly puffed-up little town fascinated her. It was so different from Lesser Wallop, lording it over the smaller village with its pretensions and snobbery and all over nothing. The main square featured an ugly Victorian fountain surrounded by impractical cobblestones damaged beyond repair by modern traffic. Planters lined the pavements but were filled with the dullest most regimented flowers imaginable, not the riotous and rebellious bursting of colour from the gardens of Lesser Wallop.

The shops here were franchises, plastic cut-outs that could be found in any high street in any town in the country. Lesser Wallop had locally owned businesses. Weird and wonderful little cake shops with bric-a-brac furnishings. There was an artisan bakery, a butcher shop with the best local farm meats, and a greengrocer who proudly advertised produce from the surrounding fields. All the things that would make a suburb hyper-desirable in London were easily taken for granted in Lesser Wallop. There was no hullabaloo about quality because quality was the norm, and to be expected.

Her meal was very good, but not as good as the pie she'd had at lunchtime at The Winded Whippet. That was an exceptional pie. Wendy had been right to boast about her mother's cooking. Renata congratulated herself once again for following her dream and buying in the valley that had captivated her all those years ago.

When Bishop Hegarty first contacted her, she had been surprised. Few men of the cloth would have been seen dead with her books, but here was a diocese bishop for the southeast corner of England engaging with her in interesting and educated dialogue. His interests were wide and varied but at their core, always spiritual. As trust grew, Andrew Hegarty opened up about the true nature of his investigations into the metaphysical world. And through that he inadvertently reintroduced her to the Wallops and stirred up memories of happier times.

Andrew had rekindled her love for the valley, and he had helped her purchase a home there. Of course, it meant she was now in some way beholden to the sly old goat, but it was a fair payoff, especially as the project he had in mind excited her, too.

She mused over the need to hide their real motives under this publicity writer-for-the-local-festival nonsense, but appreciated he had to protect himself from the ol' witchy-woo comments—at least until he retired. Then people could call him whatever kind of lunatic they wanted. That was the way it worked in her profession. You had to fly over the asinine and spit down on them from your broomstick.

She was smiling at her own joke as she left the restaurant and entered the hotel foyer. PC Wendy was loitering there, obviously off duty. She wore a nice, though slightly dated dress with a mismatched handbag and flat, unbecoming shoes. She awkwardly hung around the foyer, fiddling with tourist leaflets and glancing up anxiously every time someone came in from the street. It would be impossible to walk past her unnoticed, so Renata approached her with a friendly, "Good evening, Wendy."

"Oh, hi." Wendy blushed puce and Renata wondered what she had been caught red-handed at.

"Nice to see you again. Are you here for a meal?"

"Um." Wendy shifted from foot to foot. "Well, the truth is, I'm on a date." She flushed even more violently.

"Ah."

"Except I think I've been stood up," she blurted.

"Oh." Renata felt a little disarmed by the candid statement. "Perhaps they're running late."

"Maybe." Wendy brightened.

There was a moment of awkward silence that Renata decided to nip in the bud before it overwhelmed them both. "Why don't you join me in the bar while you wait?"

"Oh, yes, please." She sounded relieved and Renata was glad she'd asked.

Two gin and tonics ordered, they settled into a quiet corner, where Wendy could still observe the entrance.

"Can I ask who you're expecting?" Renata asked, and for a chest-clenching, achingly stupid moment, she thought Wendy was going to say Jane.

"Someone called Mike Aldershot. It's an online thing. I'm not even sure what he looks like, as the picture he posted was a holiday snap. So unless he appears wearing Bermuda shorts and holding up a sea bass, I may miss him entirely." It looked as if she didn't mind too much if her romantic evening was a washout.

"So, how long have you been a community police officer?" Renata guided the conversation onto safer ground.

"Coming up to eighteen months. It was Jane who made me apply."

"Yes, I remember you saying." Why did everything have to go back to Jane?

"And she helped Amanda set up her cleaning empire—I mean cleaning business, though it might as well be an empire, she has so many clients on her list now."

"Super." The Reverend Jane Swallow, patron saint of rural industry.

"Did you know Amanda was a doctor? Not a *doctor* doctor. She's a university doctor. But she can't find a job, so she does cleaning instead. She's also a single mum. Lauren is eight and Julie is five. They're a couple of sweeties."

"It sounds like she's got a lot on, but I don't know who Amanda is," Renata said.

"D'oh! I'm being stupid. You really need to come along to our quiz night and meet the gang. It's every Tuesday at my parents' pub."

"I think I'll be back in London by Tuesday."

"Oh, that's a pity. I thought it would take longer to fix your kitchen. Amanda has got Tipper sorting out all the trashed gardens. You should talk to her about getting your place back in order. Tipper's good with plants."

"Tipper?"

"Jane's nephew."

Of course, it had to be Jane's nephew. Her name hadn't

been mentioned for at least three minutes. "Never met him, either."

"He's okay. Nice kid, but I have to keep an eye on him 'cause of the...*you* know."

Renata shook her head. "Believe me, I don't know."

Wendy leaned in and Renata found herself following suit. Wendy whispered, "The whacky baccy."

Renata slowly straightened back into her seat. "Wow. Jane really is the white sheep of the family."

Wendy guffawed. "You're funny. I can see why she likes you."

A stab of pain nearly cut Renata in half.

"It's hard to believe she's only been here for two years. I'm so glad Bishop Hegarty persuaded her to come."

"The Bishop is a wily man," Renata said drily. Andrew Hegarty had to keep the small parish church open come hell or high water or else his retirement plans would go up in incense smoke. He needed Jane, or someone like her, to keep the place from going under. "So, he knew Jane from before?"

Wendy nodded. "I'm not sure from where, but he thought very highly of her and really wanted her for this parish. It didn't half put Colin Harper's nose out of joint."

Before Renata could raise her eyebrows, Wendy sailed straight into an explanation. "Colin is the Rector of St Dunstan's, up here in High Wallop. He wanted to have both churches for himself, but I bet he'd hardly ever use St Poe's, and it would end up being holiday homes or church storage or something."

Renata shrugged. "Looks like a 'use it or lose it' situation to me. It's up to the parishioners of Lesser Wallop to save their own church."

Wendy looked a little guilty. "I know. But the big supermarket is here and most people go to St Dunstan's on a Sunday morning, then on to do their shopping."

"Do you do that?"

Wendy squirmed. "No, but I don't go to the morning service, either," she confessed. "I go to evensong, though. I like my Sunday morning lie-in, then I meet Jane at The Winded Whippet for lunch. Mum does a wicked Sunday roast." She looked Renata directly in the eye and asked, "Is it mean to skip the morning service? Jane would never say so, even if it was."

"I don't know. You have to live your life, and it's hard to get people into church these days, anyway. Attendance is falling all over the country. I bet St Dunstan's isn't packed either despite the supermarket."

"Colin's sermons are boring," Wendy said, and giggled. "He's a pompous ass, truth be told. He wants everything for himself and his parish. Like the Beer and Cheese Festival. Every year he tries to get it moved up to High Wallop. He can be very sneaky."

"Tell me about this festival." She might as well use the opportunity to find out more about the event that was to be her cover story. Andrew could hardly admit he'd brought her here for his own uses. When Wendy looked surprised, she added, "It's a word-of-mouth technique. Lets me see things from the inside. An investigative journalism thing."

"Excuse me, but you wouldn't happen to be Wendy Goodall?" A chubby man in a too-tight navy blazer stood beside them. He was perspiring but smiling eagerly.

"Yes. Are you Mike Aldershot?" she asked.

He nodded. "Yeah, sorry I'm late. I missed my bus."

Renata acknowledged his hello and left them to it. She was tired now. A night spent on a short couch with a long dog was not conducive to good rest, especially when it was followed by such a weirdly disturbing day. She looked forward to her acres of big, soft hotel bed.

Removing her mascara before her bathroom mirror, she examined her tired eyes. She was exhausted, but it went deeper than that. She was emotionally wrung out, like some limp old dish rag. It was hard to believe only twenty-four hours had passed since she had arrived in the valley. An intensely unsettling twenty-four hours. A lot had unfolded, and she still didn't know what to make of it all.

Her deeply engrained image of Jane had been completely deconstructed and was slowly being rebuilt into something else, something new, and she wasn't sure what that was yet, only that it was affecting her profoundly. She did know one thing, though. She had been brought here, and not just by Andrew Hegarty.

Three faces looked up earnestly at her. The other parishioners were rustling about in their pews with their psalters and hymn books, and in some cases, she suspected, a bag of sweets.

"Let us join together in singing hymn number one seventy-one, 'Can You Count the Stars'." A discreet nod to Mrs Agnew soon had the old organ wheezing out the opening chords as all twenty-two of the congregation heaved to their feet and frantically flipped pages to the correct hymn.

It was the last song of the morning service, and even with Mrs Agnew's flourishes and garish musical ornamentation, it went quickly. Jane gave the last prayer while they were still all on their feet, keeping in mind that the majority of her elderly congregation had trouble standing and sitting repeatedly.

The main door gave its distinctive creak partway through her "glories above" and she cracked open an eye to see Renata Braak slip into the back pew beside a surprised but obviously pleased Wendy. The fact that Wendy had turned up this morning was a delight, but now it was tarnished. Had she planned to rendezvous with Renata? Jane decided she was being paranoid. Who plans a rendezvous in the back pew of a church? Renata was just being weird and stalker-ish. Another flash of paranoia ran through her. Renata was freaking her out.

Prayers done, she turned her attention to what was becoming, for her, the most depressing part of the morning service.

"Now we'll conclude by reading out the Praise be for our Blessings for this past week." She reached for the small wooden box with its postal slit in the lid and opened it. This box was kept near the door, and the idea was for parishioners to deposit a small note giving thanks for something good that had happened to them that week. Then Jane would read it out from the pulpit on Sunday and people would support and congratulate each other in life's little victories.

A simple, pleasant idea. It had worked well in Jane's previous posting, but the residents of Lesser Wallop were an unimaginative bunch at best. Jane read the first note.

"Mrs Braddock gives thanks that her sister in Brisbane had a successful hysterectomy." Mrs Braddock beamed up at her, while the rest of the congregation was noncommittal. "Yes, that is good news, Mrs Braddock. I'm happy to hear it," Jane said. There should have been a chorus of "Praise be" from those surrounding Mrs Braddock, but it only came forth when Jane patiently pressed for it. "Let's hear a praise be for Mrs Braddock's sister's good health."

The next note was from Mrs Agnew, who always had a blessing to share. "Mrs Agnew is thankful that her recipe for lardy cakes worked so she can make some for the Conservative Society's open day." She'd have to remind Mrs Agnew—*again*—not to bring politics into it. "Praise be," she said quietly. Mrs Agnew rewarded her from her seat by the organ with a regal bob of the head.

"Mrs Mars, chairwoman of the local WI, also gives thanks for the éclairs and canapés she and her Women's

Institute sisters were able to provide for the local Labour candidate's visit," Jane read out the next note.

"Praise be to you, too, Mrs Mars," she said, but Mrs Mars and Mrs Agnew were engaged in a glaring contest and ignored her. The rest of the congregation, however, happily chorused "Praise be," confirming their political allegiance as Labour.

Definitely no more politics. She'd add an addendum to the next church newsletter.

Jane sighed. She could feel the pressure building inside her, self-consciously aware of Renata watching this hopelessly ritualistic humiliation from the sidelines. The last piece of paper had a child's handwriting.

Jane's heart fell as she recognised it. She took a deep breath. "Emily Mars would like to thank God that Momo, her hamster, ate only three of her babies before she could get there and rescue the last five. And she hopes the three eaten hamster babies are now in heaven. Also, she has hamsters to give away to a good home if anyone wants one." Oh, Lord.

Eight-year-old Emily Mars shone with happiness from her seat beside her mother. She gave Jane the most beautiful, generous smile she had received in a long time, and Jane remembered what the weekly blessings were all about. She smiled back and opened her mouth to speak, when from the back of the nave came the singular and very recognisable voice of Renata Braak, barely disguising her laughter, saying, "Praise be."

"I invited Renata to join us." Wendy slid into the seat beside Jane and checked out the specials blackboard. "I don't know why I look," she said, almost apologetic. "It never changes."

"What?" Jane started in her seat.

"It never changes," Wendy repeated, pointing to the blackboard. "It's been the same menu since I was eleven."

"I meant about Renata joining us for Sunday lunch."

"Oh. Did you see her in church? That was nice, wasn't it? We wanted to support you."

"Yes, I saw that. Thank you. But you don't have to invite Renata to everything we do."

"I like her."

Of course she did. Jane fought not to show her exasperation. "It's just that she's a busy woman and I don't want her to feel obliged, that's all."

"Hi." Renata appeared by her elbow, and Jane had no way of knowing if she'd overheard her plaintive bleat. It bothered her that maybe she had and knew about her discomfort. After the words they'd exchanged the last time they'd met, she wondered why Renata was hanging around. What was she up to? Something about it made her uneasy—an uncomfortable echo from their past and the understandable lack of trust she had for her.

Completely ignoring the go-away vibe Jane was emanating, Renata pulled out a chair and sat down beside her.

"I enjoyed your sermon this morning."

Jane gave a soft snort. "You were only there for the last ten minutes and I heard you laughing."

"C'mon. That hamster thing was hilarious."

"Emily is genuine," Jane said, trying not to sound like she was lecturing but she knew she failed. "She wants to participate. Unfortunately, she wants to participate every week." She was torn between defending one of the youngest in her flock and accepting that the weekly Praise be's were becoming a little ridiculous.

"Remember how cut up she was when she found out what slug pellets do? How they poisoned the birds? That was a tough Sunday." Wendy shook her head ruefully. "She told me today that she wants to be a nun."

"Last month she wanted to be a missionary," Jane said.

"Looks like you have an admirer," Renata said.

Jane fought a glare at her. "Oh, soon she'll discover ponies and gymkhanas and that will be that." She wasn't sure if she'd imagined a certain slyness to Renata's words or not. She looked as innocently engaging as ever. She was a handsome woman, and she was not unaware of the interest they were receiving from nearby tables. News of the famous and attractive writer who had just moved into the valley had everyone agog.

A hand on her shoulder actually made her jump. "Sorry, Jane," Amanda was by her side. "Didn't mean to startle you. I just wanted to tell you I have an interview for the Open University job. The one you sent me the details for." Her smile was a mile wide and her fingers tightened into an excited squeeze on Jane's shoulder.

Jane reached up to cover Amanda's hand with her own. "I am so pleased, and not a bit surprised. When is it? Do you need a babysitter?"

"Next Monday, and I have the kids all organised, thanks. Moira will collect them from school with her own mob. I'll be back by teatime, anyway." Her gaze fell on Renata and she hesitated awkwardly and Jane sighed internally.

"Oh, you haven't met Renata yet. Renata, this is Amanda Crane, a good friend and someone who loves your books."

Amanda grinned and held out her hand. "I do love your books. I have them all."

"Wow. Thanks." Renata shook hands.

"The one on dealing with separation and not being afraid to be alone really helped me when my relationship broke down." It was a very genuine and blunt admission and caught Jane by surprise. She hadn't known Amanda when the father of her children left her for a woman he had met at work. She only knew he had moved away and wasn't in touch anymore. She hadn't considered how Amanda had coped at the time.

"I'm happy to hear that," Renata said.

"Well, I better be getting back to the kitchen. I'm your dishwasher this afternoon. Nice to have met you, Renata," she said. "See you guys at the quiz on Tuesday." And with a final cheerio for the table, she headed for the kitchen.

"She's lovely," Wendy told Renata. "She's so smart. *And*

she's a doctor."

"So you said," Renata confirmed.

When had Wendy and Renata had that conversation? Jane shoved down the shimmer of jealousy beginning to taint her world. "A doctor who washes the dishes in your mother's kitchen?" Renata continued, almost tsking.

"She has a doctorate in classical history. She's not a medical doctor," Jane explained, trying to keep the defensive tone out of her voice. "Academic work is hard to come by, so she does what she can."

"Of course she does. She's got a family to feed. Wendy already told me." Renata's reply brought another spike of what Jane decided was not so much jealousy as insecurity. She didn't like Renata circling her life like this. It reminded her of a boa constrictor looping around its prey before its coils tightened.

"Roast chicken for me." Wendy had moved on to the food. "What do you want to drink? Jane and I usually share a bottle of wine on Sundays."

"A rector who drinks on a Sunday. Oh, my," Renata joked. "If you don't mind, I'll join both of you in a bottle. And I'd like the roast beef, I think."

"The beef for me, too," Jane said, and Wendy went over to the bar to place their order. Once they were alone, she turned to Renata and spoke in a low voice, well aware of the nosiness of Lesser Wallopians. "What are you doing?"

"Hanging out with my new friend, PC Wendy. Bedding in with the local community. Trying to fit into my new home. What did you think I was doing?"

The reality of it struck Jane. Renata Braak was back in her life. She had moved in beside her and would slowly take over all her friends until Jane's existence became so uncomfortable, so unhappy, it would be over for her in this valley. She briefly imagined St Poe's closure, and her last sermon and the final padlocking of the old oak doors. She saw herself packing up her office and solemnly shaking hands and saying goodbye to Bishop Hegarty. She would have to move away to another parish somewhere else. Probably someplace where everyone was a drug addict and she'd be mugged in the church carpark. Somewhere that was not here, not her dream, somewhere that was not the Wallops.

And for all the nights she had lain awake imagining it, this time it didn't feel quite so bad because of the woman sitting next to her. Renata hated her. She wanted revenge for Jane leaving in order to prop up her feigned innocence. For all that it hurt to lose everything and pack up and go— and it probably would happen this year, if not the next— Jane would be glad to move away from Renata and this tempered trap.

"Where did you go?"

She blinked. Renata was talking to her. Had even been staring at her. She hadn't realised her mind had drifted. She sat up straighter and began to play with her cutlery.

"Where did you go?" Renata asked again. "You looked troubled."

And why the hell not? You're here, my father's here, my job is on the line. "I'm fine," she lied. "I was just thinking." She looked around for Wendy, who was yakking away with someone at the bar.

Renata looked disappointed at her answer. "Amanda seems nice," she said, in a pathetic attempt at social mores. She obviously had Amanda in her sights next, now that Wendy was a pushover. Jane turned on her.

"I know what your game is."

"You do?" Renata sounded surprised. "Please share, 'cause I don't have a fucking clue how I ended up here. This is not what I envisioned for my happy ever after, and believe me, that's what I was aiming for." Her voice became harder.

"What exactly is your problem with me? Is your ego so gargantuan it can't cope with being dumped? Do you normally stalk your exes around the globe until you get a satisfactory answer as to why you were unsatisfactory?"

Renata snorted. "You really are a mean little troglodyte, aren't you? I didn't follow you. You just got here quicker. Remember when we hiked through this valley and got caught in that rainstorm?"

Jane blushed violently, much to her annoyance. It had been a spectacular afternoon in so many ways. Thunder and lightning that blended with the most amazing orgasms…They had fallen in love with the valley, and a little with each other that day. That afternoon was the start of it, their summer of love, and from there it just grew—until it popped.

Renata was talking quickly, as Wendy headed back to the table. "I said that I wanted to live here. *I* said it *first. Me,* not you. You dumped me in Greece. Left me penniless with no explanation, nothing. You simply disappeared. You were a bitch and I'll never—"

"I ordered the merlot. Dad says it's nicer than the shiraz." Wendy slid in beside them.

"Okay," Jane said.

"—forgive you."

Wendy frowned and looked first at Renata then at Jane.

"You know what? I just remembered I had something to do," Jane said, struggling to keep her voice calm. "I'll call you later, Wendy." She stood.

"But I just ordered—"

"I know. I'll get my food take away. Here's some money for my share of the bottle. Sorry to be a bother." She set a couple of bills on the table and went to the bar before...before what? Before she cried, maybe. A few minutes later, she had her food and she slipped out, willing herself not to look at the table where Renata and Wendy sat, her eyes blurring with tears as she emerged onto the street.

"There's a gentleman waiting for you." The receptionist at The White Pig nodded discreetly towards a tall man patiently examining the tourism leaflets in the foyer. Renata didn't recognise him.

"Do you know who he is?" she murmured and collected her key.

"Reverend Harper." The answer revealed nothing.

Renata approached him. "Excuse me. I'm Renata Braak. You wanted to speak with me?"

"Ah, yes. Colin Harper." He stuck out a hand and gave her a cool handshake. "The Reverend Colin Harper. I've been wanting to meet you for some time. Shall we?" He gestured to a table in the corner of the foyer.

Renata was reluctant to be herded along, so she stood her ground. "Can you tell me what this is about?" she asked, though she had a good idea. "Do you want me to sign a book?" She delicately informed him of her celebrity, and that she could not be manhandled easily, and that she was certain her time was more precious than his.

"Oh." He looked surprised at her question. "No. It's...It's about the project you're doing with the Bishop. Bishop Hegarty."

She hadn't expected the Bishop to share his plans with anyone, so she was cautious. "What project?"

"Why, the Beer and Cheese Festival. You *are* going to do a piece on it for the national papers, aren't you?" He sounded alarmed that she wasn't.

"I've just begun gathering information," she said carefully. She slowly moved towards the table he had indicated.

"Then I'm certain I can be of help." He ordered a pot of coffee before asking if she drank it. "Oh, I'm sorry. Perhaps you prefer tea?" The thought suddenly occurred to him. A man used to getting his way and not by considering others, especially women. She disliked him at once but refused to show it.

"Coffee will do," she said graciously, but only because she did prefer it, and took out her Moleskin notebook and pen, pleased that he noted the Montblanc. Little smatterings of wealth mattered to men like Colin Harper, and gave her the upper hand.

"So, Colin." She used his first name and he preened. "Tell me about the festival."

"First, let me tell you about the cricket field we have here, so much better than that cramped little village green..."

CHAPTER 7

Monday morning, Renata returned to the cottage to meet with Bill Gerrard and assess the damage after the water had been pumped out. The Sturry was back to its normal level and the washed-out lane had been hastily repaired. Her backyard still looked like Swamp Thing vacationed there. Not that it mattered when a third of it was marked off for laying the foundations of her garage. An idea she was actually beginning to question.

Jane's garden was so much improved since her last visit, she could only imagine she had been out labouring in it night and day. And when she took time to appreciate the gardens strung out on the other side, the holiday home gardens with their absentee owners, she realised this was truly a lovely stretch of property. The long flow of colourful gardens nestled sweetly beside the ambling stream made a garage seem more and more alien to the harmony of the place. More ruinous somehow. She'd break the news later to Bill Snr that she'd changed her mind. Best to keep him concentrated on fixing her kitchen first before demotivating him by stripping away his work expectations.

She had already gone through her to-do list with him and decided—given his obvious disgruntlement—that it was time to leave him to pass his unhappiness on to his son, who was skulking somewhere on a mission of high avoidance.

Several gardens down, Amanda waved up at her. This surprised her, as she'd barely been introduced to her. She waved back, and Amanda waved again, signalling her to come down to her. It looked secretive and urgent. Renata frowned. This was unexpected.

She walked slowly down the lane, keeping an eye on Amanda to see what she would do next. As she got closer, Amanda ducked into a greenhouse and signalled for her to follow. It all seemed very stealthy and Renata was intrigued. Village life was anything but quiet.

"Look," Amanda said as soon as Renata stepped foot inside the door. She was pointing to rows and rows of tiny little Hessian pots with small green shoots beginning to emerge inside each one, and seemed very unhappy at the sight.

"So?" Renata would have expected as much in a greenhouse.

"Do you know what that is?"

Renata shrugged. "Something green. I'm not a gardener."

"What is green and *not* a good thing to find in a client's greenhouse?"

"A Martian?"

"What?" Amanda glared at her. "Are you serious? This is no joke."

Renata laughed. "You're right. I'm dicking around. Sorry. It's grass. Anyone can see that." She was not averse to a toke once in a while. It was relaxing in her more stressed-out moments, which were a little too frequent recently. "You got a little weed factory going on here, Amanda. Some Londoner's cottage industry, I'd imagine."

"Not *some* Londoner. He's been out of London for a year now. This is Tipper's work," Amanda said, and immediately began chewing on her fingernails.

"Tipper? Jane's nephew?"

"Yes," Amanda hissed as if Jane could pick the name on the wind at several hundred paces.

"How do you know?"

"Because I just do. He's a little ferret. No one in this village does this sort of thing. Oh, they'd all smoke it given half the chance, but no one is stupid enough to supply it. Except for Tipper. He's got a record. And he's helping me with the gardens, so he's had opportunity."

"So? Go tell Wendy."

"I can't. She'd have to arrest him, and it would break her heart to hurt Jane."

Renata had never heard anything so ludicrous in her life. Unless… "Do Jane and Wendy have a thing?" She felt stupid the minute she said it aloud.

"What?" Amanda looked at her as if she'd grown two heads.

"Never mind."

"No. Tell me what you mean," Amanda persisted.

"Nothing. It was a stupid thought. So what are you going to do?"

"What are *we* going to do. You're in on this now."

"Oh, wait a minute."

"No. I'm stuck with this, and I'm angry, and I need help to get rid of it."

"And I look like a dealer? Just dump it in the bin, for God's sake."

"I can't do that. It has to completely disappear, and you have a car and I don't. Take it away and dump it somewhere. Please," she added as an afterthought.

"Where? Behind a hedge? I don't know this valley. What if I get some sheep high?" She laughed. This was a ridiculous conversation.

"It's only seedlings. You could fill 'em with helium and they wouldn't get you high."

"Ask Tipper to get rid of it. Or better yet, ask Jane for help. He's her stupid nephew, after all."

"I can't. I don't want to hurt her, either," Amanda said. "And that doesn't mean we're in a lesbian relationship." She glared at Renata. There was no doubt she'd deduced what Renata had meant earlier. Renata could have kicked herself. Then she immediately wondered why. She was not part of the We Love Jane gang. She couldn't give a damn if people found out their curate, or pastor, or rector, or whatever the hell she was, was a dyke. It might open their sleepy little eyes a little wider.

She turned to go, not wanting any part of this. Amanda grabbed her arm.

"I thought you were her friend. If you were, you'd know how hard she's tried to keep Tipper on track."

"Tipper has his own choices to make. Jane can't do that for him."

"You're the great problem-solver, so ask the bleedin' Universe to fix this one. I have a job interview this afternoon and I don't need this shit." Amanda was wound tighter than a spring, probably more to do with the interview than this mess.

Renata looked up and down the lane. There was not a soul in sight. She looked at the little trays of Hessian plugs with their blobs of greenery, and sighed. She did not understand it. Even as she nodded her affirmative, she did not understand it. What was wrong with this bloody valley that everywhere she turned, Jane Swallow and her various dramas reared up to poke her in the eye?

"Fine. I'll bring the car around the back and you grab some bin bags and help me load it, and we'd better be quick."

Amanda nodded. "We will."

Renata strode away, irritated that she had agreed to this, but even more puzzled that she had so readily caved.

What the hell was wrong with her?

She grimaced. Damn the Wallops, anyway.

High Wallop Library was an ugly building, but its local history section did confirm what Colin Harper had already told her. The current festival had derived from a license granted to the village of Lesser Wallop by none other than Edward III in 1348, the year the first Great Plague devastated fifty percent of the English population. It seemed the valley was impervious to the pestilence, until High Wallop fell victim and a third of the parishioners died in one month.

Lesser Wallop fared better, where "*Nay nonny a man hath perished up his soul unto the Almighty twixt midsummer unto midwinter.*" Its reprieve was attributed to its healing waters, and for the next few years, it became a place of pilgrimage and sanctuary. The plague ended and soon after, the valley returned to normal.

The good King did not forget the little haven. Rumour had it one of his sons was saved by the waters, and so a special annual market was set in place where the water could be bought in phials, along with other local merchandise like wool and cheese. Renata could only assume that somewhere along the way, the wool trade died off and the healing waters were eventually replaced with local ales and beers, giving birth to the newer Beer and Cheese Festival.

It was all very interesting, but she could feel it in her gut, as much as Bishop Hegarty had done, that there had to be more. There had to be some connection to St Poe's, even though the church wasn't mentioned in any writings from the time of the Black Death. In fact, she desperately wanted to find a connection. Any link between the church and the ancient festival might just save it and allow both Andrew Hegarty and herself the time they needed to research the Bishop's ley line theories and write that book. If there was a healing spring in Lesser Wallop, Renata would lay down her last red cent it was near, or even under, the village church. That's how these things worked.

She widened her sphere of research and turned back to the stacks much to the displeasure of the lazy, part-time librarian behind the desk. As she waited for her books, she began making notes. This was going to be good. She could feel it in her bones. Her phone vibrated on her desk with a text from Wendy.

"Don't forget. Quiz night tonight at WW."

Renata raised an eyebrow. Quiz night. Was that something she wanted to dip into? Jane would be there, after all. And she probably wouldn't leave this time, since there would be more people around. She had to admit, that had stung a little, when Jane had left the pub on Sunday. Why it bothered her, she didn't know, but it did. The rest of the dinner had passed happily enough with Wendy prattling on about this and that. Amanda had even reappeared and had her coffee break with them after they'd eaten.

Jane's friends were nice, and they seemed to adore her. Renata reviewed this glumly, unsure how she felt about the dynamics surrounding Jane, her friendships, her life. But compelled to follow in minute detail anyway. She found herself in a stew that was forever thickening.

And then she and Amanda had ended up driving Tipper's weed to the other side of the valley, where they had tossed the garbage bags into a gully behind a low stone wall. How classy was that?

Could law enforcement find fingerprints on seedlings?

And plastic bags? Damn. She should have worn gloves.

Her phone notified her again of Wendy's message.

Fuck it. She liked Wendy and quiz night sounded fun. Jane could go to another table. She replied in the affirmative, then returned to her reading.

What the eff is she doing here? Jane couldn't believe it when Renata entered the barroom.

"Yoo-hoo, over here." Wendy had her hand in the air waving her over.

"We kept you a seat." Amanda slapped the chair beside her. Jane struggled to stop her jaw from dropping. She looked at Moira to see if she had any fond words of welcome, but she was too busy gazing hungrily as the latest news item in the village joined them. She's brainwashed them all, Jane decided. Zombified them. They'll all be reading her books next.

Renata reached into her bag and pulled out a book and handed it to a delighted Wendy. "Here. Signed as promised."

Wendy "oohed" and opened the cover to show off the signature to Amanda and Moira. "Whatever you want is whoever you are, best wishes, Renata Braak," she read out. "Isn't that wonderful?"

Jane struggled not to gag.

"Damn right. Will you sign mine? I have about twelve," Amanda said.

"Sure," Renata said.

Jane seethed. Her predictions were coming true.

"Where can you get them?" Moira asked.

Jane stared at her. She had never known Moira to read a book in her life. She was an abuse of a team seat, next to useless at the quiz night, except for the odd, trite celebrity question. She only came along for the "girls' night out," as she told Barry, her husband.

"I'll have more to give away when I move in properly," Renata said. Jane's blood ran cold. This was only an extended weekend visit. Imagine what it would be like when Renata moved in permanently. Heart sinking, she determined to start looking at *The Church Today*'s vacancy listings. Last time, she'd been lucky, and Bishop Hegarty had come looking for her. He had pointed her in the right direction and sponsored her throughout her job appointment. This time, it would be different and though she didn't relish it, clearly it needed to happen.

"How did the interview go?" Renata asked. Jane was surprised she'd remembered. Amanda had already told them that she felt confident she'd be at least short-listed, and even if she didn't get the job, she'd been pleased with her performance. Anything that increased her confidence had to be good, Jane had told her.

"Anything that increases your confidence is brilliant," Renata said after Amanda finished her story, and Jane shot her a look for possibly reading her mind.

"That's exactly what Jane said." Amanda sounded pleased.

Renata threw Jane a lopsided grin. Jane made a point of calling over to Una so she didn't have to acknowledge it. Then there was no more time left to dodge pleasantries with Renata. With a hum from the microphone, the quiz began.

Steve blared out his questions as usual, as if they were all sitting two streets away from him. "Sports round. Question one: Name the South American countries the Dakar Rally runs through."

"It's a trick question, right?" Jane asked. "Dakar's in Africa."

Renata shook her head. "No. The Dakar Rally is now in South America for security reasons. Too much war in Africa." Everyone groaned except Renata. "Come on guys, think," she said. "Argentina and Chile for sure, and maybe Peru?"

"They might as well just hand this round to Piston Broke," Wendy moaned, but she wrote down Renata's answer.

"Who captained England in the 2002 World Cup?"

"I'm going to throw my chair at him," Moira grumbled.

"David Beckham." Tipper pushed past their table and dropped a whisper for the team and a wink at Amanda, who scowled at him.

"We can't use that. It's cheating," Jane said.

"Shut up and write it down," Moira instructed Wendy, who quickly did as she was told.

The round dragged on until the break, when they could refill their glasses. "Would you get me a rum and Coke while you're up, Wendy?" Amanda pressed a fiver into Wendy's hand. "I don't want to go to the bar while she's there."

"Who?" Wendy asked loudly.

"Shush, don't look."

Wendy sat down again. "Who?" she asked again and leaned in to whisper. Moira butted heads as she ducked in to listen, too.

"Zoe Blair. Tipper's girlfriend." Amanda nodded discreetly towards the bar. "She came in right after him and has been glaring at me ever since."

Moira snorted. "As if you'd give that lout the time of day. Oops. Sorry, Jane, but he is a troublesome whelp if ever there was one."

Jane shrugged. "I'm not denying it. But he seems to be behaving himself these days. I only wish he kept better company."

Amanda and Renata exchanged a secret look that Jane caught. It made her chest clench. She felt an immediate resentment towards Renata and disappointment with Amanda. Had Tipper made a nuisance of himself and, for some reason, Amanda confided in Renata and not her? She thought Amanda could talk to her about anything. She always used to. Again, paranoia reared its ugly head and she decapitated it at once, but it was a Hydra and grew more heads.

First Wendy, now Amanda. This was all the working of Renata, the thin end of the wedge she had been so worried about. She found herself scowling at Renata, and she couldn't help it. It was just for a split second, but Renata noticed and scowled back, except her frown looked troubled and a trifle hurt, as if she was surprised by the scowl and, at the same time, upset. Jane wasn't sure what to make of it.

Moira went for a smoke and Amanda decided to go to the loo, leaving Jane and Renata alone at the table.

"What was that look for?" Renata asked.

Jane didn't want to have this conversation. She'd talk to Amanda first chance she had to make sure Tipper hadn't overstepped a mark.

"What look?"

"You really are a woman of mystery," Renata continued. She leant across the able, so as not to be overheard. "All those dark sultry looks. You're impossible to read."

"I feel the same about your books."

Renata blinked. "Just for that, I'm sending you the boxed collection," she said with a somehow playful smirk that only served to irritate Jane even more.

"You look cosy." Amanda reappeared. She shared another look with Renata, one that Renata seemed uneasy with.

Jane looked at Amanda, confused. There was more subtext swirling around here than on a fanfic site. Could Renata and Amanda be attracted to one another? She found the idea appalling and was trying to remember the last time Amanda had a boyfriend, when there came an almighty crash from the pool room. It silenced the conversation in the bar and fixed everyone's attention to the doorway between the two rooms. Even the smokers came in from the cold to investigate.

Moira scuttled over and joined them. "What was that?"

In answer, a red pool ball came flying through at head height. Thankfully, it hit nobody but it did crash into the

jukebox and dented the casing. This was followed by a hail
of expletives in a growl all too familiar to Jane's ears. Oh,
no. Her chest clenched in panic.

"Ah, come on, Pops." Tipper's voice could be heard
pleading with his grandfather. "You lost fair and square.
Pay the man."

Tipper was told in no uncertain terms to shut the fuck
up, and then a chorus of other men's voices began to
protest that a bet had to be settled. Above it all, Zoe's shrill
jeering could be heard. Jane blanched pale. She knew she
had because her cheeks felt pinched and her lips tingled as
they did when she was about to lose her temper. She didn't
want to, but she knew she was resting on a knife's edge.
From the corner of her eye she could see Renata watching
her intently, then reaching out for her. Just then came the
hard slap of a punch landing home and her father came
skidding out of the pool room on his arse.

She stared amidst a chorus of laughter around the barroom and then she was on her feet. Renata rose to follow
her, but Moira pulled her back down and shook her head.
Jane was thankful for that.

She advanced towards her father as he staggered to his
feet, grabbing for an empty pint glass as a weapon. He was
ready to advance back into the pool room when she slapped
his forearm hard, forcing him to drop the glass. Then she
spun him on his heels and yanked the back of his trousers
so high he was on tiptoes. Her other hand took his shirt
collar in a grip of steel.

"Out, Dad," she said quietly. "I'll drive you home."

He started slurring insults at her, but they sounded half-hearted. Humiliation was the overriding factor, and he wanted to get out, too. Wendy appeared at her side with Jane's handbag and draped it wordlessly over her friend's shoulder.

"Thanks," Jane said. "Talk to you later." It was no problem to remove him from the bar and out to the street where she had parked her car. Wendy returned to the table and the rest of the barroom seemed to have been holding a collective breath that was slowly released once Jane had left with Winston. Steve then returned things to normal with his booming announcement about the second round, which was geography.

Renata stared after Jane, astonished, then looked back at the others at the table with her.

"Did you see that? She went all Kung Fu on his ass. Where the hell did she learn to do that?"

The other three looked at her strangely. "In the army," Wendy said. "She can kill you stone dead at three hundred paces, can our Jane."

Renata couldn't sleep. The wedding reception going on downstairs was driving her mad. Drunk people were running around the corridors giggling and flirting badly outside each other's rooms, and the seventies disco beats were making her want to punch the wall in time with the Bee Gees.

It wasn't that she wanted to sleep. She wanted to lie still and think, and she needed some quiet to do that. She wanted to think about Jane Swallow the soldier—the army chaplain, of all things. Think about Jane Swallow, who had spent these last few days throwing curve balls and laughing up her sleeve. Did she even know this Jane Swallow? Apparently not. The woman she had known had melted away over time, like snow leaving a new landscape. All these years, she had a lie in her head. The person who she thought she hated most in the world no longer existed. And Jane had the cheek to call *her* a charlatan!

This left a different kind of loss in her gut. Even her memories were junk. The person whose hurtfulness towards her had been unquantifiable, whose callousness had plagued her most plaintive dreams, didn't even exist as she remembered her. It was as if she'd died and been resurrected as super-trooper Swallow, a phantasm from some superhero comic book capable of throwing a two-hundred-pound man out the door.

Giving up on rest she picked up her mobile phone and texted Andrew Hegarty. *Can we talk soon?*

Then, out of curiosity, she opened the browser and Googled *British Army Chaplains.*

Jane fought a sigh. "This is an unexpected visit."

Amanda waved a bottle of wine in her face. "With booze."

She stepped back from her front door to let Amanda enter. Wendy followed hot on her heels, wide-eyed and nervous. Jane felt nervous, too. What were her friends doing, arriving at her door at 7 p.m. on a Wednesday night? Or more like, what had her father done now? Her mood darkened.

"Come on in," she managed. "I was just watching telly." Then an idea struck her and everything brightened. She spun around to face Amanda. "You got the job! You're here to celebrate!" She could have squealed with delight.

"No." Amanda shook her head and immediately deflated her. "I was close, but no cigar. Upside is, it was a good opportunity to brush up on my interview technique. And they gave me very positive feedback even though they gave the position to someone else."

"Oh, Amanda. I'm sorry. But at least you know you were a serious contender."

"Something like that," Amanda said. "But enough about me." She looked awkward despite the casual words.

"So what's the occasion?"

"This is an intervention," Wendy said glumly. "Not a celebration."

"An intervention? About what?" Jane led them into her sitting room and switched off the TV, uneasy. Whistlestop gave them all an alarmed look, then sneaked away to the kitchen, making her wonder if he knew something she didn't.

Wendy reddened and looked embarrassed. "I'm not sure what it's about." Her sideways glance at Amanda told Jane who the ringleader was, and that Wendy knew exactly what it was about.

"Don't you back out on me now," Amanda told her. "We agreed. You're in on this all the way. We're all friends here."

Wendy's face blazed and her eyes took on a scared rabbit look.

"What's going on?" Jane demanded.

Amanda held up the bottle. "Corkscrew first, then we talk."

She started to protest, but at Amanda's expression, she stopped. She could use a glass of wine, anyway.

After it was poured, they all settled into the comfortable couch and armchairs. "Fine. We've got wine. So what's this all about?" Jane asked.

Amanda took a big sip of wine, then a deep breath, and said, "You and Renata. Your old friendship."

"And?" Anxiety built inside her.

"And exactly how friendly were you?"

Her chest tightened. "I'm not sure where you're going with this."

"I think you know where this is going," Amanda said. She was digging deep for courage. Jane could see this in the big gulps of wine Amanda was rapidly sinking.

"Not really. You'll have to spit it out," Jane said.

"Yeah. Spit it right out of the closet," Wendy blurted, surprising even herself.

Amanda glared at her before saying, "What you have to remember, Jane, is that we love you, no matter who you are. Every little inch of you."

"Yes," Wendy said, a slightly panicky quality to her voice. "Every inch. We love you."

"What?" Jane said. "Where did all this nonsense come from? Who's told you this rot?" Her mind swung to Mrs Agnew but immediately rejected the idea.

"It doesn't matter," Amanda said. "All you need to know is that you have friends who love and support you."

"Renata told us," Wendy blurted again and then looked mortified.

Amanda turned on her angrily. "We agreed no names."

"That cow," Jane said in a low growl. "What has she been talking about?"

"See what you've done?" Amanda remonstrated. "You've made her feel threatened. When we make a plan, stick to it."

"This was a plan?" Jane asked, horrified.

"The book says anger is positive and should be expressed constructively," Wendy counter-accused.

"That two-faced Dutch ruminant," Jane ranted, and it felt cathartic. She needed to somehow verbalise her anger and shock at seeing Renata bounce back into her life like a dose of double pneumonia.

"Does that sound constructive to you?" Amanda asked Wendy, even as she shot worried glances at Jane.

Wendy looked panicked. "What does it say in the book about redemptive arcs or positive energy application?"

"Redemptive whats?" Amanda slipped a book from her handbag and opened it at a particular page. Jane caught a glimpse of the cover and her jaw dropped. *Intervention: Breaking the Negative Cycle and Saving a Loved One,* by R. B. Braak. She practically howled with anger.

"You're running an intervention using a book written by the person who outed me? Are you insane? Even you can see the insult in that."

Wendy was on the verge of tears. "We just wanted to love and support you."

Jane ignored her and turned to Amanda. "I'd have thought you'd have more sense. What did she say? Tell me right now."

Amanda looked very uncomfortable. "No one has outed you. It was more an indication than a declaration," she said. "I can't tell you the exact circumstances, as it was…private."

"And *my* privacy counts for nothing?" What had Amanda and Renata been up to for a subject like this to arise? Again, she found herself reviewing Amanda's love life. Was Renata manipulating everyone around her? And, again, she was angry at the wave of paranoia that engulfed her.

"And what exactly do you mean by indication? What did she say? What did she do to *indicate* you could come around to my house and *intervene*?" Her brain buzzed with panicked thoughts as she tried desperately to get a handle on this.

"I've never wanted to run away so much in my life." Wendy burst into tears. "Jane, we love you, really we do. Everyone in Lesser Wallop loves you and we want you to be proud and not worry about your job." She sniffled into a tissue.

"Everyone in Lesser Wallop?" Jane's blood ran cold. Just how many people had Renata informed?

"Well, me and Amanda," Wendy said between sniffles.

"Wait. What about my job? What do you mean I shouldn't worry about losing my job?"

"Like in the army," Wendy managed. "We didn't want you to worry your sexuality would lose you your job like in the army."

At that, Jane sat back and sighed, trying to calm down. She took a gulp of wine while her mind worked overtime. What to say, what not to say. And how much she loved the two people before her.

"Look, guys," she said. "This is how it is. I did not lose my job as an army chaplain because of my sexuality. It had nothing to do with it. And Renata and I... Yes, we were together, but it was a lifetime ago, and it ended badly. I really wish you wouldn't talk to her about it. In fact, I think I need to go and talk about this with her face to face. What I don't need is for you to stress about this."

Wendy looked immensely relieved and Amanda's face softened. They both looked a lot happier.

"We didn't mean to snoop," Amanda said. "Wendy and I were worried. You were trying so hard to disguise whatever is going on—was going on—between you two and we didn't want you to feel uncomfortable around us. It must be so hard for you both. And she didn't out you, in that she really did say nothing. I kind of guessed. The clues were in the way she is around you. Anyone with eyes can see she cares."

Jane nearly choked on her wine but she managed to swallow. Neither of the other two seemed to notice her temporary respiratory distress. What the hell were they talking about? Renata Braak hated her. *That's* what anyone with eyes should see.

Right?

She needed more wine.

CHAPTER 8

Renata was pleased with the backwards progress her kitchen was making. The Gerrards had ripped it all out and chipped back the plaster up to the tideline. Tomorrow the walls would be re-plastered. The unfortunate part was it would take several days for the new plaster to dry out before the cabinets could be installed.

She locked the back door of her cottage and paused to admire Jane's garden, something she was doing a lot these days, pausing to admire Jane's garden. And her friendships and her life—though not her family. Jane's family left a lot to be desired.

Jane's lawn, however, had a new lushness now that the excess water had drained away. And hard work on the flowerbeds had restored them all to order. The little greenhouse was bursting at the seams with foliage, and this made Renata glance down the rows of gardens to the greenhouse she and Amanda had recently denuded. Sure enough, Tipper and Zoe were lurking nearby in furious discussion.

She pocketed her keys and strolled down to meet them. As she got closer, she could hear Zoe's whine and Tipper's weary response. It looked like the bloom had well and truly left their relationship.

"Hey, guys," she called cheerily. Zoe scowled and Tipper looked ill at ease. They were loitering around the garden where their secret nursery had once been. "How're things?"

"Okay," Tipper answered warily. "You're Aunt Jane's new neighbour, right?" He may have been wary, but his look took her in from head to toe. Renata was used to this, from a certain type of man. Zoe glared back and forth between them, from her slacker boyfriend to the perceived threat. Renata was used to this, too, from a certain type of woman.

"Yes, I am. And you must be Tipper. Amanda has told me so much about you." She idly dropped the name of Zoe's perceived number one threat into the conversation, something she knew was evil. She also knew she would one day probably burn in Hell for all her naughtiness, but she didn't care. Tipper was stupid enough to visibly brighten on hearing Amanda's name, before Zoe shot them both one last poisoned look and stomped off.

"Did I say the wrong thing?" Renata asked as they watched Zoe storm down the lane and disappear around the corner. Tipper shrugged and turned away, his interest in his departing girlfriend over, probably on every level.

"So," she said. "You like to garden?"

He grabbed a rake and leisurely began to drag some leaves about. "Yeah. It's okay," he said, trying to sound nonchalant, but she could tell he was anxious and moody. The disappearance of all his little seedlings must have been alarming.

"Well, you must be good if Amanda has you helping her tidy up around here."

"Yeah." She got the impression he wanted her to go. To trip off down the lane and disappear, like Zoe.

"Not used much are they?" She looked at the rows of gardens around her. "The owners come…what, once, maybe twice, a year?"

He shrugged. "Dunno."

"Amanda's got a nice little business going here, hasn't she? Looking after all these holiday cottages."

"S'pose so."

"Of course, she'd be fucked if someone had found the pot you were growing in the greenhouse." She nodded towards the one he'd been using. The one that was now empty, and he and Zoe had been arguing in front of. He almost dropped the rake.

"She'd lose her business," she continued, unstoppable in her rising anger. "There'd be police, possibly court, maybe a huge fine and a police record. Then Social Services might visit her and the kids. Not good for someone applying for lecturing work, now is it?"

He started, and her anger topped out. "You are the most selfish little turd I have ever met. Not only would you shaft Amanda, a friend who offered your sorry ass a paying job, but you'd do it on your Aunt Jane's doorstep so she gets splattered, too. If I ever see you do crap like this again, I'll go to the police myself and get you tossed out of this valley and into prison where you belong, you wretched little runt." She was as tall as him and her finger was millimetres from jabbing him in the eyeball. She turned to leave.

"But—" he began to speak, his face white. She held her hand up.

"Don't even talk to me," she said. "I helped Amanda dump your gear. You're a shit, Tipper. Now go and do an honest day's work for once."

She left him standing. If a shovel had been handy, she'd have whacked him with it. How dare he endanger Amanda? And Jane? How dare he not even think about the repercussions of his actions on others?

Part way down the lane, she met Zoe returning. Zoe shot off such a spiteful look that Renata wished her on him wholeheartedly. She'd never seen two such useless, selfish people deserve each other more.

She drove down to the village green and parked opposite The Winded Whippet. It was a lovely fresh summer morning and she needed a coffee after blowing her top, and maybe some cake. Sugar for those in need of sweetening. She deserved it after rattling Tipper and Zoe's respective cages. And then she stopped and stared. "What the…"

A few pedestrians had slowed down before the pub to watch Bill Gerrard Jnr hammer plywood boards over the broken window.

Wendy stood outside, grim-faced.

"Hey. Who did this?" Renata asked as she joined her on the pavement.

"Not sure. No witnesses so far," Wendy answered tightly.

"It was Winston, wasn't it?"

"We don't know for sure," Wendy said. "If we did, then

he'd be banged up in High Wallop station by now." She shrugged. "It's not as if we've CCTV in this village. Only the ducks see it all and they're not telling."

Patrick Goodall, Wendy's father, came out and pinned up a "Business as Usual" sign. He seemed remarkably cheerful, but that seemed to be a family characteristic. Except maybe for today because Wendy did not look cheerful at all.

"All right, pet?" he called over to his daughter.

"Fine, Dad," she called back. But she didn't seem to be. "When's the glazier coming?"

"It's one for the insurance, so it won't be quick," he answered and ducked back inside.

"Fancy a quick coffee?" Wendy asked Renata.

"Sure. That's what I stopped by for."

"Let's go down to The Potted Crab." Wendy moved away. She seemed distracted and Renata wondered what was up. She fell into step beside her.

Coffees ordered, Renata asked, "So, what's going on? I can see something's bothering you."

"I read your book and I don't think I should be a community police officer, or any sort of police officer for that matter."

"What? But you love it. Look at you with your bike and your uniform. It suits you."

"Oh? Thanks. But seriously, nothing ever happens here. I'll never make my mark. Your book is all about making your mark, and I can't. Not here."

Renata sipped her coffee and tried to quell her anxiety.

Would Jane blame her if Wendy changed jobs because of her book? Jane was the one who had pushed Wendy to be a community police officer. What else was there for her to do in the Wallops?

"What else do you want to do?" she asked, thinking maybe she could help Wendy see that community policing really was a good thing for her.

Wendy shrugged. "Dunno. There's no work around here," she said, confirming Renata's worst fears. "I suppose I could help out at the pub, but I hate it. That's why I wanted to join the police in the first place. To go my own way." She looked miserable.

Renata felt uneasy about the pot seedlings she had tipped in the countryside behind a stone wall. Would it have been better to let Wendy find the haul after all? But then that could have exposed Jane to very bad publicity at a delicate time for St Poe's. Not that she was worried for Jane, Renata reminded herself. She needed the church to survive so she could write her book with Andrew Hegarty. There was gold in "them thar Wallops," and she intended to mine it. Jane didn't care about her, anyway. She sipped her coffee, more as a distraction than anything else because she didn't like that thought.

"To be honest, is this really a good time to leave the village without a representative of the law?" she asked. "I mean, once you go, what with cutbacks and everything, do you think you'll be replaced? I think not. And look at what happened at your parent's place. Things happen, Wendy. Even in the

Wallops. And someone has to look out for all the old dears, like in Rectory Row when the Sturry flooded." She had Wendy's attention now. "I can't see anyone coming from High Wallop to check on the old age pensioners next time there's bad weather, can you?"

Wendy had no answer.

"Why don't you write a New Life versus Old Life style sheet?"

"What's that?"

"A sort of pros and cons of what you have now in your life and what you want. Once it's down on paper sometimes the balance looks different. What you want may actually already be in the pros list, but you don't know until you see it in black and white."

Wendy looked interested, so Renata spent the next half hour showing her how to prepare her style sheet and desperately hoping it would sideline the mental slump Wendy was currently in. Part of her wished Wendy could nab Winston Swallow for the windows he'd no doubt broken. There were only so many times a man like him could be ejected from a pub without some sort of cowardly reprisal. Then again, that, too, would reflect badly on Jane, and she needed that situation to remain stable. They all needed the situation to remain stable, at least until Renata's research was done. The more she learned about Jane Swallow these past few days—and it was a lot—the more enmeshed with her life she became.

J ane was nervous. Renata didn't look very comfortable, either.

She had been more than surprised when the bell rang and found Renata standing on the doorstep.

"Hi, sorry to call unexpectedly," she said, shifting her weight from foot to foot. "But Andrew told me that we really need to talk about this article I'm doing on the festival."

Jane had exactly the same conversation earlier that morning when the Bishop had phoned her. She knew Renata had dropped in to see how Bill Snr was getting on, so she supposed it made sense for her to call here, too.

"Come in." She led the way back to her study where she'd been working. She didn't really want Renata in the lounge, the heart of her home. It already felt too intrusive that she had slept there that first night. She may be imagining things, but the throws and cushions still held the faint scent of Renata's elegant perfume. Now the skin on the back of her neck prickled. She was super sensitized to Renata and she didn't know when she became so, or if she'd always been and the years of separation had made her forget.

"Where do you want to start?" She indicated a comfortable armchair and sat down at her desk. It was all rather formal, but she wanted it that way. Except Renata didn't sit down. Instead, she went to the bookshelves and casually perused the contents as she talked.

"I was wondering if you know of any connection with the festival and St Poe's." she asked.

"Only what everyone else knows—that the festival was

originally granted under license by Edward III in the 1300s. It was a place of refuge during the Black Death." She noticed Renata wasn't as casual as she pretended. When she reached out to pick up a knickknack or examine a book, her hand shook slightly. She was nervous. And that puzzled her.

"It's just that…" She paused for a split second when her gaze fell upon her own paperback on Jane's shelves. Then she carried on, almost seamlessly except Jane noticed the hesitation. "It's just that it's hard to believe there is no correlation between the two. Healing water, sanctuary, and a place of worship all seem to go hand in hand. We just need to find the link."

"And what happens when you find the link? I thought you wanted to write about the festival."

"I do. I have friend who's an editor on the *Sunday National Review* and she'd be interested in an article, but it has to be ready by next week for a special they're doing on neglected Old English fetes and fairs."

Jane was impressed. The *Sunday National Review* was very fancy.

"The Beer and Cheese Festival is *not* neglected," Jane said, put out. "Why, on a good sunny day, we can have as many as eight hundred people coming into the village."

"Colin Harper thinks the High Wallop cricket ground could take well over a thousand. All it needs is more publicity."

She bristled. "Colin *would* think that. It's all about money for him and he never considers the tradition, or the value this festival is to our local shops and community. High

Wallop is as institutionalised as any British town, but Lesser Wallop still retains its heritage. It needs this annual influx to make ends meet."

"No offence, but eight hundred on a good day is not really an annual influx, now is it?" Renata pointed out. "Colin is right in that the festival could do better."

"Sure. In High Wallop," she said bitterly. Renata was coming after her festival now. First her friends, then her job, and now the Beer and Cheese festival. She should have guessed as much. Her temper flared and she struggled to remain calm. There was nothing worse than feeling all hot and bothered when Renata always managed to look cool as a cucumber.

Renata shook her head. "Not necessarily."

Jane caught herself. That was *not* what she'd expected to hear. "And all these questions about St Poe's," she continued. "Is that somehow connected with the work you're doing for the Bishop? I know you've been asking around town."

"Can Wendy keep no secrets?" Renata said, maybe a little frustrated but resigned to it.

"No, unfortunately, she can't." She smiled ruefully. "You'll learn that in time. But actually, it was Jenny Coombs. She works at the library in High Wallop, and she told me all about your reading habits. She's on the Page Turners quiz team."

"I see. It really does all go on at that quiz night, doesn't it?" Renata smiled and Jane stared for a moment, remembering the first time she'd seen that smile. It was a wonderful smile, yet somehow now, it made her sad.

"I'm getting the hang of the names, too," Renata continued. "Grey Matters is the paint shop, Piston Broke is the garage, Let's Get Quizzical is the doctor's office. You're all named after the jobs you do. And your team is—"

"God Only Knows. Yes. It's the quiz theme. Quiz night is where most Lesser Wallopians meet up." It certainly wasn't at Sunday service. She shrugged and stood. "But I don't think I can help you with any of this. I don't know any more than anyone else." She also wanted Renata to go before they moved into forbidden territory. She had invited her in under the silently acknowledged pretext that they spoke only of festival business and not their own. She had no energy today to confront her about the "outing" to her friends. That conversation was still to be had, but she did not feel ready for it. Maybe she never would. She intended to move on, so did it even matter?

Then Renata wrong-footed her. She turned to directly face her and said, "Could I see your medal, please?"

Jane started then stared at her. There was an overlong silence before she answered, "How did you know about that? Bishop Hegarty promised—"

"I Googled you. He never said a thing. Did you really think something like that could stay anonymous?"

"It's not something I want generally known." There was warning in her voice. Here she drew a definite line.

"I had to dig deep. When I say Google, I mean several hours going through the Ministry of Defence public records."

She had a curious, small smile on her lips. "I'm glad you decided to accept it."

"It was the appropriate thing to do. It meant something to the people who gave it to me."

"Can I see it? Please?"

She cleared her throat, greatly ill at ease. Slightly red-faced she reached for a small, oblong, velveteen box on the top shelf of the nearest bookcase.

"It's not hidden away, then?"

"No. It's not on display, either, just close to hand. My regiment meant a lot to me. They were my family, my flock, if you like, in that they were in my pastoral care. For me, this medal doesn't represent what it says on the back. It represents my family, and my army family's care back." She handed the box to her.

Renata opened it and stared for a few seconds with a kind of reverence. Her fingers moved towards the medal, then she hesitated. "May I?"

Jane nodded, not at all sure why she was doing this. But, then, Renata always had that effect on her and, sadly, still did.

Renata lifted the Conspicuous Gallantry Cross from its case and read the inscription on the reverse. "Capt. Jane Swallow, Chaplain 4th class, The Royal Wessex." The silver cross hung from a red, white, and blue ribbon. "What's the story behind it? The records just said gallantry under enemy fire."

"There is no story, Renata. And please, you cannot write about this, okay?"

"I promise I won't write a word."

Jane stared at her, wary, not believing she could trust her.

"Please tell me, Jane." Her gaze was soft, pleading. "You were under fire, for God's sake."

"Why? Why do you want to know?" Her voice held a hard edge. "Why are you constantly snooping around me and my friends? Can't you see how unnerving it is?"

Renata held her gaze. "It's a small village. We brush up against each other."

That brought another memory that Jane had tried to bury and she glanced down at the floor, suddenly finding it difficult to keep looking into Renata's eyes.

"I'm not snooping. Could you give me some credence?" Renata looked down at the medal and let it slowly slip through her fingers back into the box. It nestled into position and she closed the lid and handed it back. She had an air of defeat, as if she hadn't expected to hear the story, as if she'd expected to be shot down but asked anyway.

Jane held the box in her hands and thought for a moment. It was heavy in her palms and carried so much more weight than the grams of silver in the cross. It carried the belief of her former comrades in her, and her love and respect for them. It carried loss, too. The loss of a family. Not her birth family, but the one that mattered. It held the weight of forced change upon her life.

How could she explain all that to Renata? Why should she expose herself like that? It was not as if she trusted her. Well, not anymore. Once, maybe. Once. When things were different. Once, she had trusted Renata—and suddenly she was talking. Words tumbled out of her mouth. Things she wanted Renata to know about her, about how much had changed, about how far apart they were, and had maybe always been.

"It was during the Iraq campaign," she said, her mind made up. "We were in convoy moving across a supposedly safe corridor. I was in the second Fox-box—that's the Foxhound protected vehicles we used. Sturdy things. Little metal boxes on wheels." She kept staring at the box, remembering. "Only the corridor was no longer safe. The first Fox ran over a mine and that was that. We weren't directly hit, but we were pinned down for several minutes by sniper fire, though it felt like forever. The men on either side of me were hurt, so I grabbed an assault rifle and started shooting in the direction I thought the sniper fire came from."

Her fingers began to tingle with adrenalin, she still remembered the weight of the weapon in her hands as it belted out bullets. "I kept them pinned down long enough so our guys could get to us. It was only about fifteen minutes, really. I hit nothing, I killed no one. It wasn't really heroic at all when you think of some of the things that happened over there. But because I was an army chaplain and not meant to carry arms, and because I had minimized the rate of fire on our convoy, I got a medal—but I also lost my job because chaplains shouldn't bear arms, never mind fire them in anger." She stopped then, and looked at Renata.

"You didn't lose your job. You resigned," Renata said quietly.

"I was in an impossible position. The church is very clear what it expects from its pastors. The army, too." She placed the box back on the shelf. "So it's not that great a story, after all. No heroics, no mad dash across no-man's-land, no tourniquets under fire. Just me firing so wildly at a hilltop that no one with any sense dared raise his head above it. The snipers got away, so I didn't even help capture the enemy." She turned back to Renata. "My regiment's head honcho was Lieutenant Colonel Davis, and he liked me. He was a Christian, and even though he knew I had to go, he fought hard for me to leave with this." She indicated the small black box. "So I could leave with honour."

"Jane, during the Iraqi War, chaplains were an acknowledged target for Al Qaeda. Killing one hurts morale and they knew it. You were a woman, unarmed, and an easy target. Just being there was a brave enough thing to do."

"I followed my regiment, and I was never anywhere truly dangerous," Jane said. "Except for that last time. Sometimes danger finds you."

Silence descended between them for a while until Renata broke it.

"I feel like I barely know you," she said. The words came out quickly and Jane went immediately on the defensive. Here was the conversation she did not want.

"We've both changed over the years," she said. "It's only natural." It was a glib response and she could see disappointment flit across Renata's face.

"We both seem to want to help people," she pointed out.

Jane stayed silent at this.

"Ah. I see. You don't think I help people."

"I suppose they feel helped by your books and courses and whatnot," she answered carefully.

"Do you think Christianity is helping them, with its failing congregations and churches closing all across the country? People are evolving. They need spiritual options that the churches can't always provide because they burned those options at the stake centuries ago. Religion doesn't own the divine all-knowing. It's not a franchise."

The fight Jane didn't want was brewing and she was desperate not to engage. "I'm not going to argue with you, Renata. Say what you have to say and then leave."

"Why didn't you do that all those years ago?"

"Do what?"

"Say what you had to say and then leave? Instead of disappearing when my back was turned? That was cowardly, Jane." She indicated the box with the medal. "And obviously not like you. And it really hurt."

Jane closed her eyes. This could no longer be avoided. "I found the credit card," she said, and sat back down.

At last, Renata took her seat opposite. "Credit card?" She looked genuinely confused.

Jane nodded slowly. "The one you'd used to fund our trip. It was stolen. That's why you always sent me off on an errand when you had to pay for something, so I wouldn't see you forge someone else's name."

Renata flushed a dull red. "It was my aunt's. I didn't steal it." And after a short pause, "Not technically."

"Technically, she didn't give it to you to use, either. Please don't lie. I was raised by lies. I know them all. My mother left when I was six, and I was dragged up by my father and whatever woman he happened to have in tow. We moved around like the people down in Tinker's Field. I know all about thieving, shoplifting, pickpocketing. I was groomed in all of them. The minute I could get away from him, I did. I hated him and what he stood for so much, and I couldn't bear it when I found out you were…the same."

"It was all paid back," Renata said, tone flat. "Apologies given and accepted. All wrongs righted, and I've never acted like that again. In fact, it was a pivotal point for me. The intrinsic sense of shame made me look hard at myself." She looked past Jane, out the window so as not to meet her eyes. "I knew it was wrong, but I was young and stupid, and I wanted you to have a great holiday. The greatest one ever. You'd never even been abroad, and I wanted you to remember it forever."

"Well, I did," Jane said. "I worked hard for my holiday money. I earned my holiday, every minute I spent on the beaches or in a taverna or climbing over some ancient ruin was hard-earned by me. But you casually stole for it and that tainted everything. I didn't want to live like that. Not ever. I'd had enough of it."

Silence descended again and oh, how Jane wished this conversation had never started.

"How did you end up a rector?" Renata suddenly asked.

The question surprised her and she had to consider how truthfully she wanted to answer. Renata had a way of making her feel exposed and raw. She unerringly went for the raw spots and Jane shut down in order to protect herself. This time, she didn't. This time, she chose her words carefully.

"We'd stopped in a carpark somewhere or other," she said. "My Dad and me. I was about ten years old, and I was kicked out early one morning to amuse myself while he amused himself with his latest conquest. There was a church across the road, and I was hungry, so I went into the kids' Sunday school class and sat quietly waiting for the juice and biscuits at the end. Except I liked the stories and the teacher gave me a special comic about Moses and the Red Sea, and I was hooked. I read and reread that thing until it fell to pieces. Then my dad went to jail and Social Services took me. You already know that part, though."

"Yes. You told me. You liked your foster family."

She rubbed her forehead. "They saved me. I grew up in a steady home environment. I went to college. I got a job… I met you," she said so softly, she wondered if she would have to repeat it.

"And you left me." The bitterness was still in her tone but there was little Jane could do about it. She had given her reasons for leaving, and maybe she had behaved like a coward, but when you grew up with a violent father, you learned to pick your fights.

"When I came back from Greece," she continued, "I wasn't sure what I wanted to do. So I went to Bible College and then directly into the army. Bishop Hegarty offered me a stab at this job when I was discharged, and I got it. I'm happy."

Well, she had been until recently. Now it seemed she'd been living in a dream and the hard realities of her father and Renata Braak had returned with a wake-up call. Maybe there was a fight out there she was destined not to avoid.

"I'm glad you're happy." Renata said it in a way that indicated she herself was not happy, and expected never to be.

Jane sighed. "Look, I'm sorry for the way I left. It was a cowardly thing to do and I'm not proud of it. I wasn't then, either. I can't really hope you'll understand how deep it went, what you were doing with that credit card. I grew up in a thieves' household and it left a lot of wounds. I can't stand being around it, and I had to get away."

It had been a terrible journey, leaving. Standing on the ferry watching the island slip away and knowing she had done something intrinsically awful, yet knowing she had to do it for her own survival, and for her own hard-won terms and life values. She refused to be a living magnet for dishonest and unsavoury things. She refused to be a pawn in other people's ill doings. She'd been surrounded by people like that all her young life, be it her father, cousins, uncles, or aunts. Everyone had an angle and everyone was abusive and dishonest. And she had been heartbroken that Renata, the one person—the first person she had ever loved in her short life—had embraced those same qualities, had exemplified all those lazy, heinous, dishonest things she'd spent years trying to escape.

The experience had left her shaken at her inability to see people for what they were, and to distrust her emotions. She'd been so careful around people ever since. None of these were good memories, and she pushed her thoughts away.

Renata's eyes sparked and Jane worried there was going to be a massive flare of anger and accusation. She was so beyond all that, but was wary that Renata might still need to vent. She supposed it was only fair.

The memories Renata had dragged up reminded her of how far she'd come since those early days, and what a sham she was currently feeling like. Here she was, sitting in a cosy little home provided by her job as pastor to this small community. Lecturing them from the pulpit, leading by example, living an exemplary life. She constantly proved how "exemplary" she was, with all the little good deeds she performed in the name of kindness towards her fellow human beings. What if she was a sham? Scared of being lesbian. Scared of what crap her family might do next. Scared of failing St Poe's.

And now her safe little life was unravelling because of those fears. She would always be Winston Swallow's daughter, and Winston was crooked, cowardly, and deceitful, and in her own worst moments, wasn't she exactly the same? She had a medal for gallantry, yet she was afraid of everything. She had hidden her sexuality from her friends, her community, her church. She had judged, condemned, and then run out on someone she truly cared about all those years ago. Someone who, despite it all, had perhaps given her love.

She was craven to the bone, and today she felt it deep in her marrow.

Renata was studying her face, and whatever she saw there, the blaze of anger melted away and was replaced with something Jane couldn't transcribe.

"I'm done here." Renata's voice was tight. She went to rise, then realised Whistlestop had crept into the room while they were talking and had his long nose buried deep in her handbag. "Hey, sneaky snout, get out of it."

"Oh, I'm so sorry." Jane dragged him away by the collar. "He's a bit of a klepto. Guess it runs in the family." It was bad joke and they both forced a smile. There was a current of sadness passing between them and Jane was unsure how it had started and what it really meant. The promise of something wonderful rotted away, she supposed. Perhaps this was the closure they needed. If so, then it surprised her with its quiet intimacy and the melancholy that came with it. They had been young and foolish then, so why should it hurt so much now?

She opened the door and Renata stepped out into bright afternoon sunlight in the airy hallway. It seemed artificial after the temperate coolness of the study.

"Goodbye," she said, holding the front door open. The irony of the word was not lost on either of them. It came fifteen years too late.

"Goodbye," Renata replied. "I wish..." Her words failed and her expression fell slightly, and she quickly turned away and stepped outside.

Too despondent, too unsettled to return to her study,

Jane moved down the corridor to the kitchen to make a cup of tea in the hope such a banal activity might ground her. Her head felt light and her heart heavy, an unfortunate imbalance. She stopped dead in the doorway. Whistlestop lay flat out on his belly, back legs splayed, a position he only held when he was in the throes of deepest delight, chewing on a lump of expensive-looking red leather.

"Oh, no. Don't tell me…" She snatched it out from under his nose. At the same time the doorbell rang. Jane knew exactly who it would be.

She opened the door to find Renata had indeed returned, and was rifling through her handbag franticly looking for something.

"I think—" she said.

"Your purse—"

They spoke over each other. Renata stopped groping through her bag and eyed the chewed wad of red Italian leather Jane held out to her.

"I think he made another foray into your bag before he was found out," Jane said apologetically. "I really am sorry. I'll pay for it. Don't worry about that."

There was a moment's silence and Jane wondered what Renata would do, if she'd be angry.

Renata blinked a little stupidly, then as if snapping out of a trance, stepped into the hall and pulled Jane into the deepest, sexiest, most toe-curling kiss she'd ever had since the moment they'd parted.

CHAPTER 9

"What do you think you're doing?" Jane pushed her away, noting that Renata was white-faced, her dark eyes huge, as if the kiss had shocked her, too.

Jane's metaphorical toes slowly uncurled but her heart still pounded, and her ears burned with the hot flash that had swallowed her body whole.

"What exactly do you think you're doing?" she repeated. Then, suddenly aware they were standing in her hallway in full view of the street, said, "For heaven's sake, close the door."

Renata reached blindly behind her, her gaze not leaving Jane's face, and fumbled the door shut.

"What do you think you are do—" Jane began again.

"Something I should have done the moment we met in that rainstorm. Something I should have done all those years ago. I should have hunted you down and found you, and made everything right."

"What?" Jane sputtered. Actually sputtered. "Are you mad? You called me a bitch the moment you clapped eyes on me. You outed me to my friends. You have done nothing but spit venom from the moment you arrived. You're insane."

Renata reached for her. "Could be. Insanity is the only explanation I have as to why I still care so much about you.

This week has been an epiphany. I hated you so much for abandoning me but now I realise it's representative of how deep my original feelings went."

"And I've just told you why I did it. You can be angry, but at least be responsible, too." She avoided Renata's touch.

"I understand that now. I really do. I get it. But I was young and stupid. We were both young and stupid, for God's sake. But I loved you like crazy. I was mad for you and so angry when you left. I couldn't understand why and I wanted to...and I've been chasing that feeling ever since, when I should have been chasing *you*."

Loved her like crazy? "Don't you dare chase me. I live here, and do so very happily without you. Why can't you just walk away and forget? People our age don't behave like this. Like besotted teenagers."

Renata started to reach for her again then stopped. "Yes, we did fall in love as besotted teenagers," she said. "And people our age can do whatever we want. We can afford to. We can afford to be foolish in a way young people can't."

"What are you talking about?" This conversation was scaring the hell out of her.

"There's a reason we ended up back in this valley after all these years, Jane. I think we were supposed to meet again, talk, and fall in love all over."

"Oh, my God. You really are insane. Are you listening to yourself—"

Renata pulled her into another kiss and they fell against the wall where the coats and hats hung and sent them spilling to the floor. Jane's knees gave out and she very nearly took them both down with the garments, but the wall kept her upright even as her knees and mouth and hands betrayed her. She clung to Renata, her hands bunched in the back of her blouse. The buttons tore open at the front, exposing creamy flesh and ample cleavage. The smell of her skin was overpowering. Now pale and subtly scented, Jane remembered a time when it was bronzed and smelled of the sun and tasted of sea salt and heat. She had kissed that flesh until her lips were hot and swollen. They had rolled entwined in the surf, and lay spent and exhausted on starlit sand dunes.

Jane moved her lips to kiss the secret place just under Renata's ear, nose buried in her jasmine-scented hair. She laid the flat of her tongue against the thrumming pulse point just under the skin and heard Renata's sharp intake of breath. Nothing had changed, yet everything had. They had come full circle and yet they still managed to miss each other.

And...she remembered where she was. Reluctantly, Jane pulled away, flushed and dishevelled and amazed at how chilled she suddenly felt removing herself from Renata, even in the heat of the day. Her hands shook as she gently pushed her away from her.

"No," she said. "I'm sorry, but no. I don't want this, Renata. It's the wrong time. We've done this before. We had our time and it's over now. It has to be."

Renata smiled. "I always wondered where you went and what you did. I've missed you as much as I cursed you. And to come back to this valley that always held sweet memories for me, and actually *find* you here." Her voice was shaking so hard, her words tripped over each other. Her face was so earnest, so open, so real that it hurt to look at her.

"Jane, that means something. At least in my belief system it does. This was meant to be, meant to happen. We were destined to meet again. And I truly believe that is why part of me kept loving you when that should have faded away."

But Jane was shaking her head even as she spoke. "No," she kept saying. "No." And finally. "This is where you're wrong. This is where you make it up as you go along. This is the easy answer." Why couldn't she just go? More importantly, why didn't she want her to?

"I love you," Renata said softly. "That is not easy to say. It was a shock for me to realise it and to accept it."

"No. *I* don't accept it. I'm sorry. I don't love you. You're a shadow from a life I don't own anymore. I can't love you. All you're talking about is dreams and memories that no longer exist. This is real life with real problems, not some mumbo-jumbo Universe claptrap. This is who I am. This is where I live and where I belong, and I won't let you take that from me."

Renata stared at her as if she'd been slapped. "You're scared."

"Please go." Jane stood rigid, refusing to bend, to acquiesce. Pushing down all the emotions screaming at her. Pushing them down and shutting them out. And Renata saw it all.

Without another word, she turned and the door clicked shut behind her with a terrible finality, leaving Jane to stare at it through eyes blurred with tears.

Renata drove back to The White Pig barely registering the road, the countryside, or the beautiful day. She was on automatic, her mind elsewhere, in a bitter place, where it tortured her relentlessly. She was a fool. Somewhere between Greece and this fucking valley, she had begun hiding from her true feelings, wrapping them up in anger and unending hurt, only to discover how flimsy her convictions were when she was finally face to face with her accused. How had she been so stupid as to waste all this time in self-aggrandized chagrin?

When she got back to her room, she would pack up and leave. She trusted Bill Gerrard to finish off the kitchen now that the water damage throughout the house had been remedied. If she was honest with herself, she could have left a few days ago. Instead, she'd used the festival article as an excuse to linger and moon over Jane Swallow from a distance, like some love-struck herbivore. She was disgusted with herself. She was a silly, foolish woman. She was everything she hated and Jane Swallow had made her this way. Had made her and kept her this way for years and years. The best years of her life wasted by her own ridiculous ego. Wasted on a cowardly woman. A scared, stupid church mouse.

A cowardly woman with a war medal, her inner conscience reminded her. *Oh, shut up.*

She must have verbalised the thought because the receptionist looked at her strangely.

"Good afternoon, Ms Braak," she said as Renata passed through the foyer to collect her key. "Mr Harper has left these messages for you." She handed over several sheets of notepaper.

"Thank you." Renata collected them and dumped them in the bin as soon as she entered her room. She sat down at the small dressing table acting as impromptu desk and logged on to her laptop.

First thing in the morning, she'd leave this valley of the damned, but not before she'd written her bloody promised article and be done with the lot of them. She could do her research from London and let Andrew Hegarty do the legwork here. He was the one mad enough to want to retire here, anyway. Let him go snooping around St Poe's looking for a bloody miracle. She sure as hell had none up her sleeve.

She opened a new document and her fingers flew over the keyboard.

Welcome to the Wallops.

There were seventy-two parishioners in the congregation today and Jane was confused. This was more than treble her usual assembly and some of those attending she knew preferred St Dunstan's because of the shopping. Nevertheless, they all looked up at her with shiny-faced expectation as she curbed her surprise and delivered her sermon with a little more gusto than usual.

She could feel their enthusiasm flag towards the end, which also made her reconsider what was happening. She felt very behind the curve at this sudden allegiance to St Poe's. Wendy smiled and gave her a thumbs-up from the back pew she now favoured on Sunday mornings. Jane smiled back, hoping it would all become clear when they met for lunch.

She went straight into the "Praise Be for your Blessings" section and reached for the box. It was the usual fare. Mrs Greene still missed her mother on the third anniversary of her death. "Praise be." Mr Harold was grateful to be in remission from his bowel cancer. A huge "Praise be" for that one from everyone. Mrs Agnew was happy her granddaughter in London had announced her engagement to a lovely man that Mrs Agnew actually approved of, though it was not quite worded like that, but Jane was happy to "Praise be," especially as Mrs Agnew had dropped the politics as asked.

Emily Mars' curlicue scrawl was next, and Jane was in a good mood and looked forward to seeing what was happening in her young parishioner's world. She opened the tightly folded notepaper and the room began to tilt. The smell of incense was suddenly too strong, her collar too tight. She set the note aside and asked them all to rise for the final prayer and avoided looking at Emily's crestfallen face.

Heads bowed and eyes closed they followed her into the final litany, but Jane was on autopilot, her eyes glued to the paper at her elbow.

I'm grateful that Rector Jane is a lest bean.

"She must have heard her parents mentioning it or something." Jane fretfully pulled her bread roll to pieces, then grabbed her glass of wine for another healthy gulp.

"'Lest bean' could mean anything." Wendy was wide-eyed and rather fretful herself, picking small holes in her napkin. "I mean, kids today can hardly spell anyway."

"Exactly. She meant lesbian and couldn't spell it," Jane hissed. Never before had she felt so exposed. It was as if the nearby tables were full of spies. People who had been her friends and neighbours suddenly seemed dual-purpose and sinister as they passed by and said hello.

"Did you say anything to anyone?" she asked.

Wendy blinked.

"Oh, Wendy. You promised. You put your hand on your heart."

"I didn't tell anyone." Wendy protested. "Honest."

Jane pointed a finger at her and then at the kitchen doors. "Go get Amanda right now. She must be due a break soon."

Wendy glanced at the clock. "It's not three yet. She usually takes her—"

"Go get her!"

"Okay, okay." Wendy slid out from her seat and slunk towards the kitchen. Amanda appeared in seconds flat and took a seat at the table.

"Wendy told me." She reached over and took Wendy's wine glass and took a generous sip.

"This will sink me," Jane said, ducking her head so only Wendy and Amanda could hear. "If Bishop Hegarty gets wind of this, St Poe's will be holiday flats before Christmas, and I will be working in a mission for meth users somewhere north of the border. Did either of you breathe a word of it to anyone? Anyone?"

Amanda shook her head fervently.

"Only Moira." Wendy prised Amanda's fingers off the stem of her wine glass and hung onto it for herself. "What?" she asked when she noticed they were both staring at her. "Moira's one of us. One of the gang."

"You told Moira? For God's sake, Wendy, the woman whistles like a hard-boiled kettle," Amanda said in disbelief and snatched for the glass.

"Get your own wine." Wendy grabbed the glass back. "And I told her it was super-secret."

Jane slapped the table. "There you go," she said, the world crumbling around her. "That's it. All over and done with. I'll be assigned to some far-flung, faith-based rehab centre and have to explain to Whistlestop what crystal meth is."

"Someone was eating dogs in Birmingham," Wendy said and halted the conversation in its tracks. "It's illegal." She explained under the glare of her companions. "Dog meat is illegal in the U.K." She huffed. "I found it interesting."

Jane put her head in her hands. She was doomed and no one got it. Perhaps it was right that she was doomed. Perhaps it was her punishment for not being honest with Renata, for being cowardly towards her yet again. But Jane could not truthfully say what her feelings were towards her long-ago ex.

Oh, the physical attraction was still strong. Renata was a beautiful, charismatic woman. The young Jane could hardly believe it when she managed to win her attention at a party, never mind take her home to her ratty old studio for a night of raucous sex. Judging by the kisses they shared only a few days ago, that raucousness could easily be resurrected if her tired old thirty-something bones allowed it. But she couldn't go down that road. The last time she trod it, it led to nowhere, and it would still lead to nowhere she needed to be.

Renata had returned to London soon after, taking the tension out of an untenable situation. For that, Jane was thankful.

"Hey, Sis." Will was at his sister's side holding out a folded newspaper. "Have you seen the piece Renata Braak did on the festival? The whole village is talking about it. Great timing."

Wendy unfolded the paper and laid it on the table. Both Amanda and Jane leaned in to read. The article had a half-page of the Sunday broadsheet. Renata had really pulled in a favour to get this much space, Jane decided. And it was great timing. The Lesser Wallop festival was less than two weeks away, and the other events mentioned were further into the year.

It was part of a special edition on little-known events to go to this summer throughout England, and it rubbed shoulders with some very fancy contenders. The Old Herring Fair at Saltfleet. The Jazz Man festivities in Whitchurch, and a Woodcrafters' Fete at Ironbridge, with countless music events for all tastes. But Lesser Wallop had the only Beer and Cheese Festival listed. It seemed to be a unique combination, and Renata wrote about it like this was the gateway to a gourmet heaven in a valley geographically designed for the making of such fayre with its luscious green slopes for sheep farming and abundance of pure spring water for micro-breweries.

"You have to admit, she's done a great job," Amanda said. "No wonder she makes a fortune selling books."

"Are you sure you don't still fancy her?" Wendy asked. "'Cause she's rich, and if you married her you wouldn't have to go and work in a meth lab."

"Meth *mission*. And are you mad?" Jane shook her head in despair.

"Well, *I* would marry her in a blink, if I were that way inclined," Wendy said, and then blushed beet red. "Wouldn't you?" She turned to Amanda, who looked at her as if she'd grown two heads, both brainless.

"Not if I didn't love her," Amanda answered, a little flustered.

"But you do love Renata. You have all her books. You said she was the most beautiful woman you'd ever seen up close," Wendy persisted.

"That's fandom. It's hardly the same thing," Amanda said. "I enjoy talking to her, same as you do. It's not exactly like what Jane and Renata had, now is it?"

"Guys," Jane interrupted, "can we stay focussed for just a few more seconds on my problem, please, and then you can go back to your imaginary lesbian relationships?"

"What can we do if Moira blabbed?" Amanda said. "We can't go around denying it. Unless you want us to. Let me text her and see exactly what she said." Amanda got furious with her phone, leaving Jane and Wendy to chat.

"Plus, church attendance is up. That has to be a good thing, right?" Wendy asked.

"How can that be good if people are only coming to look at the lesbian?" Jane said. "You've turned my church into a zoo."

"It's not that at all." Amanda tutted as she waited for a reply from Moira. "I think people are showing their support."

"Praise be." Wendy giggled into her wine glass.

Jane glared at her. "And what happens when Colin Harper hears about it?" she said. Wendy immediately sobered up. "It won't be 'Praise be,' then, will it? It will be 'Piss off.' This is the opportunity he's been waiting for. He'll be on to Bishop Hegarty faster than a rat down a hole."

"But the Bishop likes you, Jane," Wendy said. "And no one likes Harper."

"It will embarrass Andrew, and probably in his last year

of office. By rights, it's a conversation I should have had with him on appointment, but didn't, as I was celibate and felt it was my own business." Shame washed over her, another act of cowardice. "And now I've wrong-footed him when he's struggling to keep St Poe's solvent. Colin will push for me to go and St Poe's to close. I've played right into his hands. This is awful."

"Ah," Amanda said as she read the texted reply. "You may well be right. It is awful. Moira openly admits to the first wave of indiscretion, but says it was embellished a thousand times with…" She squinted at the small screen, "…cherries on top by Mrs Agnew, who saw Renata leaving Jane's house in the early hours of the morning." She looked up from her phone. "Well, that hardly helps. Not looking very celibate now, are you. Did she really stay over?"

Jane groaned, a low animal sound like a birthing ewe in a fogbank.

"This is awful." Wendy wrung her hands. "What would Renata do?"

Jane could hardly believe her ears.

Then Wendy perked upright in her chair and said, "Oh. Let's ask her. Here she is now."

Jane groaned again.

Renata knew exactly where to find Jane at lunchtime on a Sunday. She drove straight to The Winded Whippet.

She knew she should stay away but she secretly wanted to see Jane's reaction to the article. She was very proud of it and if it didn't bring in the masses, then nothing would. Plus, she had arranged to see Bill Gerrard Snr. He'd called about some last-minute business with the cottage.

Every eye turned to her as she entered the bar, and every eye was shining, so she knew the article had been a success. Not that she ever doubted it, but you never knew with the Lesser-spotted Wallopian, curious, inbred bunch that they were.

Accepting smiles, warm welcomes, and even the occasional handshake, she moved across the room to Jane's table under a canopy of avid interest. Jane, she noted from afar, did not seem that enthused to see her. *Oh, well. Hard luck, darling. I'm here now, and dripping with laurels.* Wendy and Amanda, however, looked positively relieved to see her. It was nice to be missed.

It was not until she was sliding into the empty seat opposite Jane that she realised all was not as it seemed. The surrounding interest did not abate, instead it seemed to increase to fervid proportions. Their table was the suspenseful focus of the entire room. Wendy and Amanda looked ill at ease now she had arrived, and Jane borderline apoplectic.

"What's up?" she asked, genuinely confused.

"Emily Mars says you're a Lest bean," Amanda answered drily.

"A what?"

"Jane's been outed." Wendy jumped in. "Someone told everyone she's gay."

"Was it you?" Renata asked.

"No!" Wendy looked miffed.

"More to the point, we're worried that St Poe's is stuffed," Amanda said.

Jane glared at her, ensuring Renata knew exactly who was to blame. Her. "Colin Harper will think all his Christmases have come at once. This is the gift of everlasting leverage."

"With a thousand cherries on top."

"Thank you for that, Wendy." Jane's tone was cool.

"So, why am I getting the glad-eye from everyone in this room, except you?" Renata asked her.

"Because you told *them.*" Jane hissed, and pointed at Wendy and Amanda. "And they decided it was their business, and now look what's happened. Morning service was a circus."

"I did not tell them anything about you," Renata said back, voice barely above a whisper. "What the hell is there to tell? That you were a delinquent youth who became a priest? It's hardly an indictment. I mean you only have to look at the rest of your family to see you're a bloody marvel of nature."

"She didn't," Amanda broke in. "I sort of surmised it. I mean…" She spread her hands as if her conclusions were obvious.

Wendy shook her head vigorously. "It's true," she chimed in. "You look very cute together. Anyone with half an eye—"

"Half a brain." Jane gave her such a hard look, she wilted.

"She's impossible when she gets into one of these moods." She turned to Renata. "You can't say anything nice and it's batted straight back."

"How long ago since you pair were an item?" Amanda asked, "Seeing as how we're being open about it and everything."

"Yeah. I'm curious, too," Wendy added. The initial interest in the room was waning and they were relaxing accordingly. Renata shrugged, and on seeing Jane's hard, slightly panicked glare, strode right on into her story.

"We met at a party and hung around for a few months before we went on holiday to Greece," she said. "To this sweet little island where there was a wonderful lesbian-owned hotel, above the beach. So we stayed there for a week and pretended to ourselves that we were on honeymoon." She watched with satisfaction as Jane's cheeks scorched. "Of course, this was in the days before civil partnerships and same-sex marriage," she continued. "What was the name of that mad woman who owned the place?" She turned to Jane, and deliberately asked the seemingly innocent question. "Benny Freak or something?"

Jane started as if she'd been stung, but then her eyes took a distant look and Renata knew she was reaching back in time for the answer and hopefully reconnecting with that long, hot summer of love…and betrayal…on both their parts.

"Friske." Jane came up with the right answer, as Renata knew she would. Jane had a mind like a steel trap. Honed by all the card tricks her dad had taught her. Renata had never won a game of Rummy against her.

"She was called Benny Friske," Jane said. "A Swedish woman. Mad as a hatter."

"Remember how she threw us all out in the middle of the night?" Renata began to reel Jane deeper into the memory.

"It was a fire drill, to be fair."

Renata snorted. "No, it wasn't. Her girlfriend had run off with another guest and she flipped the fire alarm to clear them out, except she cleared the lot of us out along with them," she told Wendy and Amanda. "All of the guests—*all* of us—ended up in the ornamental gardens in the middle of the night while she had a raging row with this girlfriend of hers."

"Gosh." Wendy's eyes were huge. She and Amanda were hanging on every word.

"It's a good job you grabbed that vodka." Her attention swung back to Jane now that the other two were hooked. She may be duff at cards, but she knew how to tell a story. "Jane had a litre of vodka from duty free, and we all sat around the fountain drinking and singing 'til dawn. Great times, eh?" She gave Jane a lewd wink. Let the room suck that up. Except the room was now nose deep in its dinner.

"Wow," Amanda said. "And where did you say this hotel was? What island?"

"Doesn't matter," Renata answered. "It's gone now. There was an earthquake a day or so after we left, and it was washed into the sea."

"Wow and double wow!" Wendy was impressed.

"No, it wasn't," Jane butted in, scorn lacing her voice.

"Oh?" Renata sat back in her seat, one eyebrow quirked in challenge.

"They rebuilt it," Jane rushed to explain. "And Ioanna and Benny still run it."

"How do you know that?" Renata demanded. *And there's the mind that snaps like a little turtle. You can let go of nothing, Jane Swallow. Except me.*

Jane blushed. "I'm still on the mailing list."

Sunday evening began badly with a terse note from Mrs Agnew saying that under the circumstances, she was unable to attend tonight's service and would be going to St Dunstan's instead. She finished off with an imbecilic hope that she was not in any way inconveniencing.

"Of course, she's inconveniencing, she's the bloody organist!" Jane exploded down the phone to Wendy. "This is the start of the backlash." She sighed. "I'd better go and get ready. Maybe I can get the congregation to whistle along."

But just as Mrs Agnew's door closed on her, another one opened, and Jill Fry, Will Goodall's fiancée, walked through it with her *Carmina Sacra* under her arm and plopped herself before the organ to take off on a flight of divine preludes, postludes, and offertories. Jill taught music at Hastings Sixth Form College. Her music was nectar to the ear after Mrs Agnew's naïve plonking. Jane hadn't known the old Gray and Davison organ could produce such beautiful sounds.

"She's a good old girl." Jill patted the oak after she finished. "And if there's a position as organist going, then I'd like to apply."

"Then I'd like to take this opportunity to welcome you to St Poe's, but as we're probably closing before the end of the summer, I wouldn't bother with the pension plan if I were you." Jane smiled in gratitude. She checked her watch. "Half an hour to showtime. Fancy a cuppa?"

Evensong brought 113 parishioners to the pews. Jane was mortified. As the closing chords of Jill's prelude thrilled the air around them, and seconds before Jane began her Preces, Renata sneaked into a back pew to join the Goodall clan amid much rustlings and titillation from the rest of the congregation. Jane puffed out her exasperation. Renata knew her presence would cause a stir, yet here she was. Jane pushed her spectacles up her nose and went straight into "Gloria Patri" without so much as a howdy-do.

In the vestry afterwards, as she changed out of her vestments into her street clothes, her mobile phone rang. She saw the caller's name and her heart sank but she answered anyway.

"Yes, Colin?"

He was terse and got straight to the point. Rumours were flying up and down the valley that greatly embarrassed the church. Was it true? Was she a homosexual and, more importantly (because this would be most important thing to Colin), was the Bishop aware?

"The matters you raise are of a private nature and I will be discussing the situation with Bishop Hegarty in due time. I really have nothing to say to you on this, Colin."

It was exhausting brushing him off, but she finally managed to. But not before he had accused her of bringing not only the church, but the whole community into disrepute by insisting on being head judge of the Beer and Cheese Festival. The whole thing was now a debacle, especially when that wonderful Ms. Braak had gone to so much bother to write such a lovely article about it in the *Sunday National Review*, a very reputable paper. He pressed on her that she should consider stepping aside and he would willingly volunteer to replace her as head judge at such short notice. It was the only possible way to save the festival.

Jane patiently explained she would not be stepping aside, there absolutely was no need to, and with great relief, finished the call. Well, at least he'd not heard that her erstwhile homosexual cohort had been the wonderful Ms. Braak. That news had escaped him, so far.

She dithered in her office, clearing up small pieces of paperwork that really could wait. She straightened up her desk and even dusted a little. She admitted she was reluctant to leave this little sanctuary and find Renata waiting for her outside, or Wendy full of anxious good intentions, or maybe Mrs Agnew with a crowd of torch-wielding villagers. Meeting Renata filled her with the most trepidation.

Her army training had taught her how to fend off worse than Mrs Agnew, but it did nothing for dealing with the feelings Renata still engendered.

An hour later, she finished up her game of solitaire and switched off the computer. On leaving her office and entering the darkness of the nave, despite her protestations, she was ridiculously disappointed to find it empty.

"Let me take care of Colin." Bishop Hegarty placed his cup and saucer on the kitchen table and reached for a biscuit. "He's been choraling in my ear for the last week about this. You'd think it was the second coming."

Jane was surprised at his sanguine attitude. She'd offered her resignation twice, and each time, he'd batted it away like so much cherry blossom.

He took a bite of a lemon crunch and examined the remaining half appreciatively. "Did you make these, Jane?"

"Yes. But…" She needed more than platitudes where Colin Harper was concerned. The man was as dangerous as a viper in a woodpile, yet Bishop Hegarty seemed totally untroubled.

"Could I have the recipe for Susan?" he asked. "I'm sure she'd love these."

Jane finally took the hint. He wanted to deal with this in his own way and there was nothing she could do but wait and see what that involved, and how it would affect her. It was a fair deal because she had not been honest with him from the outset when he had approached her after her resignation from the army. He had stuck his neck out for her. She had left with the kudos of a war hero, but the impiety of failing in her role as chaplain. And she had repaid him with hiding a truth that could damage his last year of office.

He had told her of his impending retirement, and she wondered if all these years of sitting on the fence over St Poe's versus St Dunstan's closure had all been a charade. With the scandal she had dumped on him, he could easily leave the good fight for his successor to worry about. A nice little gambit for a man who heartily disliked confrontation.

"I hear that tickets have been selling hand over fist for the festival?" He changed the subject. "Best year yet, I was told."

"Yes. It was sold out in under a week. We had to get more tickets printed."

"And, of course, Colin was upset about that, too." Bishop Hegarty gave a knowing smile. "There're a lot of things Colin is upset about these days. His congregation has depleted terribly in favour of St Poe's."

"And we all know why."

Bishop Hegarty raised a shushing finger and smiled. "And now all these rumours that the supermarket is moving from High Wallop down to Cross Quays."

"I haven't heard that." Jane was not surprised. Cross Quays was the larger town with a higher footfall.

"Oh, yes," he said with a sparkle in his eye. "Your friend

has been doing a series of articles for the newspapers about British traditional fayre, and supporting rural businesses. She's pointed out that local people prefer local produce and that they should keep their own family-run farms and shops going rather than use the larger conglomerates. It's a fight for survival for rural communities these days and her words had a deep effect on our fellow Wallopians, given that they now see themselves as the gateway to gourmet beer and cheeses, thanks to her previous article."

"Ouch. I bet Colin isn't happy about that. Half the valley uses his church for the easy shopping afterwards." She felt immediately mean as soon as the words came out.

"Oh, Ms Braak has fallen very far from his prayers," the Bishop said, and took another biscuit. "I've been privy to a lot of Colin's disappointments recently."

"It makes sense," Jane mused. "I mean the local businesses rallying. Wendy told me the micro-brewery where her brother Will works just got a big order from a London chain of bistro bars. They were very chuffed."

Bishop Hegarty beamed and rose to leave when loud hammering began next door.

"Oh. I thought the workmen were finished." Jane said. She peeped out the window but couldn't see the Gerrard & Son van anywhere along the back lane. She escorted the Bishop to the front door and handed him his coat.

"Thank you, Jane."

On opening the door, the hammering became even louder. A man was erecting a "For Sale" sign by the front picket fence of Renata's cottage. Jane stood, stuck in the doorway, staring blindly at the garish sign so that Bishop Hegarty had to squeeze around her to exit. He also paused to look, and sighed.

"I will miss Renata," he said. "I'm sorry she decided this wasn't the right place for her after all. I imagine it won't be long until you have a new neighbour. Goodbye, Jane."

"Goodbye," she murmured, barely registering his departure. Her gaze was glued to the sign, her heart a hard, lumpen thing in her chest, squeezing cold blood around her ice cold body.

CHAPTER 10

The morning of the Lesser Wallop Beer and Cheese Festival dawned bright and clear. The booths, erected the day before, were now filling up with the vendors and their various wares. Red, white, and blue bunting fluttered in the breeze, the tea tent was already doing a brisk trade in breakfast cuppas and bacon rolls, and the PA system was being tested, tested, one, two, three.

There was excitement in the air. A feeling of expectancy. Those locals involved bustled about, full of importance and industry. Jane wandered among it all in her white judge's coat and carrying her clipboard. Underneath, she wore a floral day dress befitting the warm weather promised by the weather forecast. She was feeling good, cheerful even, for the first time in weeks. The first time since the "For Sale" sign had gone up. Today was the ultimate distraction from thinking about the cottage next door and her neighbour, who had not moved so much as a stick of furniture before leaving again. It made her sad to see a dream crushed and know she had contributed.

She'd used the last few weeks to think about Renata. About their talk. About their kiss. And she'd watched in trepidation as a succession of Londoners were escorted to and from the house next door by the estate agents. Any one of these strangers could be her new neighbour. Not that she was staying that long herself. She hadn't been joking about the new mission. Change was in the cards.

She should contact Renata and tell her to stay. Tell her to take the house off the market. After all, Jane was the one who'd be moving soon, and Renata should be the one living here. She loved the Wallops. A few times Jane had actually reached for the phone to do just that, and hesitated then changed her mind.

"I hope she comes to the festival," Wendy said. "After all, she's the one who made it such a huge success. Maybe you could offer her a job as a judge?"

"Why do you always have to take things one step too far?" Jane answered. "If she turns up, I'll buy her a pint of the winning brew as a thank-you. How about that?"

And now she was subconsciously looking for Renata's sun-gold hair. Or a glimpse of her slim, elegantly dressed figure drifting gracefully through the crowd.

By mid-afternoon, she couldn't have seen an elephant moving through the crowd. The green was packed, and everyone seemed happy, especially the vendors, who were doing a brisk trade.

"Jane!"

She turned around to see a young man approaching her, arms opened wide.

"Chubby?" she said, perplexed, snatching his name from fond memories long past. "Chubby Benson?"

"Padre Jane!" He grabbed her up in a huge whirling hug, much to bystander amusement. Over his shoulder, as the word spun past, she saw more guys approaching, guys she knew, and knew well. Guys from The Royal Wessex, her old regiment.

"Padre Jane. Look at you in your civvies."

"Hiya, Padre Jane. You've got fat!"

"She's gone soft, too. Look at her all teary-eyed."

She was surrounded by twenty or more young men, dressed like any other young lads on a hot day, in shorts and tee shirts and all taking turns to hug her, or slap her gently on the back and kiss her on the cheek. Except these were exceptionally fit young men. Tall and lean and well-muscled with close-cut hair and strong tans. They were all from the county regiment, just back from a stint in Cyprus and the locals knew it.

The crowd around them grew as more and more people paused to watch their vicar being cheerfully greeted and congratulated by her ex-flock. Suddenly, at the back of the crowd, she caught a glimpse of sun-gold hair and a satisfied smile on a beautiful face. Renata caught her gaze and for a moment they locked in shared understanding. This was a gift. She had somehow arranged this, for friends from her old regiment to be here and share in her special day. Then Renata turned away and was lost to Jane's sight.

Why had she done this? Jane was caught up in another hug, her face buried in a meaty shoulder. Why? Was it a kindness? It had to be. The pungency of Paco Rabanne swamped her. Someone was laughing too loudly. Someone slapped her back and she staggered a little. All the guys were pleased to see her and she was overwhelmed at seeing them again. A flood of love and comradeship swirled around her. Renata had known it would be like this, and had arranged it. Arranged it for her.

"So, gov, where's all the beer, then? This is supposed to be a beer festival, ain't it?" Chubby said.

"Follow me, you big booze hounds. Why am I surprised to be showing you where the beer is?" Jane led them to the beer tent, the massive marquee dominating the green, and bought them all a pint of whatever competing beer caught each one's eye. She passed half an hour in small talk, catching up on all the news, good and bad, but mostly good. The lieutenant colonel had somehow learned of this festival and organized transport for them to come over and see their old Padre. So many had wanted to come, they'd had to draw straws. She finished her own pint and tactfully withdrew when their attention started to drift towards the local girls who had descended in flocks all about the handsome soldiers.

Outside, the afternoon was warm and muggy and she was glad the beer tasting was a morning event and over and done with. It would be too easy to get drunk in the headiness of a hot afternoon, as a lot of visitors seemed hell-bent on doing. The cheese tasting would begin at three o'clock, so Jane began to make her way over to the other large marquee.

On the way, she stopped by the tourist information booth to say hello to Amanda, who was working there. She gave Jane a huge grin in welcome.

"You look happy," Jane said. "Usually you want to punch the tourists by mid-afternoon."

"Oh, I still do," she said. "I'm happy because Renata's offered me a job."

"She has?"

"As research assistant. She wants a gofer in the valley, as she's not going to be staying." A flicker of disappointment crossed Amanda's face.

"So, she's still going to work with Bishop Hegarty, then?" Jane asked.

"Yes. She says she can do it remotely from anywhere as long as there's someone here to do the groundwork. She's paying me a fortune." The last bit came out a little breathlessly, as if she could hardly believe her luck.

"I'm really pleased for you," Jane said. "I can't think of anyone better to do the research. You'll be excellent at that." She had to concede Renata had made a smart move there.

"Thank you." Amanda gestured at the green. "I wish she wasn't going, though. I mean look at this place. She has the Midas touch."

"That she has." Jane looked around her at the throng, pleased to note the smiles and waves she was getting from her own parishioners. There were still a few glares from those who favoured St Dunstan's, but these were in the minority. She was happy to note that while they may disapprove of her sexual orientation, few had followed their pastor's lead and boycotted the festival.

"Where is she? Have you seen her?" she asked. They needed to talk. Especially about the sale of her cottage. That had to stop.

"Oh, she's around somewhere but she'll be heading back up to London soon," Amanda said. "Shall I tell her you're looking for her?" She gave Jane a curious look she couldn't quite interpret.

"Yes. If you see her, tell her I'm at the Cheese tent and I'd like to have a word. If she's free, that is."

Amanda nodded, satisfied.

"Renata! There you are." Bishop Hegarty descended on her. "I've been looking for you everywhere. Susan and I hoped you'd join us for a Pimm's at the beer tent. They sell civilized beverages, too, you know. It's not all beer."

He indicated for her to accompany him and she gladly fell into step alongside. "I'd love to, Andrew."

She was glad for the distraction. Since seeing Jane caught up in a million manly bear hugs, she had been meandering around the green feeling rather lonesome. Amanda was busy at her booth, swatting off tourists, and Wendy was on duty and nowhere to be seen. She'd wanted to go over and share in Jane's joy, but the satisfaction was in witnessing it from the outside, knowing she had been a key instigator.

"Excellent turn out, isn't it?" Andrew looked around with great pleasure.

"I can't compare," she said, "but everyone seems to be enjoying themselves."

"Oh, this has been a very good year, all thanks to you." He led her to a small table where his wife smiled warmly as Renata settled in beside her.

"Good afternoon, Susan," Renata greeted her. They had met many times while Renata and Andrew compiled their research and ideas on his ley line theories.

"I see our head judge had a little surprise of her own today," Andrew said. "Was that down to you, too, by any chance?"

Renata shrugged. "I can't believe she earned a gallantry medal and hardly anyone in this valley knows about it. These people have no idea an actual war hero is talking to them from the pulpit. But Jane swore me to secrecy, so what's a girl to do?" She raised her glass in salute and Susan and Andrew joined her silent toast.

"You had a very inventive solution," Susan said.

"Only because your husband put me in contact with Lieutenant Colonel Davis and he was more than happy to organise the rest." Renata sipped her Pimm's with enjoyment.

"But you're still leaving us?" Susan asked.

"I'm afraid so." Renata grimaced slightly. The idea was unpleasant, but she'd thought carefully about it. There was no other option. She felt too emotionally raw to stay. "It's a nuisance, especially as I've just sold my London apartment. But timing is everything and I'm sure something is just around the corner."

"Let's hope it's something wonderful," Susan said. Renata drank to that.

The something wonderful just around the corner came forty minutes later as Renata slowly made her way towards the car park.

"Yoo-hoo, Renata." She turned to see Wendy striding towards her in her uniform, smiling warmly.

"Hi," Renata greeted her. "Had a busy day? I haven't seen you at all."

"That's because your New Life versus Old Life stylesheet is wonderful, Renata."

"Oh?"

"I filled it all in and really concentrated on it, right? Meditated, yeah? Asking for guidance with my career and all that. Remember I wanted out of the police?"

"Yes?" Renata felt a small bubble of worry rise to the surface. And because this was Wendy, it was probably a methane bubble and very explosive.

"Well, it worked. I *am* meant to be a police officer after all."

"Well...great. Not such a big leap at all, really," Renata said, deeply relieved. "So what helped you draw this conclusion, besides the list?"

"I just made a drug bust!" Wendy nearly squeaked with delight. "Well, more like I found a ton of pot plants."

"Sorry?" Renata went very still. "Pot? Here? In the Wallops?"

"Oh, yes. Half the youth in this valley are smoking weed. It's absolutely everywhere this summer, and I just found a huge supply of it. Huge! All growing in little pots. The Superintendent is very pleased with me."

"Wendy, when do you get off duty? Can we go for a drink?"

"I'm not sure if I can. I have to go up to High Wallop for a briefing. I might be going on a raid!" She grabbed Renata by the arm and squeezed. "Imagine. Me. On a raid. Busting up a cannabis farm."

"Wow. I can't. I mean…a raid." Renata leaned in and whispered. "Who do you suspect?"

Wendy shrugged. "Dunno. High Wallop detectives have some suspicions, though. Not sure who."

"Okay. Well, I'd better let you go. You have important places to be." Renata stepped back. "Be safe."

"Thanks, Renata. Thanks for everything."

She watched until Wendy was well out of sight then ran for her car as fast as her kitten heels would let her.

"Where do you keep it?" she demanded. Tipper looked vague. He'd only just surfaced from his bed, even though it was three thirty in the afternoon. He stood looking at her, befuddled, scratching at his locks. She wanted to shake the stupidity out of him and a modicum of sense in.

"What you on about?" he asked around a huge, rude yawn.

"You have seconds to ingest what I am about to tell you. Then I'm turning around and leaving, because the truth is, I don't give a rat's anal gland about you and your scabby granddad." She spoke swiftly and quietly and, unfortunately, inches from his ear. "There's a police raid brewing and I bet it's directed at this field and all the little hijinks that go on in it." She registered the widening of his eyes and continued in a hoarse whisper. "So, if you have any funny farm business going on here or in the immediate vicinity, I suggest you pack it all up and get the hell out of this valley 'cause half the kids are off their sweet little apple-cheeked faces and the law is none too pleased about it. Can I make it any plainer?"

"Shit!" He snapped into full wakefulness.

"I've often been told I have a tongue like a Taser, but in this instance, it's all about you waking the fuck up and moving out. Do you understand?"

He blinked. That was enough understanding for her. She swung around ready to leave when he caught her elbow.

"Look," he said quickly. Then, noting her glare, dropped his hand immediately. "Look. I don't sell it, okay? I'm a producer. I grow the stuff and harvest it. That's my thing. Zoe and Winston, they sell it on. I don't even get a cut from the street stuff. I just trade with them."

She was amazed at his stupidity. He even did business badly. "If it's on your property, then it's your problem. I bet it's not sitting in either Zoe's or Winston's laps," she said, and watched as his gaze swung towards the scrappy old caravan behind his camper. "Oh, my God. Don't tell me you're so dense, you're growing it on your own doorstep. You have a hydroponic nursery in there, don't you?"

He started. "How do you know tha—"

"I'm Dutch, you idiot!" She raged and pointed at the caravan. "Get that thing out of here, and fast." She had no more time for him. She swung on her heels and marched down the field back to her car, giving off such negative vibes, even the dogs left her alone.

How had she let herself get involved in this mess? She had some nerve calling Tipper an idiot, since she wasn't much better herself. What if the police had found all those seedlings she'd dumped? There were hundreds of them. And why hadn't she asked Wendy for more details on her big find? *Because you are freaking out, that's why. If you weren't so bloody moonstruck over Jane Swallow, none of this would have happened.*

She berated herself all the way back to her hire car, which she turned sharply towards Cross Quays and the route out of the valley. She'd go straight back to London tonight and get the hell out of here.

A mile down the road, she screeched to a halt and sat tapping the steering wheel. With a hiss of frustration, she did another sharp turnaround and headed back the way she'd come, back towards Lesser Wallop and whatever madness that entailed.

Amanda was just packing up the tourist booth as she entered the green. The majority of the stalls were closing as the crowd began to dissolve. People were either heading home or moving on to the pubs and local restaurants for their evening meals.

"Have you got a moment?" she asked. Amanda was surprised to see her.

"I thought you'd gone back to London. Jane was looking for you earlier."

Pleasant news as that was, Renata had no time to dwell on what Jane might have wanted. "We may have a small problem. Is there somewhere we can talk?"

"Um. Here's as good a place as any. You can help me pack up." Amanda looked curious. Renata moved inside the small canvas booth and helped pile pamphlets into boxes, moving as fast as possible.

"I caught hold of Wendy just before I left," she said.

"Oh? I haven't seen her all day and she promised to drop by. You're putting those in the wrong box."

"To hell with the box. She told me there'd been a drug bust. *She'd* found some pot plants. A huge number, she said, and there's going to be a raid."

"Holy fuck!" Amanda dropped her armload of literature all over the ground.

"Yeah. I pray like that, too," Renata said drily. "I think we need to go back to where we dumped Tipper's little party treats and check those weren't the ones Wendy found."

"That is the maddest thing I've ever heard. What if the cops are lying in wait?"

"I think we'd see them from a mile away. Anyway, we're

meant to be out and about doing research for Bishop Hegarty. No one can prove any different."

"And we just stumbled across hundreds of baby cannabis plants?"

"Yes. Yes, we did, because Wendy says this valley is full of it."

"Wendy's full of it. I'm not going." Amanda bluntly refused.

"Fine. I'll go myself and make sure that nothing can be somehow traced back to you. Like your sudsy palm prints, or any incriminating household rubbish in the bags you gave me to dump the dope in."

"Your prints are on the bags, too."

"And that would be why I'm really going. Like I give a damn about you and your incriminating Toilet Ducks."

"Okay, okay." Amanda sighed and dragged her mobile phone out of her pocket. "Let me tell the babysitter I'll be a little late."

The drive up the back lanes to Gyfu's Coyne was quiet, as nearly every valley resident was over in Lesser Wallop enjoying the festivities. The shadows were growing longer on the eastern side of the valley, but the air still retained its warmth.

They both knew exactly where they'd dumped the bags. It involved parking the car and heaving themselves on foot several yards up a slope. There was a wobbly, dry stone wall, and behind it a gully, and in it, the two large, black bin bags lay undisturbed.

"There's no way Wendy could have found them unless she rolled down this hill head over tit," Amanda said, and there was relief in her voice.

"Then this valley must be stuffed to the gills with weed," Renata answered, "because she found loads of it somewhere. Just how much of the stuff does Tipper produce? Have you any idea?"

Amanda shrugged. "Not my weapon of choice. Gives me a gods-be-damned headache. I'm a *vino rosso* woman. But if he's been using my gardens again, I'll gut him."

"He uses the derelict caravan behind his camper as his centre of entrepreneurial excellence."

"Bloody muppet."

"He swears he just grows and harvests it and leaves the selling to Zoe and Winston."

"Jesus, what a crew. Poor Jane being manacled at birth to that shower." Her face twisted in distaste. "I wish they'd all fuck off back to London and leave her in peace."

Renata grunted. "So, what do we do with this?" She indicated the bags.

"Nothing. It's rotting away nicely in the plastic."

"So just leave it here, even though the police are aware of a load of cannabis in the valley and are actively looking for more?"

Amanda snorted. "Believe me, the local coppers are pig lazy. They'll do little more than pick up a few kids and deposit them with their parents for them to deal with."

"Wendy reckons there's going to be a raid, and you can

guess where they'll focus, especially if they're as lazy as you say."

"Tinker's Field," Amanda concluded. "It's a dead cert. Well, if he's smart, he'll get that caravan out of the way."

"That's what I told him to do." Renata stood and dusted down her dress. "Okay. Looks like we're through here."

"Good," Amanda said. "My feet are soaking."

"Mine, too." Renata looked down at her expensive mud splattered shoes in surprise. "These cost a fortune."

"Why is it so wet here?" Amanda looked around her. "It's been dry for weeks now. They're talking about an early summer drought, for heaven's sake."

Renata moved away to where the ground was less boggy. Looking back, she could see the gully was very wet, unnaturally so, considering the land surrounding it. "It looks like a runnel of some sort. Where does this gully go?" she asked.

"Dunno. It ducks underground a few yards from here. It probably links into the Wallop River somewhere below."

Renata looked up at the hilltop behind them, its face now a swirl of shadows. Amanda followed her gaze and named the mount. "Gyfu's Coyne."

"After the old goddess," Renata murmured. "Funny that it was never Christianised."

"Not here. In this valley the old names stuck. Look over there. That's Aled's Beacon. Aled was an Anglo-Saxon chieftain. Or even the Saturn Fields, where they dug up the Roman villa." She pointed to the fields opposite glowing gold in the last of the sun's rays. "The old names remained in some form or other. Even St Poe is an alteration for Pu, an ancient water sprite."

"A water sprite?" This was news to Renata, but then, that's why she'd employed Amanda. She had superlative knowledge of the valley and its surroundings. "That has to be connected to healing water and St Poe's. It just has to be."

Amanda shrugged. "I'll look into it, boss. First thing in the morning. Can we go now? My feet are freezing and I need to get home and pay the babysitter."

Renata dropped Amanda off outside her small terraced house a few streets back from the village green, which was now eerily quiet. After saying goodbye, she pondered what to do next. Return to London? Her overnight bag sat on the back seat, and if she wished, she could go on to The White Pig, where she'd pre-booked a room, but it was probably wiser to head back up to London, far away from the Valley of the Dolls. At least until all this drug-bust talk was over. She could work remotely with Amanda and Andrew. But she was tired now that the adrenalin running through her for the last few hours had drained away. And it might look suspicious to book a room on the busiest weekend of the year and not show up.

Yeah, sleep first, then back to London tomorrow. Her mind made up, she put the car in gear. She'd go home first thing in the morning. Except that London was no longer home. London was a sold apartment filled up with packed boxes heading straight for storage until she found somewhere else to live.

She ignored the clenching feeling in her chest and tried to ignore the voice in her head that told her this was where she belonged, here in this crazy little valley. *You've got to move away from here,* she told herself. *You've got to move away from* her.

She circled the green and headed out on the North Lane that eventually hooked up with the main road to High Wallop. It was a moonless night and clouds obscured the stars. The darkness felt lonely and empty. Or maybe that was just her own feelings projected onto it.

Up ahead, a small red light blinked from out of the grass verge at the side of the lane. It hazed a wobbly red streak across the tarmac. Renata slowed down. It was an odd place for a light to be. As she drew nearer, it became obvious she was looking at the rear light of a bicycle lying on its side, partially under a hedge. Then she saw the flash of pale legs scrabbling weakly for purchase. Renata stopped the car immediately and jumped out. There was a furious scrabbling from under the bicycle as the rider tried to detach herself from it and the hedge she'd fallen into.

"Jane! Oh, my God! Are you hurt?" She ran to help her up. "What happened? Are you all right?" She was aware of the hint of panic in her voice. Jane dragged herself onto her feet and wobbled on the uneven ground. Renata reached for her elbow to steady her.

"Jane, what the hell happened?" she demanded.

"I don't know," she said crossly, and tugged her arm

away only to tip backwards and have to scramble for Renata's hand again. "I fell over. Must've hit a pothole or something."

Renata looked around. The road surface was smooth. There were no potholes anywhere. Then she became aware of something else. "You stink of booze."

"Of course I do. I'm the beer judge. I probably smell of cheese, too."

"Yes. Well." Renata decided to let that slide. "Are you fit to be out on the highways and byways on your bike?"

"Of course I am." Jane whipped away her arm again and stumbled onto the road.

Renata followed, observing her closely. "You're not steady on your feet. Keep still and let me examine you. Did you hit your head?" she asked.

"I'm fine." Jane spun full circle. "Where's my bike?"

"Over there." Renata pointed to where it was lying partially in the hedge. She continued to watch Jane suspiciously, trying to decide if she was drunk or concussed. Jane went over and tried to pull the bicycle upright.

"Here, let me." Renata reached past her and righted the bike. The back wheel was bent. "You're not riding this any further tonight," she said. "Look, let's fling it in the boot of the car and I'll take you home." Even as she said it, she could see Jane's face fall into a sullen mask. A blunt refusal was on its way, but Renata held up her hand before her offer could be dismissed. "You need to get home, Jane, and this bike isn't going to take you anywhere."

The sense of her words seemed to sink in because Jane stood undecided looking up the road then down at her buckled wheel, a perplexed frown on her face, as if she couldn't understand how she got there.

"I've lost my glass— No, here they are, in my pocket." She pulled her spectacles out, then put them back into her pocket.

"Come on." Renata gently prised the handlebars from Jane's grasp and half-carried, half-wheeled the bike to the rear of her hire car and popped the boot open. She was surprised she managed to do so without any further objections. After stowing the bicycle as best she could, she found Jane dithering near the passenger door, looking lost.

"Here." She opened the door for her. "Let's get you home, eh?"

Jane obediently slipped into the passenger seat without a word, immediately raising Renata's suspicions that she was not her normal self. She scrutinised her carefully but with a sly sideways glance. Where was the local doctor's office? If it were a Tuesday, she would have found them all at the quiz night. Then Jane placed her head against the cool of the car window and hiccupped.

"You *are* smashed," Renata said. And relief washed through her, she wouldn't need a doctor, just a lot of hot coffee. She did a nifty three-point turn and headed in the opposite direction back into the village.

"No-*hic*-no, I'm not." Jane hiccupped. "It's j-just-*hic*-ugh." Jane gave up trying to communicate and waved a hand ineffectually at Renata, indicating that she should shut up and drive.

Renata drove silently the ten minutes it took to arrive at Rectory Row, the only noise the quiet purr of her engine and the hiccups of her passenger. A smile played around her lips and she had to fight to stop from reaching over and giving Jane's hand a comforting pat. Apart from several wet hiccups, the mood in the car was peaceful and relaxed with only the thin light from the streetlamps and the illumination from the dash highlighting the curve of Jane's cheek each time Renata looked over at her.

"Does this happen every year?" she asked. "The head judge gets poleaxed? Is it part of village tradition?"

"I am not-*hic*-drunk. I simply fell off my bike. A car passed too close and I wobbled-*hic*."

"A car?" Renata didn't like the sound of that. "A car forced you off the road? Do we need to call Wendy?"

"No." Jane's answer was blunt.

"Are you sure?"

"Let me out-*hic*-here. I can walk from-*hic*."

"No." Renata was equally as blunt. "I'm taking you and your bent bike home and that's final." She swung around the final bend with more gusto than intended and Jane fell against her with a disgruntled "Oof."

Despite the narrow lane, Renata parked partially on the pavement, not caring that she was blocking it. No one would be traipsing down Rectory Row this time of night, and she suspected her stay would be minimal if the symphony of hiccups and tuts beside her was anything to go by.

Jane lurched out of the car and zigzagged up her garden path to her front door. Renata followed several steps behind, eyeing her cautiously. A few seconds were spent fumbling in her pockets for the door key, then came the rattle of the key finding and losing the keyhole. After several futile attempts, Renata's fingers itched to take the key from Jane and get them both inside and out of the night air, which was turning chilly. The rattling continued for a few moments more until it mercifully ended with a decisive click and the door swung open.

Jane found the switch with ease and the hallway flooded with light. Renata made to follow her.

"Stop right there." Her nose was inches from Jane's flattened palm. She stopped immediately, wrestling an absurd feeling of hurt at being sent away so soon. Then Jane pointed to her feet. "Not on my carpet with those mucky shoes." Then she spun away up the hall.

Renata looked down at her feet. Her shoes were indeed muddy, right up to her ankles from her earlier adventure up Gyfu's Coyne. Well, at least she wasn't being denied entry point-blank. She kicked off her dainty heels and after a slight hesitation, reached up under her dress and pulled down her pantyhose, kicking them off her damp, bare feet onto the doorstep.

Jane glanced back and spluttered in disbelief. "You can't do that," she squeaked as she reached out and pulled Renata into the hall. Then, with a quick glance up and down the street, she slammed the door shut after them. "What will people think if they see you pulling off your tights at my door?"

Renata shrugged indifferently. "That we couldn't wait?"

Jane flushed brightly.

"There, I cured your hiccups." Renata moved on into the lounge.

Whistlestop looked up from the couch and reluctantly dragged himself off it, stretching his long legs and arching his bottom at her in a languorous yoga pose, presenting her with a view of his bony backside.

"Everyone has an opinion in this house," Renata muttered and made for the kitchen. "I'm going to make you some black coffee, okay?"

"I take mine black."

Renata shook her head. "Okay. Where do you keep the coffee?" She began opening cupboard doors, looking for the tin.

"I can't drink coffee at this time of night. I'll not sleep." The answer was more a mutter and Renata had to strain to hear it. Jane was becoming sleepier and sleepier.

"Herbal tea, then." She was determined to prolong her stay by being useful and making sure Jane was comfortable before she left. "Where do you keep it?"

"Top shelf." A big yawn—or maybe a sigh? "By the coffee."

She was surprised Jane wasn't at her shoulder, bossing her about. After switching on the kettle, Renata drifted back to the door to see Jane lying on the sofa occupying the warm spot Whistlestop had made. That wasn't like her. Renata frowned. Whistlestop whined at the back door to be let out, so she tended to him. When she returned to the sofa, Jane was fast asleep. She lay on her side, her dark hair a muss all around her face, and her pink mouth softly pouting in a troubled sleep.

"Jane?" Renata gently removed the glasses that had somehow reappeared and perched lopsided on her nose. "Jane. You can't sleep here. You need to drink some water, then go to bed." Maybe she should leave her. Pull a throw over her and go. She prised off Jane's shoes and considered the coat she was wearing for a moment. Could she manage to slip it off and not disturb her too much? Probably not.

"Jane, honey. Can you sit up for just a moment so I can get your coat off?" She gently touched her shoulder. Jane moaned, her mouth made little kissy noises and she murmured something indistinguishable.

"What was that?" Renata leaned in, her ear close to Jane's lips. The temptation to turn her head, just a teeny-weeny bit, and kiss her, was incredible, but a no-no. A definite no-no.

Jane muttered again.

"What do you need?" Renata asked and leaned in even closer. Jane's breath stirred her hair. Jane raised herself on to one elbow and Renata leaned back, feeling a little embarrassed at being caught so close.

"I couldn't hear you," she said a little defensively. "What

were you trying to say?"

In answer, Jane leaned over the edge of the couch and vomited all over Renata's feet.

Wendy arrived just as the doctor was leaving.

"Hi, Dr James." She awkwardly greeted the doctor at the door and stood far back to let her exit. Then she turned to Renata, who was showing the doctor out.

"I came as fast as I could." She looked anxious. "How is she?"

Renata showed her into the lounge. "Okay now. She's fast asleep in her bed. Dr. James says it's a mild concussion. She gave her some tramadol and a list of instructions about rest and recuperation that we can wrestle about with her tomorrow. Because you know Jane won't do a thing she's told."

"Dr James is nice," Wendy said, and reddened. Then, "It smells funny in here." She wrinkled her nose.

"You can help me clean up. I only had time to give the carpet a quick swipe and wash my feet before the doctor arrived."

Wendy looked down at Renata's bare feet and frowned.

"She puked on me." Renata offered by way of explanation.

"Is that why your shoes and tights on the doorstep?"

"No. That's a lesbian thing. You wouldn't understand."

Wendy gave her a weird look and Renata laughed.

"Joke. Come on, grab a cloth and some disinfectant and help me."

Wendy obeyed and followed her into the kitchen. "You said you found her lying on the road?"

"On the side of the road. Almost under a hedge. I saw the bike lights first. Otherwise, I might have driven past her." She didn't like voicing that possibility.

"Is her bike still out there?"

"It's in the back of my car." Renata knelt by the sofa and began scrubbing with her cleaning cloth. "Honestly, Wendy, I thought she was tiddly. After all the beer she must have drunk at the festival, I mean."

"She doesn't drink that much. It's like wine tasting. Most of it ends up in a spittoon."

Renata scrubbed harder. "I feel really bad I missed that she was ill."

"It's easily done with a head injury. Especially if it's not a bad one." Wendy offered genuine sympathy. She raised up off her knees. "Is your car open? I want to bring the bike around the back."

Renata reached in her pocket and tossed the keys over. "It's parked badly."

"I'll drive it around to the back lane. I imagine you're not going to The White Pig tonight, are you?"

Renata shook her head, unsurprised at Wendy's astuteness, and too tired to pretend that Jane didn't matter to her. Renata was still reeling from the backswing of the pendulum. When she'd first seen Jane, she was filled with rancour and self-victimisation. That had now spun her the full one hundred and eighty degrees and washed away down the cosmic plughole. Life was like that sometimes. It had her facing west, then came up behind her from the east like an effing train. She had tracks all the way up her back to prove it.

She was rinsing the cleaning cloth in the sink when Wendy came in through the back door. The grim look on her face stilled Renata's hands under the running water.

"What?" she asked.

"Her bike," Wendy said. "It has paint on it from another vehicle."

"Like scratches? Like she scraped against something?" Was Jane in trouble?

"No. Like someone hit her, out on the road."

Renata's face went numb. It actually went numb, even as her hands cramped with the pins and needles from the adrenalin racing through her. "She was knocked off her bike? By a car?"

Wendy chewed the inside of her lip as several thoughts flitted across her face at once.

"Jane always looks after her bike," she said. "It is—was— pristine. She loves it. She would not ride around on a dented, scratched bike. It's called Sissy Sparkles, for God's sake."

Sissy Sparkles was news to Renata. She stayed silent and waited for Wendy to continue.

"Plus, I saw her bike this morning and if it had been all scratched up, I'd have noticed for sure. The paint from the other vehicle is even on the rubber of her back tyre. I think she was hit while she was riding home. Did she mention a car to you when you found her?"

Renata thought back. "She told the doctor she remembered nothing about falling off her bike. But at the time—I mean when I picked her up off the grass—she did say something about a car, though she was very cranky with me."

"Cranky?"

"She was more interested in scolding me than telling me anything useful." Renata felt anger and agitation swelling inside of her now. "Show me the bike," she said. "Do you get a lot of drink driving at festival time?"

"Yes, but usually we're all over it with police checks. Tonight we were...you know."

Renata nodded. "Any luck?" She tried to sound casual as they went out to the garden shed the bike was now housed in.

"Yes. But you know I can't say anything until they're charged."

"Sure. I understand." Renata was raging to know if Tipper or Winston had been lifted. Surely, Wendy would say if that was the case?

Wendy found the pull cord light switch and the small shed flooded with too much light from the overhead fluorescent. The bike stood out in stark relief. It was propped against the wall, the rear wheel buckled into a sharp angle. Now that she knew what she was looking for, Renata could clearly see the smear of white paint over the pearlescent red framework. Poor Sissy Sparkles. There could be no doubt the bike had been hit from behind.

Renata let out a long breath of frustration. "They could have knocked her under the car. They could have killed her."

"Was the rear light on when you found her? You mentioned seeing a red light earlier."

"Yes, it definitely was on. That's how I noticed her."

"Okay," Wendy said. "I'll have the lads from High Wallop drop by in the squad car tomorrow morning. They'll need to take the bike away. You'll still be here, won't you?"

"Yes," Renata said. "I'll make sure of it." *I'll be here until Madam summons up the energy to toss me out herself.*

But until then, she was planted.

CHAPTER 11

The doorbell chimed pleasantly at exactly seven thirty in the morning and Renata struggled from under her throw and leapt from the couch in seconds flat before the visitor rang again and disturbed Jane.

Andrew Hegarty stood on the doorstep eyeing her shoes and pantyhose. Renata cringed inwardly. She had totally forgotten about them with all the brouhaha last night.

"Don't tell me," he said. "It's a lesbian thing. I wouldn't understand." He took one look at her face and burst into gales of laughter.

"Come in before you wake the whole neighbourhood." She drew him into the hall, sweeping up the shoes and tights as she did so. "I take it you've already been talking to Wendy?"

He chuckled all the way past the lounge and went directly into the kitchen. Renata surmised it was his habit to go straight there when he normally visited.

"Yes. PC Wendy told tales. What would we do without her?" he said.

"Keep some secrets, I should imagine," Renata replied and clicked on the electric kettle.

"I know she had a career crisis and you helped her

enormously, Renata," he said and pinned her with a clear blue stare from over the rim of his glasses.

"I did nothing. She sorted it out all by herself. Sometimes people just need to relax and contemplate where they are before making their next move. So many live on automatic pilot. It helps to turn the pilot off once in a while and sit down with a map."

"Wise words indeed. Now tell me, how's our patient?"

"Conked out and I'm hoping she'll stay that way for another couple of hours. Dr James is coming back to see her later this morning."

"Well, let her know that I am taking the service this morning at St Poe's, and I've sent word out that the evensong will be at St Dunstan's. We might as well put Colin's shoulder to the wheel for a change. He needs to be seen contributing more to this community." His words were light but his eyes darkened with what might have been anger.

"I take it he boycotted the festival? Never mind. I know he did. Otherwise, he'd have been at my shoulder complaining about everything all afternoon."

"Oh, that he did anyway, but in a long letter. And funnily enough, Susan and I had the best time without him glued to our side. But perhaps that's a little unchristian of me?"

Renata snorted. "More like a sensible conclusion. I haven't heard a word from him since the article hit the papers, and that's a blessed relief, if that isn't too Christian for me?" She poured boiling water into the teapot.

Bishop Hegarty laughed again, a big, booming sound that

filled the kitchen. "He does bend the ear once he grabs it."

"He rips it right off and keeps it in his pocket. Have you had breakfast? I'm about to make some toast." Renata looked around for the bread bin.

"No, thank you. Susan always sends me out with a full stomach." He patted his paunch contentedly. "She says it eases the load on my parishioners' pantries."

Renata poured the tea and idly wondered if Colin Harper bore such a grudge against St Poe's and Jane, and just about anything Lesser Wallopian, that he'd knock her off her bike. Immediately, she squashed that thought. The man was a vicar. A pain in the ass, but still a vicar. So that made him a holy pain in the ass. She suppressed a chuckle at her awful joke.

"The police are collecting her bicycle later this morning for forensics," she said.

"Yes. It's a pity one of the side effects of the Beer and Cheese Festival is irresponsibility and drink driving. Usually, there's a big police presence, but I heard they were conspicuously absent last night. Something to do with that drug raid at The Dancing Bear in Cross Quays. Apparently, they apprehended quite a few ne'er-do-wells down there."

Cross Quays. Renata felt the slightest relief that Tinker's Field had been bypassed, combined with the begrudging thought that Tipper and his ilk had got away with it. It was a mixed response and the root of it was Jane being spared the embarrassment of a drug arrest in her immediate family. Renata knew it was only a temporary reprieve and that conviction was inevitable. It always was with the criminally stupid. Tipper and Winston would forever be a millstone around Jane's neck, which pissed her off. Jane would never escape them with their constant financial leeching and odious life choices.

"Have you ever heard of an ancient deity called Pu, a water sprite?" she suddenly asked, determined not to think about Tinker's Field and its inhabitants.

"Pu? Not that I recall."

"Amanda brought it up yesterday. She told me there used to be an ancient water sprite worshipped in the valley, and St Poe's was named for it. I just thought it was too coincidental not to mean something."

"I thought Poe was the early Christian saint who drowned off the coast near Cross Quays?"

Renata shrugged.

"That would be the water connection, I suppose. Amanda's idea is intriguing, but then she is an expert on all things historical around here. She once told me she gleans a lot of old folklore from the oral history of the old people she cleans for. Isn't that fascinating?"

"She's a clever woman. I'm glad I had the bright idea to hire her."

From overhead came the sound of footsteps moving from the bedroom towards the bathroom.

"I think your patient is on the move," Bishop Hegarty observed and drained his cup. "I'd better go before I end up in a tug of war over who is going to do the morning service. You know what Jane can be like."

Renata escorted him to the door wondering at his comfy assumption that she knew what Jane could be like. He'd heard the rumours about Jane's sexuality—everyone knew that by now—but how much did he know about her relationship with Jane, and their parting? She bit back a sigh. No one seemed to know, though, how much Jane despised her.

"Please keep me in the loop with whatever Amanda comes up with, will you?"

"Of course."

Once he said his goodbyes she headed upstairs to Jane's darkened room. The curtains had been pulled against the early morning sun and Jane was curled up on her side in bed with Whistlestop sprawled out at her feet. He raised a lazy head to acknowledge her arrival before swooning back onto the bedspread.

Jane had clearly gone back to sleep and Renata perched on the bedside behind her and examined the pill bottles on the side table trying to determine if any had been taken during Jane's trip to the bathroom.

"Wha— Get off my bed!" Jane suddenly snapped awake. Renata sprang to her feet. "Bad boy," Jane continued groggily. Renata glared at Whistlestop as he slid off the bed and slunk out of the room. Slowly, Renata sank back down onto the bedside, embarrassed at her knee-jerk reaction.

Jane rolled onto her back and slowly propped herself up against her pillows. She glanced over and registered Renata with a look of surprise. "Have you been there all night?" she asked, alarm punching through her grogginess.

"Don't worry. The doctor said no contact sports." She waggled a bottle of pills. "Did you take any more of these since last night?"

Jane shook her head and held out her hand obediently as Renata shook a couple out for her. She swallowed them down with the glass of water Renata passed her.

"How are you feeling?" Renata asked.

"Like an elephant sat on my head and farted in my ear." She smiled. "Is that a haiku? You elevate crankiness to an art form."

"And you elevate my blood pressure to a blood spatter. What time is it?"

"Nearly eight. Andrew is taking your morning service and evensong will be in St Dunstan's. No work for you today."

"But—"

"Nope."

"I—"

"No can do. It's all organised, so shut up and sleep. Unless you'd like a cup of tea?"

Jane sighed and leaned back, then nodded. "I'd like that," she said quietly. "Could you also give Whistlestop his breakfast, please? There's a tin of dog biscuits near the bread bin. He gets three or four in his bowl and he likes a drink of tepid water with them."

"What, no Earl Grey?"

"Don't give him any ideas. Every time you set foot in

this house his manners go to the wall. But Earl Grey for me, please. Black, no sugar."

Renata gave a mock curtsy and left the room, a half-smile playing on her lips. As she descended the stairs, another rap sounded at the door and she received the first "Get Well Soon" bouquet of the day.

By mid-morning, the house was awash with cards and flowers. Renata had run out of vases long ago and was improvising with milk jugs and jam jars, which she spread around the house. A particularly lovely bouquet from Andrew and Susan Hegarty sat in Jane's bedroom by the window she had insisted on opening to let some fresh air in. Jane remained in her bed after a small fight that Renata won, at least until Dr James's visit, when it was declared she was fit to rise and mingle with the rest of humanity again.

Two High Wallop constables came and removed the bicycle from the shed. After a quick chat with Jane, they admitted they didn't hold out much hope of finding the car, which was probably back in London by now. Everyone knew the mad way Londoners drove around the valley.

Renata wasn't surprised at their negative prognosis before they'd even collected the evidence, given their lazy attitudes. She was damned if she was making them any tea. They could gasp all the way back to the police station. They made Wendy with her eager get-up-and-go attitude look like a human dynamo. It became apparent to her why Wendy had her momentary career wobble. It would be hard working with asshats like that and seeing them take all the icing on the cake. Debilitating indeed.

The next visitor came to the back door. Tipper stood on the back step and looked extremely surprised at seeing Renata there. She stepped back and let him enter.

"How's Aunt Jane?" he asked, eyeing all the flowers cluttering the table.

"Having a shower. She'll be down in a moment." She moved away. He was another one she'd not be making tea for. He could dehydrate, desiccate, and blow away, for all she cared.

"Hello, Tipper." Jane appeared at her shoulder and Renata decided to drift off into the lounge and leave them to talk in the kitchen. The less time she spent around that turd, the better.

"How are you doin', Aunt Jane?"

"I'm feeling a lot better. Not as bad as all the flowers would suggest." She smiled. "Would you like a cup of tea?" She was touched he had come over to see her.

"Can I have a coffee instead?" He settled into a seat at the kitchen table.

"How's Dad?"

He shrugged. "Okay. Talking about going back to London."

"Oh. Already?" She wasn't surprised. Winston never stayed anywhere too long. When she was a kid and he dragged her all over the country, he used to say it was his Traveller blood. It made his feet get itchy and he had to move on. She'd always supposed it was because the police came sniffing around and his collar got itchy, so he up and ran somewhere else.

"He asked me to ask you to talk to those Hackney guys for him. The Prison Fellowship ones."

"Tell him he'll have to come and see me himself. I'm not sure that offer is still open. You have to talk to them directly from jail." This was annoying but typical Winston behaviour. Kick the gift horse in the mouth, then afterwards try and count its teeth.

"I wanted to talk to you about something, Aunt Jane." He glanced cautiously towards the lounge, where Renata could be heard on her phone. "It's about Zoe."

"Sure. What's up?" *Please don't let her be pregnant. Please don't let her be pregnant,* she silently chanted.

"We split up."

Thank you, Lord. I owe you one. "Oh, dear," she managed to say aloud, then noticed the scratch marks on his neck and cheek, mostly hidden by his dreads. It must have been a nasty goodbye.

"She's gone off for a bit," he mumbled. "Thing is, my caravan is on her pitch and she says I have to get it off right now. Like, immediately." He tugged gently at his dreads, always a sign of stress with him. "Would you mind if I parked it behind the church, just for a few days until I can get somewhere else?"

"That scrappy old caravan? Can you even move it or is it rusted into position?"

He nodded his head vigorously. "Oh, yeah. I can move it easily."

"Why don't you just dump it? It can't possibly be habitable anymore."

"It's good for storage." His cheeks flushed a dull red and she relented. He hadn't much in this world and who was she to judge what was precious to him?

"You know that no one can stay in it if it's on church property. And it can only be for a few days, max."

"Sure. Sure. No one will be sleeping in it. It's only full of my stuff. And I promise to move it again in a few days."

"Good. Because I'm having enough trouble with Colin Harper without him accusing me of using church property for personal storage."

"I promise it will be gone in no time. I just need to pop up to see some mates in London and arrange somewhere for it to stay, then I'll come and get it, okay?" Tipper sprang to his feet and kissed her on the cheek. "Thanks, Aunt Jane. Tra-ra" He was out the door before the kettle had even boiled.

"He was quick." Renata stuck her head around the doorway.

"Yes, he was," Jane said trying not to sound aggrieved. "Here, you can have his coffee."

"What did he want?" Renata moved into the kitchen and accepted the cup she was offered.

"Just to let me know he was heading off for a while. So is my dad." She took a sip of coffee and thought about it. "In fact, they're all on the move."

"The ship must be sinking."

"Don't be mean. And why is your pantyhose on my washing line?" Jane frowned out the kitchen window at the offending article flapping in the breeze.

"You puked all over my feet last night and do I make criticism? You'll find my shoes drying on the back doorstep."

"Your feet are ugly. They obviously offended me in my delirium." She turned back to find Renata bemusedly examining her bare feet. "Why are you still here?" she asked, then felt a little bad about demanding that kind of answer.

"I'm waiting for my pantyhose to dry."

"You know that's not what I mean. Your house is for sale and you have Amanda working for you remotely. You don't need to be here." She tried to sound a little more gentle.

"You're ill. I'm trying to be useful." A stubbornness had crept into her voice.

"Renata, you're about as useful to me as my appendix." Jane took another sip of coffee and muttered into her mug, "And you grumble more."

"I found you under a hedge, and not in a fairyland sort of way," Renata came back at her. "What was I supposed to do, dump you on your doorstep and drive off? You'd probably be dead in the dahlias the next morning if I hadn't called Dr James."

"It was a very mild concussion. I would have coped fine."

"My pantyhose begs to differ. So do my beautiful Stella McCartney shoes."

"Stella McCartney shoe—singular." Jane glanced back out the window. "I'm afraid it looks like Whistlestop has eloped with one of them."

"Nooo!"

"Well, you did leave them lying on the doorstep," she shouted after Renata, who was running barefoot down the garden after Whistlestop. He immediately dropped his bounty and fled behind the greenhouse.

"Poor boy." Jane took another sip and waited for Renata to come stomping back up the lawn. "He probably thought Christmas had come. All that expensive leather and the smell of ugly feet."

Renata held out a well-chewed shoe. "That dog is costing me a fortune. He's lazy, spoilt, and overindulged. I mean, tepid water, for God's sake."

"Shush. He's watching." A long snout leading up to a pair of worried eyes peeked at them from around the side of the greenhouse. "You'll upset him."

"Aw, gee. Why don't I give him my other shoe and he can chomp on the entire six hundred quid's worth? That'll cheer him up." Renata waved the shoe at her. "Your hound has done nothing but eat money since the moment I arrived."

"You spent six hundred pounds on shoes? That's indecent." Jane was aghast.

"It's tax deductible. Also, I'm rich and single. What else would I spend money on?"

"I would have guessed lap dancers, but your knees are too knobbly."

Renata stared at her. "Are you winding me up?"

"Like loose yarn." And she was. She was teasing her, and she was enjoying it.

"You're actually joking with me. Just how hard did you hit your head?"

"To be honest, I think the pills are making me a little high. I don't think I want any more."

"You're bloody well taking them until Dr James tells you to stop." Renata had steel in her voice. "I don't care if you're so high you're floating above the house. You're taking your tablets."

"Don't tell me what to do."

"Dr James is telling you what to do. And I'm telling Dr James if you don't. That'll teach you."

"Wait." Jane stared at her. "Are you flirting with me?" The thought had streaked into her head and she almost convulsed in getting it out. The moment the words hit the air, she experienced a combination of mortification and fascination as to what the answer would be.

Renata tensed. Denial flashed through her eyes, then it was as if her whole body relaxed into an honest surrender, and she smiled, sheepish. "Yes. But you started it."

Jane blinked. True. She had. A fleeting sensation of power filled her. Power and satisfaction, and she set her cup down, then stepped up to Renata and kissed her, hard.

It was a very impolite kiss, rough and smothering, and

she wrapped her arms around a shocked Renata's waist and felt her immediately melt and mould into her. Their kiss deepened as Renata woke up to it and responded, and Jane didn't care anymore about the why and wherefores, because for whatever reasons, all she wanted was this kiss. There was more than history between them, she sensed. There was still a certain amount of care and consideration, and she had seen it since Renata had reappeared in her life. Renata, who wouldn't be here like this if she didn't care.

Jane slowed the kiss and it became softer, more mellow. After the initial intensity, it flooded with emotion, a contact beyond words, and the world simply drifted away. She felt the delicate trace of Renata's fingertips on her skin above the waistline of her jeans, and the flat of her own palms were pressing into Renata's back, pulling her closer.

"Hey guys, I— Oh!" Wendy stood by the open backdoor with a look of surprised embarrassment. Renata leapt back, flush-faced. She flashed Jane a look of panicked guilt but Jane was in the same situation. Her lips still stung from their kiss and her pulse rate felt like she'd run a mile.

"Um. I need more pills." She reached for the bottle on the kitchen table.

"No, you don't. Not until three o'clock." Renata removed the bottle from Jane's hand and set it on the countertop. Then she snatched up her handbag. "Don't let her take any more until three, okay?" she said to Wendy as she brushed past her, words falling from her mouth almost as fast as she was walking.

Wendy watched her go. "Does she know she's not wearing shoes?" she asked.

"It helps her run faster," she said, tone dry.

"And why is she running at all?"

"Marathon training." She picked up her cup, and noticed that her hand was trembling.

"Jane, what exactly is going on?" Wendy asked, expression shrewd.

"I've no idea. Maybe I have a fever." She touched her own forehead for effect.

"You do look very flushed. Your cheeks are on fire and your mouth is the colour of sin."

Jane frowned. "Are you smirking at me, Wendy Goodall? 'Cause if you are, you can turn around and go straight home. I promise not to overdose on Dr James's happy pills."

Wendy snorted and led Jane back into the lounge. "I don't think there's a pill for the kind of happy you've got." She switched on the TV and found the sports channel. "Now sit down and watch the rugby. England is playing France. But you have until three o'clock to figure out just what the hell *you're* playing at."

What, indeed? Jane sank into the chair and stared blankly at the telly, the taste of Renata's lips still in her mouth.

CHAPTER 12

"I'm surprised to still find you around," came a snide comment behind her.

Renata turned to find Colin Harper loitering partway between the dining room and the foyer of The White Pig. He was clearly on his way to lunch, but couldn't resist the chance to shoot a remark at her back as she signed out of the room she'd not even unpacked in.

"And why would that be, Colin?" She faced him, determined that he would not snipe and run. She'd had enough of unsaid things today. If the man had a problem, he was damned well going to spit it out before she shook it out of him. If she couldn't shake Jane Swallow, then she might as well shake Colin Harper, though for a completely different reason.

His cheeks glowed a dull red and he kept casting anxious glances into the restaurant at whoever was waiting for him there.

"I hear the festival was a drunken morass, full of soldiers from the county barracks, and that the head judge was knocked off her bike by a drunk driver."

It annoyed her that he referred to Jane as the head judge rather than by name. He really did have a chip on his shoulder about her. And she hated how he tried to belittle Jane's accident.

"The festival was a success with everyone, as usual. The soldiers were from Jane's old regiment and behaved perfectly. What happened later with the hit-and-run driver was unfortunate and the matter is now with the police. I'll send Reverend Swallow your best regards." She turned back to the reception desk.

"It should have been in High Wallop." She could see from the mirror behind the reception that he took a step towards her. He was obviously not used to being politely dismissed. "We have the perfect venue at the cricket ground, and you were told that."

She snapped her credit card back into her purse, the one with Whistlestop's teeth marks, and dropped it into her voluminous Gautier handbag. "The perfect venue is the village where the original license for the fair was granted. Have you any idea just how unique that is, Colin? It's a fantastic source of tourism that Lesser Wallop badly needs. And the village coped just fine with the influx of people. In fact, I see lots of room for expansion and none of it needs a cricket ground." She was walking towards him now, on the way out. As she drew level, she could see only one other person in the restaurant, an Asian gentleman, who was obviously waiting for Colin but with less and less patience.

"Expansion! You're talking nonsense, Ms Braak. The damn thing needs to be moved for health and safety's sake."

"But all the regulatory requirements are met each and every year."

"Not if people are getting run over by drunks."

"Don't be ridiculous. Drink driving is obviously outside the remit of the local council's health and safety measures. I think you'll find it's more a criminal action. Now, if you'll excuse me, I need to get back to London."

"And that's another thing. It didn't take you long to flip the cottage in Rectory Row that Bishop Hegarty helped you buy. It's positively indecent to turn a profit like that on church property."

"*Former* church property, so it's positively none of your business." The man was infuriating. He simply had to have the last word. Even his guest looked uncomfortable as their voices carried.

"And now, I really must get a move on. If you have any suggestions, then please send them to the festival committee. They meet the third Thursday of every month." She made a point of looking into the restaurant and giving a gracious nod of farewell to the abandoned guest before sailing out the door, leaving Colin spluttering in her wake.

Jane spotted Amanda and Wendy in the back corner as she entered The Potted Crab. She waved at them and walked briskly to the table.

"Sorry I'm late. I can't walk down the street but everybody

stops me and wants to know how I'm feeling." She dropped her cardigan on the back of her seat and sat down.

"Well, everyone's worried about you," Amanda said. "You could have been another little furry blob at the side of the road with tyre marks all over it."

"I certainly feel like roadkill with the drugs Dr James has me on. I'm really woozy. I was walking around like a zombie all day Sunday."

"Maybe that's why you were eating the face off Renata?" Wendy said with mock innocence.

Jane flushed. "I told you, it's not like that. I don't know what you thought you saw, but—"

"I'm a police officer. I'm trained to see."

"I'm sorry, Jane, but if Miss Marple says she saw it, then she damn well saw it." Amanda handed over the menu. "You were caught red-faced and red-handed. Now choose a cake. We've already ordered a pot of tea and a chocolate éclair each."

"Is this another intervention?" Jane asked, suspicious. "Because the last one left me with a hangover the following morning and emotional jitters for a week."

"And a huge congregation," Wendy added. Then she looked confused as Amanda gently shook her head at her. "What?" she asked.

"That would be part of the emotional jitters," Amanda said. "Our little friend here is in denial. She has skittered down her mouse hole and will not pop her whiskers back out until she's good and ready. Unless, of course, our Dr

James keeps prescribing tramadol. Then, apparently, she'll be a strumpet."

"I am not hooked on tramadol. Can't a person be little bit delirious around here without her best friends making massive assumptions on her moral fibre?"

Wendy's phone beeped from the handbag slung over her chair. She scrabbled to find it and blinked owlishly at the screen before rising from her seat. "It's the Sarge, I'd better take this," she said, and disappeared outside.

"This is definitely not an intervention, Jane. We've learned our lesson. Whatever is going on between you and Renata is your very own business, okay?"

Jane nodded. "Okay. Though, just for the record—nothing is. We lapsed, that's all. Just a lapse. So, how is the new job going?"

Amanda's face took on a different light. "It's wonderful. I can't believe the money I'll be earning, and because I can do it in my free time, I'm not losing out on my cleaning jobs. I need to keep those so I have something to fall back on when this little windfall finishes."

"Do you think it will finish soon?" Jane wondered how long Renata's interest in the valley would last, once her project with Bishop Hegarty was through.

"It depends on how much I unearth and how deep Renata wants the research to go. I'm already off to a running start. In fact, I'm meeting Renata and Bishop Hegarty this Friday. She's coming down for the weekend." She looked at Jane with an odd expression, then said, "I hear the cottage has been sold."

"Oh." That was surprising. "I hadn't heard." The "For Sale" sign was still up. She was unsure how she felt about it. It was obviously what Renata wanted to do, but it nagged at her that it was related to Jane's rejection. Then again, there'd been a second kiss, instigated by Jane herself, and the cottage was still to be sold, so maybe Renata wanted out, anyway? Maybe the Wallops wasn't for her after all? Maybe all that kissing meant nothing? And why did she even care? What was the point of coming into the Wallops and kissing people and then just going away again as if nothing had happened? Because things *did* happen when you kissed people. Renata ought to know that. She was the one with the "what you give, you get" philosophy. *She* was the one who'd started it. Wasn't she?

Jane studied the menu, but didn't really read anything. Everything was slipping out of control. Her job, her church, her home, even her health had taken a nasty knock-back, and now she was kissing people she had no intention of ever, ever kissing again. It had to be a form of hysteria.

Wendy reappeared and slid back into her place at the table. "That was High Wallop station," she said. Her cheeks were twin spots of excited colour. "The car that hit you has been found abandoned in southeast London. There was paint and scratch marks on it, all matching the damage to Sissy Sparkles."

"Half the valley goes up to London," Jane pointed out. "Half the valley actually *lives* in London."

"Whose car is it? I know all the Londoners around here.

I clean for most of them. Who was it?" Amanda asked.

Wendy shook her head. "It was stolen several months ago. Someone's been driving around in it with dud number plates."

"Well, that doesn't sound like any of the folk I work for. They're loaded." Amanda looked at Jane. "I was expecting you to be hit by a Lexus or a top-end Land Rover, not dud number plates."

"I feel such an underachiever," Jane said drily. "So, you're really none the wiser?" she asked Wendy.

"No," she said, clearly disappointed. "Not really." She looked down at her hands, avoiding Jane's gaze.

"It wasn't my dad," Jane said, suddenly reading Wendy's awkwardness. "I know he's a pain in the ass, but he wouldn't run his own daughter over. I'm his trust fund."

"True," Wendy agreed. "I'm sorry. His name just popped into my head."

"You're a police officer. It's supposed to."

Brenda arrived with their tea tray.

"Oh, I completely forgot to order my cake," Jane said. "Could I have a slice of the Victoria sponge, please?"

"Of course, m'dear." She placed an ample hand on Jane's shoulder and squeezed. "I'm glad to see you're up and about. Tell you what. Let's say this is my little treat, all right?"

"Thank you so much." Jane turned to her companions with a smile as Brenda ambled away.

"You'll get fat on so much good will," Amanda grumbled.

"Oh, look." Jane glanced towards the window. A young

woman walked past it outside. "There's Zoe. Did I tell you she and Tipper have split up?"

"No. That's the best news I've heard all week," Wendy said and bit into her éclair.

"I hope he stays well away from that type in the future," Amanda said. "Women like that are nothing but trouble."

Jane couldn't agree more. But she wasn't the only kind of woman who was trouble.

Renata turned inland from the coast and drove the last few miles up to the Wallop Valley. She sat behind the wheel of her rental car in trepidation, something she usually felt when she came back to the Wallops since knowing Jane lived there.

Today, she was more nervous than usual. She had been so strong all week, managing to stay away from the phone and not call her. She wouldn't have been sure what to say, anyway. For four entire days, she had thought about the kiss and how Jane had initiated it. She'd over-thought every word they'd spoken, right up to the moment when Jane's lips had touched hers. It was something Jane had wanted, no doubt about it, but once Wendy walked through that door, Jane had closed down on her.

Renata couldn't bear another rejection, so she had decided not to call. Instead, she would let Jane sit and think it over on her own and then, maybe, they would discuss it face to face when there were no pills, or fever, or intervening friends to use as excuses. She had no qualms about simply walking away and letting Jane sort her life out for herself. It was long overdue. And if there was a chance that a small sliver of that newly sorted life might include her... well, she would jump at it. But she had to be invited first.

For her part, Jane hadn't called. She hadn't sorted out anything, or wanted to talk about anything, either. No surprises there. Maybe she had done another runner. Renata imagined her hiking over the hills like a hobo with her stupid dog on a rope rather than have a hard but honest conversation. She almost smiled.

Amanda had been talking to her almost daily regarding the research she was doing on the water deity Pu, so she could surreptitiously keep up to date on Jane's recovery. Though the hidden glee in Amanda's voice left her with no doubt that Wendy had told her everything she'd seen in the kitchen.

In no time at all, she was drawing into the car park of The White Pig and grabbing her overnight bag from the back seat. The check-in was routine to her now, and even her room number was the same. She had become a regular without realising it. It took minutes to unpack and then she was straight down to business.

She called the Bishop on her mobile. "Andrew, I'm at the hotel. Where will I meet you?"

"Susan is asking if you'd mind coming here for afternoon tea. She's been baking." This was asked with such relish, she couldn't deny the man access to his wife's baked goods.

"How can I say no an offer like that? See you soon." She grabbed her car keys, stuffed them in her handbag, and headed down to her car. Andrew and Susan's new home was a few miles farther up the valley from High Wallop and Renata knew the way from previous visits. It was a house she enjoyed visiting. The view from the Hegarty's conservatory was amazing. Renata could look straight down the valley to the coast to where the diamond glitter of sea shone on the horizon. To her left, Gyfu's Coyne sat solidly on guard duty, while below it, the gunmetal grey of the Wallop River wove through the fields all the way down to Lesser Wallop. From this vantage point, the village was no more than a jumble of tiny rooftops looped by a belt of green willow, where Renata guessed the Sturry ran its circuit.

"This really is a beautiful view," she said looking out across the vista.

"Positively bucolic," Andrew agreed, and sat back smiling as his wife poured the tea.

"I sit in here most days and try to knit, but mostly I just look out at the valley and daydream with the needles in my hands. It's so restful," Susan said. "Now, if you'll excuse me, I must get back to my gardening." And she gracefully left them to talk alone.

Renata took a seat on the lounge chair opposite Andrew. The coffee table between them was filled with an array of cakes and sandwiches. She may have been invited for tea, but Renata knew there was a serious talk brewing and Susan was using her garden as an excuse to get out of the way.

"You both seem to be settling into the new house well," Renata said, accepting her teacup.

"The best move we ever made, though it does lengthen my commute, but only for several more months and then I retire," he said. Then, "Renata, I truly wish you could be as settled in your new home. How are things with Rectory Row? I hear you have a purchaser?"

Renata swallowed around the dryness in her mouth that always appeared when she thought about letting the cottage go. The Gerrards had done a splendid job restoring the downstairs rooms, and a fresh paint job had the place looking fantastic. It hurt that it couldn't be hers in the way she'd intended, but life had been hurting a lot recently. This was a summer of hard lessons and reopened wounds, and maybe she'd write a book about it someday, when she'd scabbed over sufficiently.

"It's just one of those things, Andrew," she answered lightly. "Nothing went as I'd planned."

He nodded sagely and sipped his tea. "Colin has commented on the quick turnaround of your house sale," he said.

"He's already publicly reproached me about it."

"Did he? Well, I'm afraid he's seen fit to take it further and address his concerns to Archbishop Wang Lee, my boss. It seems you and I are being accused of some sort of real estate skulduggery."

Renata remembered the gentleman Colin Harper had been dining with last week. Could he have been the Archbishop? "The last time I saw him, he said as much." Renata shrugged. "He seems intent on making mischief. What's behind all of this? He can't still be angry that this year's festival was such a success."

"It's several things with Colin. The main one being he wants St Poe's to close and leave St Dunstan's as the only church in the valley. The problem with that is St Poe's is one of the oldest churches in the county and extremely picturesque. And like any quirky country church, it has all the ailments of an old building, while St Dunstan's is the more commodious, modern structure."

"St Dunstan's looks like a category C prison," Renata stated bluntly. Built sometime in the seventies, with all the architectural allure of that era, it was nothing more than a concrete block with colourful windows.

Andrew agreed. "Even so, one of these churches will have to close in the foreseeable future, and Colin is trying to sway the odds in his favour by acquiring anything of worth from Lesser Wallop, like the festival. He tries dragging it up to the High Wallop cricket ground every year. This time, I think he thought he had a possible ally in you, but you proved false." He grinned. "So now he's punishing you with a scandal about your house purchase."

"So, my moral decrepitude is all about money and not my sexual orientation? That's refreshing."

"Not in this day and age. The church does not discriminate, that's the party line. But there are little pockets of backward thinking, and I'm sure Colin is tucked away inside one of them."

"So, he can't publicly abuse Jane on that level?"

He shook his head. "No. He can't be seen to do that at all. Not in the Anglican Reformation Church. It would cost him a lot to be seen to do so. Though Jane is effectively between a rock and a hard place. Much like when she had to leave the military. She could be an army chaplain but not bear arms, but when she did during that ambush, it placed her out of line with church philosophy and her position as Padre. She chose to retire gracefully rather than cause embarrassment to either of her masters."

"And now?"

"Now, even though the church recognises its gay clergy, it expects them to be discreet. Jane wouldn't be allowed the luxury of a public relationship such as Susan and I have. There are still a few more steps to go before any of us can crow about all-inclusiveness. It's the difference between tolerant and tolerable. People like Colin would tear it all down if they could."

"But he can't, so he's doing the next best thing. Trying to tear down St Poe's."

"And now that he knows you're working with me, he has gone over my head to a higher office to push his agenda forward. I think he has learned through the Beer and Cheese Festival that you are a formidable adversary when it comes to a war of words. Colin is a man of action. He will throw himself into the fray without a thought." He seemed to think this was a good thing. "The Archbishop has done me the courtesy of informing me that he is attending evensong at St Poe's this coming Sunday."

"Is this like a test? Does Jane know?"

"Jane knows. I told her myself. And it's not a test insomuch as the Archbishop wants to experience St Poe's for himself. Jonathan is a shrewd man. He will see how Jane interacts with the community, and he wants to feel the robustness of her church firsthand. I have no worries St Poe's will prevail."

"But it would be nice if Amanda came up with some little gem that cemented St Poe's foundations even further into this valley." Renata smiled and selected a sandwich from the plate.

"That would be very agreeable." Andrew helped himself to a sandwich, too.

Renata left the Hegarty's with fond farewells and promises to meet again soon. Driving away from that special view through the hill roads to The White Pig allowed her mind to run riot over Colin Harper and the upheaval his snitty little political games were causing. Finally, she latched onto a reinforcing thought, pulled her car over, and got her phone out of her handbag. A quick scroll through her directory and soon she was dialling. After several rings, a man answered.

"Hello? Is this Chubby Benson? You don't know me, but I'm Renata Braak, a friend of Jane Swallow's. She served with you in the Royal Wessex…yes, she's fine. It's just I want to ask a favour…"

The call ended satisfactorily and no sooner had Renata tossed her phone back into her bag than it started ringing again. She dug it out and looked at the screen. Wendy Goodall was calling her.

"Hi, Wendy. What's up? Sure. I'm about twenty minutes away. Yes, I came down early. See you soon." She hung up and put the car in gear and swung past the turnoff for High Wallop and headed all the way down the valley to Lesser Wallop.

Wendy was waiting as promised in The Winded Whippet. She was off duty and chatting to her father while sipping a tall glass of apple cider on ice.

"Want one?" She raised her glass as Renata approached. "It's really refreshing for the heat we're getting today."

"Sure." She joined her at the bar, pleased to see the place was quiet in the lull between lunch and dinner. "You said you had news?" she said, as soon and she'd been served and Wendy's dad had moved away.

"It's a bit of a long shot, but I've been thinking," Wendy began. "That car they found in London with Jane's bike paint on it."

"Yes," Renata said slowly and sipped her drink.

"Well, I could be wrong, but I think I've seen Zoe Blair driving around in a similar car."

Renata absorbed this. "Are you sure?"

"No." Wendy looked dejected. "And I'm not sure I can

convince my sergeant to push for a forensic check on her. Zoe, that is. To make a match with the recovered vehicle, I mean."

"Have you asked your Sarge?"

"Yes. And he said no."

"Ah." The picture clicked for Renata. Wendy hadn't the clout as a Special Community Officer to call the shots for High Wallop's boys in blue. She had her hunches, but her hands were tied as far as gathering proof went. "And Zoe has no police record, so no existing fingerprints or stuff like that floating around?"

Wendy shook her head. "No. She's as shiny as a Hollywood smile."

"And yet she hangs out with a load of people who have police records longer than a nautical mile. Like Winston Swallow, for instance. Strange, isn't it?"

"She must be very clever, 'cause I just know she's up to no good." She peeled the damp paper layers off her beer mat. "And she's back in town, too. Did you know she and Tipper broke up?"

"No. But I bet Jane was pleased." Everybody probably was. That relationship was tedious in several ways.

"She was. Oh, look, there's Amanda. I invited her along, too, but she wasn't sure she would be finished with work in time."

They shuffled along to make room for Amanda, who slid onto a bar stool beside them.

"Hey, guys. I just got away from Roland and Marian

Lynch. A lovely old couple, but it's impossible to break free once they start talking. Today, I was clearing out their under-stair closet, so I was well and truly trapped. Every single item I brought out held an hour-long memory for them."

"I don't suppose they had the source of Pu's healing spring in there?" Renata asked.

"No, just every possible artefact from the Indian Raj they could carry before they had to hop on back to Blighty," Amanda said with a rueful smile. "But I do have some information you and Andrew will be very pleased to hear."

"Tell me. Tell me now," Renata demanded.

"Are you sure? Won't Andrew be disappointed to be left out?" Amanda asked.

"Is Andrew paying you?"

"No, my unholy master of filthy lucre to whom I am enslaved." Amanda pulled a folder from the message bag slung over the back of her bar stool. "Order me a red wine and all this bounty shall be yours."

"I'm still not sure I see the connection," Wendy said. "So Pu and St Poe are the same guy?"

"No." Renata took a right turn and moved the car around the village green. "Pu was a mythical water deity, and probably no more than a spring renowned for its healing powers that was personified in ancient times. After the Black Death, when the spring became more popular, the

Christian Church moved in to take over the waters and changed Pu to Poe and then had to make Poe a saint to fit in with the vernacular. There was probably never an actual guy called Poe."

"Good, because it's a stupid name."

Renata decided not to comment.

"So the church can invent a saint, just like that?" Wendy snapped her fingers. "So I could be Saint Wendy if, say, I was rich enough, or did something amazing, like fly?"

"No, it takes some time to be ordained. It's a very complicated business these days. And if you could fly, you'd be PC Super Wendy," Renata said.

"That might help me pin Jane's accident on Zoe."

Renata made a sympathetic noise. "Anyway, this all happened in the Middle Ages when the King and the church were more or less the same thing. The healing waters saved one of Edward III's sons from the plague, so he made the place holy by royal decree and let it have a special feast day, probably set on the day his son was saved. Weren't you listening to Amanda?"

"On and off. When she gets into that professor mode, I kind of switch off. It's like being in school again."

"Well, it's only theory. There's still a lot to do. We need to actually find the spring and link it uncontestably to the folklore, then layer in all this ley line stuff that Bishop Hegarty has been investigating for years. There's definitely an interesting story here and it connects St Poe's with the festival. And all of that has to be good for Lesser Wallop."

"Are you going to St Poe's this Sunday for the special show?" Wendy asked.

Renata paused. "You mean the Archbishop's visit?" She wanted to go if only to support Jane by being another bum on a pew, but then again, the whole village seemed to be behind her. Did she really need the distraction of an ex who wouldn't go away sitting right in front of her? Another problem that wouldn't just lay down and die, but rose Lazarus style from the past to haunt her?

"Well, yes. She'd appreciate it. I know she would."

Renata shot her a quick look. Did Jane really need another problem? She stared out the window. Yes, bloody well she did. She also needed a rocket up her arse if only because Renata had sold out her happy-ever-after because of Jane's lack of emotional clarity. The least she could do would be to talk to her before she left for good. Well, not really for good. There'd be the odd visit back to unpick the Pu story, but in the meantime, Renata had a gig in Athens and Bucharest coming up. She'd be away from the UK for a few months and the idea was more than welcome.

"Here we are," Wendy said, and pointed out the car window at a pretty Victorian detached house. "This is where I live. Unfortunately, all my family live here with me," she said ruefully. "I'm not very grown up, am I?"

"A lot of kids have to bunk down with their parents these days, Wendy. It's the economy. You're lucky it's such a lovely house and your parents are nice people."

Wendy nodded sagely. She was a little drunk on apple

cider and Renata was more than happy to have run her home. Wendy opened the door and got out, then stuck her head back inside the car.

"So I'll see you on Sunday at church. Same place, same pew? The Pu pew?" She giggled again and slammed the door, then banged a goodbye on the roof.

Shaking her head at her friend's antics, Renata drew away from the curb. She was glad Wendy was not normally a drinker—she'd make an alarmingly animated drunk. Then it occurred to her that she now, seamlessly, considered Wendy a friend despite the fact she had known her for only a few months, if that. This valley, and everyone in it, got to her, and it irritated her that Jane was so damn stubborn.

She didn't want to go back to The White Pig just yet for an early dinner alone. Instead, she knew what she wanted to do. Her fingers itched to turn the car around and head straight over to Rectory Row. And she legitimately could because she still owned a property there. The contract had not as yet been signed. The new would-be owners were in a property chain and not free to sign, and for some reason the delay suited her.

But she didn't turn for Rectory Row. A part of her was afraid of the brewing conversation with Jane as much as she longed for it. This would be the final goodbye, and maybe that's why she'd been dragged back here—to get all the malevolence out of her system, to forgive and be forgiven, to heal into a responsible, caring human being capable of offering a loving, committed relationship. She had been accused of shallow emotions and selfishness too often by ex-girlfriends who wanted more than she had to give.

So, maybe she'd got it all back to front and Jane Swallow wasn't the love of her life after all. Maybe Jane Swallow was just a learning curve. A wound she had to heal, her lesson in the heart's humility, a person of importance in her life but not life itself.

Maybe there was someone out there for her. Someone she'd yet to meet, in Bucharest, or Athens. Yes, she would meet someone new and lovely and be open to a wonderful romance, now that she was purged of her negativity and abandonment issues. She tried to imagine herself with a sultry dark-haired beauty, but the imaginary woman kept morphing into Jane with her spectacles askew, snoring gently on the sofa before upchucking her beer and cheese all over Renata's bare feet. She chuckled. Now *that's* romance.

The rooftops of Cross Quays loomed a mile or two ahead. She had driven almost completely out of the valley and was cruising alongside the high hedges enclosing Tinker's Field, coming up on the entrance to it. Out of nosiness, and the need to turn around somewhere soon before she ended up all the way down on the coast and the heavier traffic, she turned in. The field was quiet with only a few mangy dogs lying about. She supposed on a nice day like this, most people would be about their business shopping, or taking the kids to the beach. The she remembered Jane's upbringing with Winston. There hadn't been many days at the beach. Jane would have been over by the broken play area with the dogs while Winston smoked dope, or had a shag, or went down to the pub, leaving her behind.

The thought made her glance over to where Tipper's camper van usually sat. It was gone, and, thankfully, so was the caravan holding his rolling cannabis farm. So he was on the move, as well. Smart lad. She suspected the police haul in Cross Quays had been a little too close for comfort and the Swallows had upped anchor and scarpered.

Renata did a nifty little U-turn and was pointing out of the field when the door of a nearby camper van opened. She wouldn't have noticed if the dogs hadn't kicked up a racket. She looked into her rear-view mirror to see Zoe Blair emerge and glare at her car. She was probably trying to make out if it was friend or foe. Renata didn't know if this was Zoe's own camper or if she'd moved on to another bloke. Disinterested, she pulled out and turned back the way she had come, towards High Wallop. She would have a bath and an early dinner after all. Tomorrow, she would meet with Andrew and Amanda and then she could decide if she really wanted to hang around another day for morning service on Sunday, or just get an early start on the road to London and out of Jane's life for good.

The thought left her melancholy.

"This is better than anything I'd imagined," Andrew said. He beamed at Amanda as she gathered up the maps she'd strewn over his conservatory table.

"It was my pleasure," she responded and threw Renata a very smug smile.

"And thank you for the photocopies. Archbishop Wang Lee is arriving later this afternoon. He is our guest for lunch this afternoon and I'd love to show him your research. We have invited Colin along as well, so he'll be privy to this, too, if you don't mind?"

"It's fine with me," Renata said. "I think it's about time he saw the bigger picture and understood it's not all about supermarkets and 'my church is bigger than yours'. There's a spiritual connection over the ages between St Poe, this valley, and an ancient god of healing."

"Yes," Amanda piped up. "It's about the intrinsic context history brings to the present day. We need to see the past as the backdrop for the way we live now. Both have value, and treated correctly, lay a firm foundation for the future. It's the same principal for the Royal family."

"Is it? How fascinating." Andrew's blue eyes twinkled. "So I take it I'll see you ladies in church tomorrow morning?"

Renata hesitated but Amanda's stalwart agreement seemed to have her nodding along. Okay, so she wasn't on her way to London first thing tomorrow.

They left Susan and Andrew's house on a high. Their first report had been overwhelmingly successful and there was no doubt they were onto something important. It concerned a venerated Plantagenet King of England, the Black Death, and a hidden valley with mystical healing waters that at the time were still treated with a pagan reverence. Renata tingled when she thought about all it implied.

Andrew Hegarty's own private research showed that for many centuries, this place had been a focal point of healing, his evidence of multiple ley lines crisscrossing southeastern England zoning in on a single point in Wallop Valley. Before it had been Christianized as St Poe's, this lost spring had served a prehistoric community for probably millennia. The significance of this site was mind-boggling.

"I can't believe this is happening to me," Amanda said, as they travelled down the hill road past the turnoff to High Wallop and on to Lesser Wallop. "I'm actually part of a team that is discovering something unique and incredibly historically significant. It's wonderful. It's fantastic. I can't believe it."

"You won't be coming in second best after this," Renata told her. "Universities will be headhunting you once this hits the TV screens."

"TV?"

"You bet. Once we deliver a complete package of research and have written the book, I can assure you my agent will start scouting the best people to present this in populist format, meaning television. It's happened to me before with the Universal healing book I wrote about five years ago. That's the one that made me my fortune and my name." She hammed that last bit up out of habit, but she was unduly proud of that book and the leverage it had provided her.

"I have that book. It's the first one I bought."

"See? And you bought all the rest after that, didn't you?" Amanda nodded.

"That's how it happens." Renata focussed on the road ahead. "You work and you work and one day, you hit pay dirt. And when you do, you just keep on digging."

"I may have lied to the Bishop," Amanda said after a few moments.

"What?" Renate nearly steered them off the road.

"About going to morning service."

Renata blew out a puff of relief. "I thought you meant your research was faulty."

Amanda gave her a look of abject horror. "Never! I'll have you know, I'm a professional. What I meant was, it's hellish for me to get all the kids up and out and ready for church, and then expect them to sit quietly while Auntie Jane gabbles at them from the pulpit."

"Ah. You've an atheist household, then?"

"Well, sort of." Amanda sounded very guilty. "I just agreed to go because Andrew is so lovely."

Renata shrugged. "Your kids will sort it out as they get older. Jane says she hadn't even heard of the Bible until she was ten. She thought God was a swear word, not an actual person—um, thing. Entity."

"You're not sounding like a true believer there yourself, Renata," Amanda said with a smile. "And I never knew that about Jane, but given how Winston is, I suppose it makes sense." There was a moment of silence before she asked.

"Will you go tomorrow?"

"Yes," she said. "Yes, I think I will."

Silence fell between them and Renata watched the rolling green hills, wishing she could stay on this path forever but knowing it would be far too painful.

"Have you been in love with her all this time?"

Renata started slightly then relaxed. "No. I used to hate her for leaving me. I hated thinking about her and the horrible way she'd treated me. When I saw her again, I'm sorry to say, that hate took off like a bucking bronco. Luckily, somewhere along the way, I sort of lassoed it and took a good look."

"And?"

"The anger wasn't for her. It was about being left, for being caught at being dishonest and paying for it. And I was angry about having to take responsibility when it was easier to blame her for leaving." She looked over at Amanda and gave a rueful grin. "An old and now very dead life pattern of mine."

"We all have them," Amanda admitted. "So, when you saw her again, something fell into place in your head?"

"Not at first. Remember, I was really angry. But...I don't really know what happened. I fell back in love easier than falling down a greasy slope. Though for me this is an older, wiser kind of love, not the hot, crazy teenaged stuff I've already gone through." She stopped. She had to think for a moment before she could say it out loud, here in the intimacy of the small hire car and in the presence of a new, but somehow trusted, friend. "But Jane hadn't a greasy slope to help her fall in love," she continued. "She's always stood on firm ground. She's got this inner strength, yet all she can see in herself is weakness. And the upshot is, she doesn't need me the way I need her. I look outward to the Universe to give me what I think I need but Jane finds it within herself." Her palms were sweating on the steering wheel.

"You need to talk to her before you go away."

Renata shook her head. "I think that would be the final goodbye, and I don't want to hear that just yet, though the Universe said it was okay for me to be the one who runs this time."

"I never want to take my kids to church if this is the emotional emptiness that comes out of it," Amanda said bluntly. "And I'm going home to burn all your books." She twisted in her seat as much as her seatbelt would allow.

"What? Why?"

"You are looking at a single mother of two adorable little bastards—that's what they are. Their father and I were never married. And let me tell you this, when we were breaking up, I did my best to make it work, but it didn't. It was just too far broken. But at least I know I did everything I could, and I never, ever wake up with a 'what if' hanging over my head or any of my kids' heads. I'm living out the truth of the circumstances of my life, and because of that, I am free to move in whatever direction lies open to me."

"Wow. That's wonderful." There might have been some tears lurking at what she had said.

"It's a quote from one of your books, you ass."

"Oh? Oh. Yeah."

"What I'm saying is, go after your girl," Amanda continued with passion. "Don't leave with things unsaid and your tail between your legs like some...like Whistlestop."

"Oh, that's a low blow. Dirty, low blow."

"Well, he *is* a mess."

Renata laughed. "That he is. But he's Jane's mess."

Amanda smiled. "Don't leave another one. That's all I'm saying."

She didn't respond and turned down the road to Amanda's. After dropping her off, Renata peeled back to the village green and drove slowly past the butcher's shop, the newsagent's, The Potted Crab, and The Winded Whippet, where she slowed down even more.

Zoe stomped along the street. She looked like a woman on a mission, her body language raw and angry, and she seemed to be on the lookout for someone. People avoided her, body-swerving so as not to make contact, averting their gazes.

Wendy had said Zoe was up to no good and Renata had to agree with her. She had seen Zoe twice in as many days, and each time she had been glowering. Something was wrong in her little criminal world, and Renata itched to know what it was.

She was so absorbed in her thoughts, it took her a while to realise she was minutes away from Rectory Row. One right turn and a couple of hundred yards and she could be there, outside her own pretty little cottage, with its "For Sale" sign.

Or did it have a "Sold" or "Under Offer" sign up yet? She suddenly wanted to know. Wanted to see her personal closure in the garish colours of the estate agency sign.

Renata turned right.

CHAPTER 13

Jane was in the back garden, deadheading roses. Renata watched her from the kitchen window in what was still her own house. The smell of fresh paint surrounded her, and she wished she could open the window to let the fresh air in, but she didn't want Jane to know she was there, that her ex-neighbour was watching her. She was overwhelmed with an unexpected sadness.

The "For Sale" sign still stood by the front gate—not "Sold" or "Under Offer" —so the exchange of contracts was still stalled. For the next day or so, this was still her house, these newly plastered walls and gleaming kitchen with its empty cupboards, the wood burner she'd had installed, and the lovely cream stair carpet. All hers, but never a home.

She ached with want. And when she looked out the window and saw Jane bent over the lush pink blooms, with Whistlestop stretched out on the lawn beside her, the ache grew stronger.

Amanda's message came through loud and clear, but not in the way she had intended. She and Jane were also too far broken. Renata couldn't go out there and talk to her. Words would choke her, and she knew she'd break down and cry, standing there like a fool blubbering over the garden fence. She turned away and quietly left, turning the key in her front door for the last time.

With time to kill and maudlin thoughts to pull out and gently examine, and because it was never far from her mind anyway, Renata drove over to St Poe's.

The graveyard was full of long shadows. Birdsong and the rustle of wind in the yew trees were the only sounds, and they were lulling and kind to her ear. She found a seat on a raised plinth near the graves of the two young soldiers and sat quietly with her eyes closed.

It would be wonderful if this restful little church held the secret to the healing spring water so well guarded by the old god Pu. It would secure its future forever. What a wonderful gift to offer Jane, a lifetime in this valley, safe in the work she enjoyed and surrounded by the people she loved. She was determined to provide that for her. She could still love her, but in a different way, and from a distance, quietly and gracefully, while she rebuilt her own life elsewhere. She would do right by her past and leave it at that. It was wrong to expect anything more. Jane had moved on and she needed to as well.

The crunch of tyres on gravel broke into her reverie. A black BMW drove in through the gates and halted before the old oak doors. Colin Harper emerged from the driver's seat. Renata slid off her perch and walked over to meet him.

"I saw a hire car out on the road and thought it might be you. Doing a little research are you?" There was a sneer to his voice, but then he had the kind of voice that always sounded like that. Renata decided not to interact with him on that level.

"Just enjoying the evening. It's a restful spot," she said pleasantly.

He sniffed dismissively and brought out a set of keys and opened the side door that said "Private". Renata was surprised he had keys for St Poe's, but then for all she knew, Jane had the keys for St Dunstan's. Maybe that's the way it worked around here.

"You and Andrew may think you have this all sown up with your ancient springs and heathen little idols, but there is no reason this needs to be an active church. It can store chairs, for all I care," he said as he stepped inside. "At the end of the day, the Archbishop will decide and he is more interested in community and service than historical drivel." He slammed the door, finally getting the last word, she noted with amusement.

Andrew had obviously declared himself as a Poe man over lunch, when he'd presented their opening argument of a link with the current church all the way back to Edward III, and beyond that into prehistory. It must have been a hard issue for Colin. And here he was now, most likely rifling through as much of Jane's notes as he could find, to see if she had any material on the subject. Little did he know Jane was as ignorant as him regarding the elusive background of her church.

Amused, Renata carried on walking towards her car. When she came alongside the gate, she turned to read the sign stating Jane Swallow was the rector of St Poe's. It still had the power to amaze her.

A particularly sweet trilling from an evening songbird drew her attention back to the trees at the rear of the church, and she paused. Then frowned. She took a step closer for another look, then another. Was that a...suddenly, she was in full trot towards the hitch bar she could see peeking out from behind the back of the church. On rounding the corner, Renata no longer heard the songbird, only the thunder of blood in her ears. She gawped incredulously in pure unmitigated shock at the scrappy old caravan tucked away behind St Poe's. She was looking at Tipper's caravan. Or rather, Tipper's cannabis bus.

The door was locked, and the windows blacked out with paint. Renata stepped away, but only after wiping her prints off the door. What in hell's name was this doing here? Did Jane know?

The sound of a powerful engine and the rattle of gravel told her Colin had departed, and this served to shake her out of her astonishment. Only by sheer good luck had he not seen the caravan. Imagine the consequences if he'd had it forcibly towed away, for he was the type of man who would organize the police to do that. Imagine if it were ever opened and its contents revealed? Jane had to be mad to allow this. But, then, Jane didn't know what was in it.

Renata seethed at Tipper Swallow and promised to thump him senseless if she ever met him again. She swung on her heels and marched to her car. This caravan had to go. It was a ticking time bomb right under Jane Swallow's career. Renata couldn't call on Amanda for help on this one. Amanda couldn't drive and had the kids. And if she went to Wendy, then it would become police business. That left Jane. It was time Jane became privy to what her family was up to in this valley.

Except Jane wasn't in. Renata sat in her badly parked car outside Jane's house, watching the "For Sale" sign next door swing gently in the evening breeze. This was turning into a really crappy day after such a fantastic start.

To hell with it. She needed a martini. Renata drove too fast out of Rectory Row towards the village green and grabbed the last parking spot outside The Winded Whippet.

The pub was still busy serving food, but she found a seat by the bar and ordered her drink, which was surprisingly good for a country pub.

"Hey." Wendy appeared at her side. "Thanks for the lift home the last night. I don't usually drink that much."

"You had two apple ciders, Wendy. Hardly a blow-out."

Wendy slid in beside her as a seat became vacant. There was an air of conspiracy about the move that caught Renata's attention.

"What's up?" she asked.

"I've seen Zoe Blair several times now skulking around the village. She looks like she's looking for someone, but every time she sees me, she scuttles away."

"Yeah. I saw her down at Tinker's Field and again in the village. Do you think she's looking for Tipper? Is he back already?"

Wendy shrugged. "Not that I've seen. And if he was, Jane would know because he'd be straight over to her for a handout. That's the way it is with him."

Renata mulled this over. How much to tell Wendy, how much not to? Perhaps her good intentions were going to hurt Jane rather than help her. "Do you know where Jane is tonight?" she asked casually.

Wendy looked surprised. "At dinner with the Archbishop and Andrew and Susan Hegarty. Didn't you see them? They're up at The White Pig, though the food here is better." She muttered the last bit into her glass.

"No argument here. But I haven't been there since breakfast."

Maybe that's what she needed to do. Go up to The White Pig and try to grab Jane for a moment. The second she thought it, though, she dismissed it. Jane would not appreciate being dragged away from the dinner table, especially for the crazy news that a caravan belonging to her nephew, possibly filled to the rafters with grass, was sitting behind her church on the eve of the most important day of her career. Oh, she would be interested, but not appreciative.

"What's wrong?" Wendy asked. Her thoughts must be written across her face for Wendy to pick up on them. Then, more forcefully, "If something bad is going to happen to Jane, you'd better tell me right now."

Was her face really that readable? "Um, I'm thinking Zoe is not looking for some*one* as much as some*thing*."

"What?"

"I can't tell you because of what you are."

She frowned. "Adopted?"

"What? No. But you never told me you were adopted." She swung around in her chair to face Wendy full-on.

"Oh, yeah. Me and Will are adopted. Mum and Dad aren't our real mum and dad."

"Well, blow me down."

"We don't even look like Mum and Dad." Wendy giggled. "Everybody around here knows we're adopted."

"Everyone but me. But it explains a lot. You and Will are peas in a pod, but as for your parents, they *are* your real parents and they love you. You don't need biological parents to have *real* parents."

"I know." Wendy gave a wide grin. "I've the best mum and dad in the world. So what were you going to say?" She doggedly brought the conversation back on track.

"Ah. I can't tell you because you're a police officer."

"What does that mean?"

Renata stared into her glass. Bollocks. She sighed. "I think I know what Zoe is looking for. But there's someone we both know who might be in trouble, through no fault of her own, and if I told you everything I knew, or thought I knew, you might be obliged to report it further."

"And would reporting it hurt this someone we both know?"

"This Sunday it would."

"What about on Monday?"

Renata shrugged. "It will smart, but maybe this someone

we both know needs to see someone else we also both know in a new light and understand there is nothing more she can do to help him if he refuses to be helped."

Wendy frowned in confusion and Renata whispered in translation, "We have to tell Jane that Tipper's a little shit. But not until Monday."

"Oh. Will you be here on Monday, then?"

That was a very good question and it always amazed Renata that just as she wrote Wendy off as daft, she wrong-footed her with alternative, but very pertinent, logic.

"Um."

"And by 'we' you really mean 'me', don't you," Wendy said. "I'll be stuck with the fallout on Monday, won't I."

"Well, yes. And Amanda, maybe. Though she knows even less than you."

"So, Amanda knows less than nothing, and you know it all, but you'll only tell me some of it in case I have to go to the law with what I then know?"

"Um. Yes."

"Okay. So, tell me some of it and let me decide."

Renata drained her martini, then set her glass carefully on the bar. "Okay, it's like this…"

Jane finished organizing her office at St Poe's, though it was never really disorganized. She'd been spending more time there than usual, as if she were clinging to it and trying to get as much time in its peaceful spaces as she could.

After all, tomorrow was probably it.

Her last service here.

She stared dejectedly around the comfortable space in this part of the church, its slightly crooked walls strangely welcoming rather than off-putting. No matter what Amanda and Renata had found, she doubted it would save this place, and Colin would get to turn it into a storage room. He'd be thrilled about that.

With a sigh, she locked up and stood staring out over the graveyard, thinking about the day not so long ago when Renata had shown up. Jane had assumed she was trying to run her out in some kind of revenge scheme, but now she knew that wasn't the case.

Why couldn't she just call her and tell her to stay? She clearly loved the valley and it seemed unfair for her not to be able to settle into the cottage next door. After all, she herself would be long gone and then Renata wouldn't even have to see her.

She somehow lost even more courage when it came to Renata. And to feelings. And especially to feelings for her.

No, that couldn't be. She couldn't possibly have feelings for Renata. Not again.

She slumped onto one of the benches near the church wall, knowing full well that, yes, she could and, yes, she did, and that's why she hadn't tried to contact her and tell her to take her cottage off the market. Because the matter of their last kiss still hung in her head and heart, and no matter how hard she tried to push the memory away or ignore the effect that kiss had had on her, it didn't work.

And here she sat, still a big coward. Still afraid of her heart.

Renata probably hadn't thought about their last kiss. It was all just some weird rebound thing for her, probably. A sort of closure from all those years ago when Jane had so cruelly run out on her. Another cowardly act.

She leaned her head back against the warm stone of the church and closed her eyes. Renata hadn't tried to call her since that kiss, so she, too, knew it had been a mistake.

Or maybe she was giving her some space, because if Wendy hadn't interrupted them, who knows what would have happened? She sighed again. She could imagine what would have happened. She thought about it every day, as much as she tried to convince herself she shouldn't feel these things for Renata, and instead she should be able to let go of the past and move on to the next assignment on her life's journey.

But it was proving much more difficult to convince herself than it had ever been.

Why couldn't things be simple? They used to be simple.

Jane stood and buckled on her bicycle helmet. She was using a rental these days until she could get her own bike fixed, and though it was a perfectly fine bicycle, it wasn't Sissy Sparkles.

She wheeled the rental around the church but stopped, staring into the brush behind the building. Tipper really needed to come and collect his caravan soon. He had parked it pretty well, and most people wouldn't pick up on it, but it wasn't completely camouflaged, and it did look a sight. How he had managed to even get it up here, she didn't know, since it looked like it could barely move, and it listed slightly on one side, like the suspension was sagging.

She couldn't see inside, since he had painted the windows black, but she figured it was filled with the odds and ends of Tipper's wandering ways. She had hoped that he would have been able to move it before tomorrow's service.

No such luck, clearly.

She mounted the rental and headed back into the village. There was nothing she could do but call Tipper and have him promise to move it next week. At least it was out of the way for tomorrow's service, and for that she was thankful.

The next thing on her agenda was the more difficult item. She had to call Renata and talk to her and clear the air before either of them left.

Renata drove Wendy over to St Poe's to see the locked-up caravan, looking as innocuous as ever behind the church.

"I mean, it could be empty for all I know," she pointed out, suddenly feeling she had bitten off more than she could chew.

"When did you last see Zoe?" Wendy asked.

Again, a very sensible question that Renata had to think about. "This afternoon. She was walking down the main street in Lesser Wallop. Looking pretty angry."

"Curious, because I don't think she's been into the Whippet. Mum dislikes her because she hangs out with Winston and a lot of the other bad boys. Mum always goes on about it when 'bad news' comes around. Winston is a regular every summer and there's always trouble."

"The only other place she might be hanging out is at Tinker's Field. I saw her coming out of a camper van there."

"Show me."

Renata glanced over at her, surprised at this more authoritative side to her, but did as Wendy asked and they drove down to Tinker's Field, which was lively given the time of night. A bonfire was burning and several people sat around it drinking from bottles. There was no sign of Zoe, though, and they decided not to get out of the car, especially if they couldn't see her. The camper van she had come out was gone, too, so Renata wasn't sure if that meant Zoe had left the neighbourhood altogether.

All in all, it was a disappointing night. Renata reversed out of the field and they drove back up to Lesser Wallop.

"I think the best thing is to wait until the Archbishop has gone and then have the caravan reported by a mysterious tip-off—that would be you—and taken away," Wendy said.

Renata nodded agreement. "And what about Jane?"

Wendy sighed. "She doesn't know what it contains, if anything, and if there *is* cannabis in it, then the Metropolitan police will pick Tipper up in London, so there's a chance it might not make the local news."

"A very thin chance."

"Yes, but better than no chance at all."

"And we couldn't somehow drag it back to Tinker's Field?"

"No." Wendy was adamant. "That changes all the rules, Renata. We are not going to do that. Plus, it's not fair to the decent people who live down there. Not all of the Tinker's Field residents are like the Swallows. It's a proper mobile home community once you get away from the temporary parking bit. Some of those people work around here, and their kids go to the local school with Amanda's and Moira's kids. We can't paint them all with the same brush."

Renata winced. Here she was, the great guru of universal kindness, and she was getting everything wrong. She knew better than this.

"It's in one of your books," Wendy concluded. "I've bought the boxed collection. Will you sign the box?"

Renata laughed. "I think maybe I need to reread a few of them myself."

"It's not your fault. You're all upside down at the moment."

"I'm what?"

"You're in a feedback reward loop with the neurotransmitters in your brain," Wendy said with sympathy.

"What?"

"You're awash with norepinephrine and phenylethyl-amine. These are sending wacky messages around your body, making you sleepless and horny, and making your stomach flutter and your pulse race and stuff like that. And 'cause it stimulates your brain and your brain likes it, it makes it happen again, over and over, every minute of the day, and especially when you see your stimulus."

Renata stared at her for a quick moment.

"It's okay. It happens to the best of us," she said with a shrug.

"What you're really saying is that I'm in love with Jane."

"Hmm. I think that Jane is your reward motivator. Your dopamine levels are saying the rest. Leave me out of it."

"How do you—wait. Don't tell me. You read it in one of my books."

Wendy nodded. "I'm good at remembering things."

"Clearly. And I'll think about all of that later. In the mean-time, we have a Monday morning plan for the caravan, right?"

"Yes. And I'll see you tomorrow at church."

Renata hesitated.

"Aw, come on. We have to support her. No matter what your dopamine does."

"Okay, okay. I'll see you there. Same place, same pew." She steered the car toward Wendy's place.

R enata was in the shower when her phone rang the next morning. She chose to ignore it but it cut off and then rang again. This happened a third time before she decided to cut short on her second hair conditioning and see who was in such a froth to call her.

The caller screen said Wendy, Wendy, Wendy, so Renata called her back immediately.

"Where are you?" Wendy's voice came over in an excited, distorted rustle.

"At The White Pig," Renata answered. "Getting ready for church. Where are you? And why are you talking like that? You sound like you're under a blanket."

"I'm hiding behind a newspaper."

"Why?"

"I'm at the newsagent's looking directly at Zoe Blair. She just came in, so I'm hiding behind the postcards and holding a newspaper in front of my face. I don't want her to see me. Oops. She's leaving now." Her whispering became more fervent. "She bought some cigarettes and she's going out the—a blue Ford Focus. She's just jumped into a blue Ford Focus. I've never seen it around here before, and she's driving away." There was a thump and clunk as Wendy apparently rushed out the door after her quarry. Then, "Come quick, Renata. I only have my bike. I can't keep up with her. She's heading north towards High Wallop. Come down the main road and you'll pass her."

"Okay, okay—" But Wendy had already hung up and Renata tossed on her Sunday best as quickly as she could, grabbed her handbag and car keys, and dashed out of the room with wet hair. This was ridiculous. She'd catch pneumonia, and God knew what she looked like. It usually took her half an hour or more to get her hair right.

Nevertheless, she drove out of High Wallop as fast as she was legally allowed and headed down the road to Lesser Wallop. It was more or less a straight road and she could see a blue car off in the distance coming her way, but before she could get close enough to see if it was a Ford, it turned off. Far, far behind it, no more than a speck in the road, really, Renata thought she could make out a cyclist. Surely not? She pulled over and grabbed her compact binoculars from her bag. She went nowhere without them these days, especially not in this valley.

Sure enough, a red-faced Wendy came puffing up the road towards her. She swung the binoculars around to the left and followed the roof of the blue car, barely visible above the hedgerows and saw it make another turn, to the right this time. It seemed to be heading to the church, since there was little else out that side of the valley.

Renata had to make a decision. Pursue the blue car and hope it was the right car, and that she would know what to do if Zoe was in it. She wasn't confident of either of these things, so she put her own car in gear and screeched off towards Wendy. She was the law and order around here. She would know what to do.

"I thought I was going to have a heart attack," Wendy wheezed when she slumped into the seat beside her. Renata did a faultless three-point turn and headed back towards the junction where the blue car had first left the road.

"I hope my bike's okay." Wendy unbuckled her helmet and looked back over her shoulder to where they had flung her bicycle into a hedge and driven off.

"You hate your bike. You should hope someone runs off with it." Renata swung down the lane the blue car had taken.

"But I'll be a laughingstock at the station. The copper who had her bike nicked," Wendy said in protest. "This is the way to St Poe's," she added, noting the passing countryside. "I wish I had a siren to stick on top of your car."

Renata slowed down as they approached the church. The car park was full and several cars were parked on the grass verge outside. "You underestimate the element of surprise, or the irritation of a vicar whose most important sermon ever is interrupted by blue flashing lights and a screaming siren. And it looks like we may be late for the service."

"Do you think Zoe is in the church?"

"Hell no. She has to be after that caravan. Somehow, she's figured out where it's stashed. With any luck, we'll creep up on her and she'll have the key to open it."

"And then I can make the arrest of my career," Wendy said joyfully.

"You can wrestle her to the ground in handcuffs, for all I care. I'm glad to see the back of all this." Her words were snatched away as she slammed on the brakes. Zoe, in a blue Ford Focus came haring out of the gates and missed her front bumper by inches.

"Bloody hell, she could have killed us," Wendy shouted.

"That woman is a bloody maniac." Renata puffed in relief. "You're right. We do need a siren. I'd love to pull her over and give her a piece of my mind." She glared after the fast receding car.

"Renata?" Wendy said. Her gaze was fixed not on Zoe, but on the back of the church. "Renata, what's all that smoke?"

They jumped from the car and raced to the rear of the church. Tipper's caravan was ablaze. An empty petrol container lay off to one side. Wendy kicked it well away from the flames. "That's evidence," she called to Renata. "With luck, her prints are all over it."

The majestic roll of organ music blended with the crackle of the flames rapidly consuming the small vehicle. The heat was momentarily intense, and they had to stand back, and then, suddenly, the initial combustion was over. The flames lowered and began to burn in a determined, smouldering fashion.

"Do you think there're any gas cylinders in there?" Renata asked.

"Not sure, but wouldn't they have gone up in that first flash?" Wendy said. "All it is now is a small fire and lots of smoke."

"For God's sake, don't breathe it in," Renata called.

But it was too late and they were enveloped in a cloud of thick, resinous smoke. It bathed everything around them, blotting out the carpark, the graveyard, even the church. For a blind moment they couldn't even see each other. Then a hand clawed at Renata's and together they dragged each other away to the graves.

CHAPTER 14

The pews were packed, with a few people having to stand at the back of the nave near the door. Jane felt justifiably nervous. The last few rows were filled by the uniformed ranks of her old regiment. All spic and span, standing tall with their hair oiled down and shoes shining. She felt tears well up at the sight of Chubby and his mates once again standing shoulder to shoulder with her through another battle, of sorts.

Jill Fry was playing beautifully, and Jane couldn't help but give thanks that Mrs Agnew had stormed off in high dudgeon and would never again have her toes tapping on those organ pedals, even if she begged for the chance.

She sniffed. The incense smelled weird today. The usual frankincense burned but underneath it was another layer of something stale and sort of funky. She frowned. A tension headache was forming but she expected that, as she was so nervous.

Then she noticed the layer of haze coating the rafters of the vaulted ceiling. It was more obvious to her as she was higher up here in her pulpit than everyone else. Smoke seemed to be drifting in from the open window ports high up in the stained glass windows. It clung to the lofty points of the ceiling and hung down in trembling tendrils towards the heads of the congregation.

The various scents suddenly fell into focus in her mind. She knew this smell. Cannabis! Her church was filling up with pot! What the fudge?

The organ music began to fade away as Jill hit the last resonating chords. Jane's head was reeling. What was she going to do? Already some of the stalwarts in the pews below her were looking fidgety and restless, and sort of glassy-eyed. Her boys in the back pews were pulling at their collars as if over-heated. In the pew directly in front of her, Bishop Hegarty, Archbishop Wang Lee, and the Reverend Colin Harper, were looking up at her, expecting her to begin the service. She had to do it. She had to go through with her sermon and hope for the best. Goodness, but weren't the colours of her stained glass windows beautiful?

She looked to the back of the nave and gave her boys a quick wink and salute, they saluted her back as one, even though she was no longer their chaplain and they didn't have to.

Jane gave the rest of the congregation the best smile she owned. "Friends, we are gathered here this morning to give praise with our voices. So let us begin with 'All Things Bright and Beautiful'." Even as she said it, Jill opened the organ pipes and ground out the opening bars. She grinned widely at Jane, who grinned back.

She loved Jill Fry. She loved this church. She loved this village and everyone in it. She gave Jill the thumbs-up.

Bishop Hegarty smiled at her from below, a little hesitantly, so she gave him a thumbs-up, too, then, along with the rest of the congregation, she began to sing her heart out.

"How many 'All Things Bright and Beautiful' is that'?" Wendy sighed and held her fingers in a lattice against the sun. They were lying on the grassy bank by the graveyard. "Five. Maybe six," she answered. "Isn't sunlight wonderful? Look how rosy my fingers are when I do this."

From the open windows, Jane's voice rang out loud and clear. "All together now—one, two, three…" The congregation burst wholeheartedly into yet another rendition of "All Things Bright and Beautiful."

"Seven." Wendy wove another figuration with her fingers against the sunlight.

"Jesus." Renata chewed on a blade of grass, her hands tucked behind her head. "They're all stoned." She blinked at a pink-tinged cloud and it blinked back. "*I'm* fucking stoned," she said, and turned her head infinitesimally towards Wendy. "How about you?"

"I'm gay," Wendy said.

There was a moment's silence before Renata said, "Yeah, you're totally stoned." She tried to raise her head enough to view the smouldering wreck of the caravan, but it took too great an effort. After the first conflagration, it had burned out quickly, leaving only the skeletal remains of charred and twisted metal, and a thick fug of smoke that hung around the church and its grounds, although most of that was slowly dispersing in the mild-mannered breeze. "Where the hell is this fire brigade?" she asked. "We did call them, didn't we?"

"I always kind of knew… I mean had my suspicions."

"About the fire brigade?"

"No. About being gay."

"Ah. You want to talk about that."

"I mean, I always wondered but never knew for sure, and then when I saw you and Jane—well it all fell into place."

"What did?"

"Me being gay. I could see how you and Jane cared for each other and respected each other and—"

Renata laughed hysterically for what seemed like ages. "Jane doesn't respect me. I stole when I was younger and it freaked her out. She hates that sort of thing because of… well, you know."

"I know? I know what?"

"Because of her family being as crooked as a dog's hind leg."

"No. No, Renata. She loves you. I know she does. Amanda knows, too."

"You and Amanda know nothing. You all read mush."

"We do not read mush, and Jane's lovely. You *should* love her. Look how all the village are in there trying to support her." She pointed at the church. "They even did a whip round and got the money to fix her bike. But she doesn't know that yet. It's a surprise, so shush."

"Oh. That's nice."

"Shush."

"Sorry."

"I hate my bike."

"Why?"

"I want a squad car with flashing blue lights and a siren."

"Why?"

"'Cause that's what the High Wallop boys have."

"But those guys are useless, Wendy. Who saw the paint on Jane's bike and got forensics involved? You did. Who found out that there were drug deals going on in the valley? You, that's who. And who found the caravan the cannabis is harvested in? You again. You're a one-woman force, Wendy Goodall. Flashing lights won't make you a better police officer. They'll make you a disco ball." Renata reached over and took Wendy's hand and squeezed it.

Jane's voice wafted from the church, "And again. One more time...'All Things Bright and Beautiful'..."

"We should get them all out of there," Wendy said. "They're having a Groundhog Day."

"Nah, they're having fun. Listen to them whooping it up. Praise be!"

Blue lights hazed in the distance, along with the sound of sirens heading down the lane to the church.

"There they are." Renata was incredibly pleased. "And they brought the police. That's nice."

"Blue's my favourite colour," Wendy said.

"Mine, too," Renata replied, astounded at this revelation. "Wendy, I'm so glad you're a lesbian."

"I think I am, too."

Renata laughed.

"I think we're kind of lucky the fire brigade evacuated everybody when they did. People were getting far too merry. Colin Harper kept shouting 'hallelujah' and waving his arms about." Jane sat at her kitchen table cradling a cup of tea and staring glumly at the wall opposite, glad that Renata was here but still uncertain how to interact with her.

"What about the Archbishop?" Renata asked. She pushed the plate of buttered toast across. They both had incredible munchies.

"He was fine. Very composed and mild-mannered. He just mellowed out while Andrew fell asleep in his pew. Luckily, they don't seem to remember much about it. Or else no one wants to talk about it just yet."

"And the guys from your old regiment?"

"They said it was the best church service ever," Jane said, a little shame-faced. "All they could do was fall about laughing. They were very useful with the emergency evacuation, though. They had to carry Mrs Agnew out. She got very obstreperous and refused to leave without the altar flowers." She perked up a little. "Did I tell you Chubby got Amanda's telephone number? He helped her out to the car park and they got talking. He's very chuffed. He thinks she's lovely."

"Well, she is." Renata stopped. "Wait. She was at the church? Oh, my God, don't tell me her kids were in that mess."

Jane was shaking her head. "Moira had them at her house. Amanda came on her own. Mercifully, there were no kids there this morning. The Mars family was away on holiday, so no Emily, either."

"Praise be to that. At least some things went right."

Jane sighed. "I can expect a letter any day now reassigning me to some backwater of a mission. Poor St Poe's. I've failed it badly. The little church deserved better."

"I wouldn't be so sure of that. There's been a lot of On High interest in Amanda's research. Your little church could be sitting on an ancient shrine. That has to give you more clout than that St Dunstan carbuncle. Colin Harper could well be on *his* way after all the trouble he's caused."

"I think Tipper and Zoe overshadowed him by far." She stared at the tabletop, uncertain what to do and wondering what she had done wrong to deserve family like Tipper and Winston.

"I'm sorry about Tipper and Winston," Renata said, like she was reading minds again. And it was genuine. Jane appreciated that. And she appreciated that Zoe had been stopped on her way back to London and ratted on everyone she knew.

"Zoe's not admitting it yet," Renata said, clearly in synchronicity with her again. "But I bet she's the one who whacked you with the stolen car."

Jane shrugged. "I'd like to think it was an accident and not deliberate."

Renata snorted and they fell into silence, though Renata was chewing thoughtfully on toast.

"So, what about you?" Jane asked after a while.

"Me?"

"Your plans."

"Um."

"Look, you don't need to sell your cottage. I've wanted to tell you for ages. I was hoping to see you after the service—that is, in difference circumstances. Anyway, I'll be moving on soon, and I really want you to stay here."

"Why? So you can come visit?"

"Maybe." She smiled, sad. It wouldn't be half-bad to see her, would it? She took another bite of her own toast.

"Hey. Listen. I really think it will work out okay," Renata said. From her expression, she believed it could, if the sensationalism of this morning's events remained within the valley alone. Zoe was in custody in London and most of the congregation seemed unaware they were off their faces for forty minutes. And she couldn't see Wang Lee or Andrew Hegarty welcoming an investigation into the embarrassing events. "So, why don't you wait and see what happens instead of worrying about things you can't predict?"

"Can I assume that's the title of your next book?"

"No, it's going to be 'Ganja Crash Makes Jane a Cranky Cow'."

Jane half-smiled and another silence stretched between

them until Jane said, "Thank you."

Renata shrugged. "Okay, but I'm not sure what you're thanking me for. The book title was a joke."

"For pointing out the importance of St Poe's to the right people. Promoting valley businesses. Calling Chubby and asking the guys to come over for the service today. Rows and rows of handsome soldiers always looks good in church. And I know you arranged for them to come to the festival, too. You've done a lot for me and I'm thankful."

"Wasn't hard. It was a beer festival. They'd have climbed over me to get there."

"Probably. But thank you regardless."

She nodded. "You're welcome."

"So…are you going to stay?"

"Don't worry. I'll head out after this." She indicated her teacup.

"I meant stay in your cottage. Will you take it off the market? Please? I feel awful about you selling it."

"And what will you do if I stay and you don't go? I'll be right next door. You'll have to look at me every day." Her tone was light, but there was an undercurrent of sadness there, too.

"I can deal with that," Jane said.

"I'm not sure I can," Renata responded, voice soft.

Jane looked at her, emotions she wasn't sure what to do with fizzing through her chest and stomach. "Renata," she began, her gaze drifting off to the wall again. "I know when you kissed me you were having a sort of rebound reaction at us seeing each other again."

"Wendy's already explained what happened to me. Apparently, my dopamine levels hit the top of my skull and my neurotransmitters told every inch of me I was in love."

Jane's hand stilled on her teacup. "What?"

"I'm sorry, but according to Wendy, you're my reward motivator. And according to Amanda, we're not too far broken." She shrugged. "I'll do whatever I can to prove they're both right." She reached across the table for Jane's hand and Jane let her have it, as stunned as she was.

"I've been an honest, upright, and moderately successful adult for some time now," Renata continued. "I have a good career and a nice lifestyle. I'm a complete turnaround from the person you once knew. How can you be so lenient with Tipper but so hard on me? Like him, I was young and stupid once, and you were right beside me being young and stupid, too. Why can't we just forgive each other?"

Her chest felt like it was squeezing the breath out of her lungs. "Because I'm scared." She slowly slid her hand away. "I'm not sure I can be around you and be who I want to be. Or who I need to be, for myself and for this community. I'm tired of losing the important things in my life."

Renata held her gaze. "Maybe you don't realise it, but you haven't lost a thing. The army didn't want to lose you. It honoured you the best way it possibly could with that medal in your study. And see how your comrades still support you in every way they can?" Passion made her words heated and energised. "Your father follows you wherever you go. I bet Tipper does, too, and not just to constantly tap you for money."

"What, then?"

"Because *you* hold your mangy family together like duct tape keeps their tatty vans in one piece," Renata said earnestly. "Your friends adore you and go out of their way to help. Bishop Hegarty wanted you here and wove wonders to keep you."

"I guess we'll see how that works out." She stared into her cup.

"And I—well, I'm still in love with you after all these years. Or, perhaps more accurately, I've fallen all over again."

She looked up at her, heart pounding.

"You've lost nothing, Jane. The important things follow you everywhere you go, like that stupid dog." She nodded over to where Whistlestop snoozed on his blanket. "So stop running, stand still a moment, and allow yourself to accept your blessings." She paused for a moment. "Are you crying?"

Jane sniffled into her sleeve. "I'm sorry I'm such a coward."

Renata moved around the table, knelt by her side, and wrapped her arms around her, and this time, Jane didn't push her away. "I've just told you, you're not. You've a medal for gallantry, for God's sake."

"That's not what I mean and you know it." She fought another round of tears. "I told you to go because I was afraid of how hard it would be to make things different. I didn't want to lose my job, or my friends, or my home."

"I understand that. And it's okay to be scared. It's only if you don't ever face your fears that it becomes a problem."

"Maybe I don't know how." And she dissolved into a round of tears but Renata just held her closer.

"Do you love me?" Renata asked quietly after a while.

"Yes. I do. I so do." And there was something liberating about saying it.

"Okay. Do you want us to be brave? We're older now and a little wiser. Do you want us to try again? Just a little, and see how it goes?"

"I think I do."

"Okay. I do, too."

She smiled through her tears and wiped her face with her sleeve.

"And while I can't say for certain, but I don't think you'll lose your job or your home. There are too many positive factors in your life, like your parishioners, who adore you, and the community you support, and the fact that your bishop desperately wants to keep you. And again, I can't be certain, but I don't think you'll lose your friends, either. Wendy and Amanda care too much about you. Moira, Una, Dr James—all your friends from quiz night. Basically, half the village supports you. They want you to be happy."

"But there're also people like Colin."

"There'll always be people like Colin. People so miserable in their own lives, they spew spite over everyone else. There will be many Colins along the way. But whether we're together or not, they'll be there anyway, so we might as well face them side by side and win."

Jane pulled away slightly and cupped Renata's face with her hands. "I want to try. This time, I don't want to run away." And she kissed her, lips salty with tears.

Renata pressed back into the kiss and tightened her hold. Then she pulled away and looked into Jane's eyes. "You can trust me. I promise. This time you can trust me."

Jane brushed a few strands of hair out of Renata's face. "I know. I've seen it in everything you do, everything you are since you arrived. As much as I tried to fight it, I've grown to love you again. Maybe I never quite stopped. Do you think that by running away all those years ago we never got to say our goodbyes, and we were always stuck in that one place?"

"That place is here and now. Let's forget the goodbye that never arrived." And they kissed again. Then Renata rose and held out her hand.

"Let's go to bed," she said gently and pulled Jane to her feet. There were many more kisses as she led her slowly from the room.

A moist snuffling at her ear awoke her the next morning. Renata opened a sleepy eye and got a close-up of Whistlestop's wet nostrils. As she blinked in confusion, he decided to smell her eyebrows next, and then her hairline.

"Ew, stop that, you knobbly string bean."

"He's interested because you're in bed with me and he's not allowed." Jane was sitting up in bed beside her, watching with an amused smile.

"Huh. Look at that. I *am* in bed with you." She grinned and rolled over, then reached for her hand and kissed the knuckles. "And he'd better get used to it, for I've no intention of going anywhere soon."

"I thought you had a world tour or something coming up."

"You want to be rid of me already?" She pretended to pout.

"No." She patted the pillows and Renata scooted upright to join her. They sat shoulder to shoulder in the wide bed. Whistlestop placed a paw on the quilt and gave them a surreptitious sideways glance.

"No, you don't. You know the rules," Jane scolded softly, and he withdrew his paw and slid out of sight. "He's so sneaky."

"You have to be sneaky to get into your bed," Renata answered. "Look at the hoops I jumped through."

"Not with those feet." Jane pushed the covers back and slid out of bed nude. "I'm going to make some tea. Can I bring you up a cup?"

"Only if you bring it naked."

But Jane was already tying the sash of her kimono. "And I bet that would be the moment Mrs Agnew popped over to borrow some milk." She moved over to the window and opened the curtains. "Oh. Hmm."

"What?"

"Well, so much for rumours of my celibacy." She puffed out her cheeks, struggling with her annoyance. Then she relaxed and shrugged. "Screw it. If Andrew doesn't like it, I can always go live next door because apparently, my neighbour's a bit of a trollop."

"What? What are you talking about?"

"If I lose my job because of my lewd lifestyle, I'm moving in with you. So you'd better get that cottage off the market because I fully intend to be lewd."

Renata left the bed and came to stand beside her, peering out the window to see what, or whom, had elicited this flamboyant speech.

"That's right, you stand there with your boobs out. Damn them all," Jane said, then casually turned away. "Darjeeling or Earl Grey?"

Renata crossed her arms across her chest and squinted out the window. "I don't care which," she answered. "What are you talking about? I don't see anyone." This was answered with an all-knowing tut and then Jane left the room. Renata continued to glare out the window.

The lawn leading down to the Sturry was emerald green in the bright, early morning light. The flowers bobbed their heads in the breeze, and Whistlestop lay belly down on the grass, luxuriating in the day. There was not a soul about to spy on them.

She was unsure what had made Jane so momentarily belligerent. But it had to be a good thing that she had woken up ready to face their new life together in such a feisty mood. Amazing, what a night of nonstop lovemaking could do to settle things. A little bit of Renata was smug that it was *her* nonstop lovemaking that had brought about such a particular, if confusing, change in her lover's outlook.

In the kitchen, she heard cups clinking, along with the rattle of the cutlery drawer and the pop of the toaster. She still didn't see anything, so she turned away to grab a tee shirt and join Jane downstairs. And then it suddenly clicked and she swung back to the bucolic view with a snap.

There, resplendent on the lawn, in full view of anyone who cared to pass by, Whistlestop lay in a happy belly flop, his tail thumping the grass in full appreciation of the pink lace panties he was chewing to bits.

Ha! That'd be a sight for Mrs Agnew or Colin. Would serve them right, too. She grinned and went downstairs, where she found Jane on the phone.

"You're certain?" she asked, as she motioned for Renata to take a seat at the table. "I mean, I really don't want there to be any problems—" She paused, and Renata frowned. She decided not to sit down after all and stood, waiting for more information about this call.

And then Jane smiled. "I would be honoured. Thank you for this opportunity."

Anxiety prickled her spine.

"Thank you, Andrew. I appreciate the call, and I'll see you at dinner with the Archbishop." She paused. "Definitely. Thank you. Bye." She hung up, eyes shining.

"What?" Renata said.

"That was Andrew."

"So I gathered. And?"

"I'm having dinner with him and the Archbishop again."

Renata waited, barely breathing.

"Apparently, the Archbishop loves St Poe's and said it's clear from what he's seen over the past few days that I'm meant to be here."

She let her breath out, heart pounding. "So...you're staying?"

Jane set her phone on the counter and took Renata's hands. "Yes." And she kissed her, a soft meeting of lips.

"Good," she murmured against her mouth. "Because you owe me fifty quid for my underwear."

She drew back. "Fifty quid? Who even buys underwear that cost that?"

She shrugged and kissed her again, smiling.

"My new neighbour is clearly a trollop," Jane said after a few delectable moments of kissing.

"And mine said she would like to be lewd. In my house. With me."

"She did, didn't she? Well, seems like there'll be plenty of time after all to do that."

"Praise be..."

Jane laughed and kissed her again.

The End

About the Author

Gill McKnight is Irish but spends as much time as possible in Lesbos, Greece, which she considers home. She can often be found traveling back and forth between Greece and Ireland in a rusty old camper van with her rusty wee dog. Gill enjoys writing, gardening, and, by necessity, some easy DIY. You can learn more about her on her personal website at www.gillmcknightwrites.com.

Other Books by Gill McKnight

The Plague Tree Coven Series

Borage

The Garoul Series

Goldenseal

Ambereye

Indigo Moon

Silver Collar

Little Dip

Others

Falling Star

Green-Eyed Monster

Erosistible

Cool Side of the Pillow

The Tea Machine

Daughter of Baal

Also from Dirt Road Books

Cake by Jove Belle. A sexy romance about two women, one inconvenient wedding, and a shared love of cake.

Borage (Book 1 of The Plague Tree Coven series) by Gill McKnight. A hapless witch on a mighty mission. Can she hoodwink the despicable CEO of Black and Blacker?

Big Girl Pill by KD Williamson. Two women get a second chance at love, even if one is engaged to a man.

Penny on Parade by Penny Taylor and Gill McKnight. A woman joins the British Army in the early 1970s. Based on a true story.

Fianna the Gold (The Shift Series). A woman finds a world of dragons...and her destiny.

Learning Curve: Stories of Lessons Learned (various authors). An anthology benefiting One Girl, an organization dedicated to educating and advancing the lives of girls around the world.

Wild Rides by Sacchi Green. An anthology of erotica by the award-winning author.

The Potion by R.G. Emanuelle. A novel of intrigue and secret formulas.

Little Dip (Garoul Book 5) by Gill McKnight. A prequel to the wildly popular werewolf series.

Friends in High Places (Far Seek Chronicles 1, Second Ed.) by Andi Marquette. A space opera about outlaws and old flames.

Bitterroot Queen by Jove Belle.A mother and daughter move to a small town to run a hotel and get much more.

Audiobooks

Little Dip (Garoul Book 5) by Gill McKnight. A prequel to to the wildly popular werewolf series.

Bitterroot Queen by Jove Belle.A mother and daughter move to a small town to run a hotel and get much more.